geeks,
misfits
& outlaws

D1500513

edited by

Zoe Whittall

McGilligan Books

National Library of Canada Cataloguing in Publication

Geeks, misfits & outlaws / edited by Zoe Whittall.

ISBN 1-894692-07-1

1. Short stories, Canadian (English) 2. Short stories, American.
3. Canadian fiction (English)—21st century. 4. American fiction—21st
century. I. Whittall, Zoe II. Title: Geeks, misfits and outlaws.

PS8323.E22G43 2003   C813'.010806   C2003-905279-6

Derek McCormack — "The Elf" was originally printed in *Wishbook* (Gutter
Press, 1999). Excerpt from *Cool For You* by Eileen Myles, copyright 2000 by
Eileen Myles. Used by permission of Soft Skull Press, Inc. Sky Gilbert —
excerpt from *I Am Kasper Klotz* reprinted by permission from ECW Press
and the author. Marnie Woodrow — "Why We Close Our Eyes When We
Kiss," copyright 1991 printed by permission of the author. Jonathan
Goldstein — excerpt from *Lenny Bruce is Dead* — reprinted by permission
from Coach House Books and the author. Emily Schultz — "The Mothers"
reprinted from *Black Coffee Nights* with permission from the author and
Insomniac Press. Mariko Tamaki — "Hump" reprinted by permission of
Women's Press."I Know Angelo" by Heather O'Neill originally appeared in
Blood & Aphorisms #37. "House Contents & the Big, Wild World" by Camilla
Gibb originally appeared in the *Hart House Review*. "Markéd" by Jim
Munroe originally appeared in *Adbusters*.

Editing: Zoe Whittall
Copy Editing: Noreen Shanahan
Cover Design: Suzy Malik
Cover Illustration: Gillian Bell
Interior Layout: Heather Guylar
Printed in Canada

McGilligan Books, P.O. Box 16024, 859 Dundas Street West,
Toronto, ON, Canada, M6J 1W0, phone 416-538-0945, e-mail
mcgilliganbooks@sympatico.ca. McGilligan Books gratefully
acknowledges the support of the Canada Council for the
Arts, the Ontario Arts Council and
the Ontario Book Publishers Tax
Credit for our publishing program.

ONTARIO ARTS COUNCIL
CONSEIL DES ARTS DE L'ONTARIO

Canada Council   Conseil des Arts
for the Arts   du Canada

For Pretty, Porky & Pissed Off -
the best group of
outlaws a girl
could ever run with

Introduction

> "Be nobody's darling;
> Be an outcast
> Qualified to live
> Among your dead."

> *Alice Walker*

I have a *Stella Mars* postcard above my desk that I've had for ages. It says, "Normal is a Myth" and I refer to it often, when plagued with a sense of failed normalcy. At 27, I have at one point or another, been a geek, a misfit and an outlaw. I've been ostracized and celebrated for my differences.

The idea for this anthology came to me during a lengthy shift working as a bookseller where I had a lot of time to ruminate on my literary favorites while grouping together texts for a display. The themes of my favorite works were diverse but united by one thing: otherness. Bad-ass girls. Creepy boys. Revolutionaries. Gentle outsiders. The antithesis of the Oprah table.

I tend to feel passionately about characters, and people in real life, who cause a stir, illicit stares, awe, pity and most definitely envy, while living on dividing lines: Villanelle, the web-footed gender-bending protagonist of *The Passion* by Jeanette Winterson; Lynda Barry's brave narrator of *Cruddy* with her knife called Little Debbie, the little boy who is also a red-winged monster in Anne Carson's *Autobiography of Red* all the way back to Judy Blume's *Otherwise Known As Sheila The Great*.

Geeks, Misfits and Outlaws is a collection that celebrates the eccentric in style and content. This collection of short fiction is varied, peppered with humor and sadness, but united by one thing: eclectic characters who struggle with and cherish their status as outlaw, geek or misfit.

Zoe Whittall
Fall 2003

Contents

RM VAUGHAN AND LYNN CROSBIE

A Poetic Affair Between a Cynical Queen and a Straight Woman Locked in Her Room

RM VAUGHAN
Eight Reasons for Loving a Recluse

1. My baby don't go out at night — or in the afternoon, or even at the split of dawn.
Does that make me a hermit hag?
Let's examine the concept of reclusion. Why is staying at home at all costs, including fire and flood, a bad thing?
Human contact is over-rated.
Here's two choices:

a) Go down to the bakery, forget your gloves, listen for five minutes to an intense family argument, in Portuguese, which you don't understand, pay for your $1.05 worth of bread with a twenty and get the glaring of your life, pull the Push door, get glared at again, leave the bakery haunted by snickers, and know, just know, that everyone can see the salt on your boots and thinks you are dirty and poor. Finally — make it home under a dark cloud, cut your fingers on the broken doorknob, drop your bread on the cat's head and feel guilty for an hour (petting that hateful demon feline who only loves you, only wants to touch you,

9

because you are warmer than the radiator), cry and go to sleep; or

b) Stay home, lock the door, unplug the phone.
You decide which one of us is crazy.

2.   She has a long purple cloak, ankle to chin.
She looks like the Invisible Girl from the Fantastic Four.
Out on the town.
She is a startled blush, a cool August streetcar breeze.

3.   Am I too controlling? Do I love my shut-in sugar just because I always know where she is and what she is doing? Yes.
The world is a moving, swirling, narcotic, stupefying parcel — I take comfort in her inabilities, her reluctances, her finality, her dust.
We all like to know exactly where our keys are, where we left our wallets and what time the mail comes. Am I a bad person for wanting more? When I read *Jane Eyre*, God help me, I figured Rochester had the right idea. Except for the fire.

4.   There is no health food in her home, no Nordic tracks or motivational tapes. Her body rejects vim and vigor, she'd never use that get up and go. I feel free to go to seed.

5.   Hermit, misanthrope, agoraphobic, layabout, monkish, anti-social, sabbatarian, anchorite, homebody, ascetic — say

the following words and visualize something luxurious, something you'd like to touch; such as a mother of pearl, or velveteen. Your little ostrich will become an image of love, her sand-caked head a dewy flower. It's all in the terminology.

6.   Fall in love with a recluse and you will never be jealous or worried again. You know she is not out dancing at the Matador with girlfriends who tell her you are getting fat. She is never shopping idly at Holt Renfrew, wandering the aisles and pricing escape luggage. She is not going to put your clothes on the sidewalk no matter what you do — the sidewalk is outdoors. She's not on the internet, she has no spare rooms, no fold-out beds for guests. Vacation brochures send her to bed, shivering, and hotel doors do not have enough locks. She cannot imagine phone sex.

So relax. Kiss her, she's your baby, your honey, your locked safe bet.

7.   Curiously, she has a miraculous collection of shoes. What the hell for? If you ask her nicely, she'll walk up and down the clicking bathroom tile — all sassy, foxy and way, way off the ground.

8.   Because it's like knowing Greta Garbo, or Louise Brooks, or Marlene, or Nijinksky, or Balthus, or Howard Hughes, or any Free-mason, any member of the Supreme Court, Deng Xiaoping, or Tippi Hedren. And let's face it, I need

the glamour. I like to imagine I am part of a very, very small cabal.

People who never go out start to glow, it's true, like television screens after you turn them off. Sit beside her in the dark, read a book. You'll remember the first time you went camping, staring at Tomb of Doom comics by coleman lamps — happy and comfortable and tingling with fear.

LYNN CROSBIE
Eight Reasons for Loving a Gay Man

1. When I am at home, I know he is taking the same tranquillizer: as I lift the pill to my mouth and place it under my tongue, he is tasting the same orange, its bitter pulp and sweet dissolution. Our hands release the bottle; it drops into the drawer, all its spheres singing, and we drift deep into the Pacific, breathing slowly through the same lung.

The sun illuminates his yellow hair; my hair is red in the circlet of sun.

The waves break and purple; when night falls, a familiar terror descends. Electric with distress, beauty schools and shimmers, tumbles between my teeth and granulates, until the tide runs golden, signaling my likeness, whose body places in the shadows, and batters forward.

2. I'm talking about a man of the world, making the scene in an amethyst stickpin and violet boot-knife. Sharkskin suit

and brocade vest — plum damask — empurples him a white dove who wings past my window, his silver rings shining, one lilac glove pressed to his ianthine lips, a kiss panes my window and he slips out of sight in a plume of smoke. Singing blue moon, blue tails, black and blue eyes about the man I love.

3.   I am fatter than Robert Earl Hughes and lowering into the bath, I think of him, rotting in this piano case. I toss two white hearts milkening the water and obscuring myself.

I know that he is out there unknowable, entering a bath, radiant eyes burning, fearless. I was terribly overweight, he says, revealing himself as he negotiates towels like scarves, like fans, like doves.

The bath hearts detonate, breathing violets.

My skin is hot and clean; a lustrous pomegranate in nectar. We are weightless, suspended in ripe tumbling, and unashamed.

4.   He wears a pineapple appliquéd on his blue jacket, wherever he goes it is tropical. A vision of big Tarzan-men on rafts, husking the fruit and spilling it into each other's mouths.

I pour Jamaican rum into its hollows and drink, to palmfronds, paper parasols, salt-licked hard-bodies, and drink, and pine.

5.   Sweet Sweetback, Evil Jack; Earth Angel, Home Devil; Bartok, Puccini, Bach and Ravel; The Leader of the Pack,

Big Daddy Kane, Jack Kerouac; Christopher and Philip Marlowe, Kurt Weill and Turnadot; Mallarmé, Anton La Vey; Erroll Flynn, Gunga Din; John Barrymore; High John, Prince Ali Khan; Douglas Hoftsteader, Eddie Veder; Tim Horton, Joe Orton.

My screen saver, my call-display, my E-male.

He is violet pressed in Baudelaire: "How far away, that fragrant Paradise."

6. Fall in love with a gay man and become Dante to his elusive Beatrice, Petrarch to his indifferent Laura.

Draw chest hair and a goatee on a crude cartoon of yourself. Mail it to him, madly impatient, because you have recited five pages of Honcho into his answering machine in a deep baritone, or couriered your revisionist libretto, Bellini's Norman, or started a chat-group on the internet called Post Sexuality in the Millenium: Who Needs a Cock?

Love his ex-girlfriendless phone book and photo album; sit pretty on his parents' sofa where he never gave head to someone named Tammy; enjoy his vacation slides, Fun in Acapulco, featuring him playing Dexedrine Elvis to The Memphis Mafia, instead of some fat-assed Shelley Faberes.

You are virtually in love your hand in black leather glove and eyes glamorously shaded. Preen when he calls you Red and decimates the competition.

When a beautiful girl appears on television, flipping her hair, he telephones to say: I heard she was a man, an ugly, ugly, man.

Fold his picture into a flower and wear it in your hair, flaming star.

7. In your dreams, he is barefoot and pregnant. He slits himself open, delivering two quivering plums. And offers you one, wrapped in a white linen napkin.

You bite into its flesh; its ripeness makes your stomach ache, depressing you. You dream too of the fertile Arnolfinis, their confex mirror and shoe.

8. Because it's like visiting an art gallery and being allowed to touch the exhibits. He makes miniatures: bunny plates, framed dolls' skirts, ants in amber.

Gorgeous duplicates, the way his cells mesh in rapture, making him, making you, a heart-shaped cookie wrapped in hyacinth tissue paper, he slips it under your door, to hold and taste, the grace he radiates, enfolds — like the purpose dragoned royal standard — this quiet pulsing place.

Floods

"Those pants are *floods*. Did'jya know that?"

Denise Coppins and I were walking home from school together. The sidewalks beneath our running shoes (hers: real Adidas; mine: a fake version — witness the number of stripes) were gray and damp. The lawns beside us were scuffed with pocked piles of old snow, and littered with wrappers, wet plastic bags, and decomposing dog shit. Empty picture windows gazed blankly out in the late afternoon gloom. If I looked in a window, I almost thought I saw the profile of a woman sitting in a dusted armchair, waiting.

I suddenly realized Denise was giving me fashion advice. I'd wondered why she was walking home with me; I'd long since been dumped from her hip crowd. It had been a couple of years since she'd invited me to her cottage one summer, and I — ecstatic at the idea of temporarily abandoning the hockey arena architecture of Scarborough for wild rock and sharp pine — had pleaded with my always-too-sweet mother to fiddle and fiddle with my rage-crazed father without my audience for a weekend.

And oh, the strange disappointment that followed her permission and my voyage out. At that age, I was still grappling half-hopefully with the way the profane always seemed to interrupt my idea of the sacred. I sat in a kind of shocked silence in the backseat of a tan Volvo all the way to the "cottage", while Denise's mother spun between stations and sang, "Yummy, yummy, yummy, I've got love in my tummy." That a mother might smoke and sing bubblegum songs (not that I knew they were "bubblegum songs" — Denise had not enlightened me on that nuance of propriety yet) confused me. My own mother was eternally poised. She never got angry or even vaguely aggressive — no matter how verbally abusive and hysterical my father got. My mother was prone to helping injured animals, and repeating phrases like "Ladies don't sweat, they perspire." Denise's mother, on the other hand, talked about "sweating like a pig." She lit "smokes," and yelled at her husband to hurry up and pull over so we could all "take a pee" (I squatted in the woods a distance away and couldn't let go). For the last stretch of the trip, she and Denise argued about boys, and fought over the last coke.

The cottage, when we got there, was just an extension of the suburbs we'd left behind. There was a lake, but the ubiquitous green lawns were still there, dotted with clipped hedges and squat pansies in barrels. All the cottages were close together, and every cottage had some version of a dock and a motorboat.

Inside, everyone seemed irritable and argumentative. Denise's grandfather had caught a fish, but he wasn't cleaning it. Everyone else refused to clean it too, and the fish was dumped in the kitchen sink after dinner to suffocate. It blinked there all night. I spent the long, dirty night sympathetically running water over its panting gills and extending its suffering.

I looked down at the pants I was wearing. They belonged to my older sister. She was, admittedly, a smaller, more tender version of me (something she loved to point out — extending her tiny hands beside mine and cooing about it) so my long legs poked out of the bottom and the edges of the pants floated a couple inches above the surface of the sidewalk. It took a few minutes for the critique to even make sense. These... I repeated to myself...are *floods*. I looked at Denise's face and realized that she'd decided to walk home with me because she just couldn't take my radical lack of any fashion sense anymore. It embarrassed her. Worse, it irritated her, and she was just barely restraining herself from crossing the street and communicating her contempt with catcalls and vulgar gestures.

It struck me then, that she might still retain some sense of the temporary friendship we'd fashioned a few years earlier. I only had the vaguest recollection of it. The world behind the closed door of my two-story house with aluminum siding on the second floor was both intensely regulated and wildly out of control. It absorbed me completely. I had a sense of arms and legs poking out of the windows of the family home — as if we had all ingested some fungus-infested narcotic, and couldn't fit inside anymore. At the same time, it was all *so* contained by schedules and tightly-knit agendas and long, empty, boring hours. By the time I started hanging out with Denise, my nerves were stretched to provide a helpless musical accompaniment to any raised voice, any tightened mouth, any widened eye, any shaking digit, any harbinger of a bright screaming twister in the form of my barely-functioning father and head of our horror-hunted household.

The last memory I had of Denise - before she performed the important social function I'm describing here - was not actually *of* Denise. It was of the principal coming to the classroom and calling me to the office in grade five. Denise was my friend, right? Yes, I said, sitting carefully and stiffly on the straight-backed wooden chair he'd ushered me to. I was a good girl. I was an honest, truthful, girl. Had I ever seen Denise spread her legs for the boys underneath the desks at school?

No. (Yes. Maybe...)

Nigel was a geek, and Nigel wore floods. Pink cotton floods that grazed the top of his large-boned ankles. Nigel leaped and cavorted in his pink floods, and my younger sister Charlie and I wanted him desperately. He was a wild thing — as delicate and twisted as a broken toy. Oh, we tasted his loneliness, and knew just what he was saying in his pink pants and his broken boots with the untied laces. We wanted to knock him down and sit on him and take turns kissing him. We wanted to find his tongue and hold it between our teeth, to restrain his long gangly arms over his head until he wept with frustration, and take him that way. We wanted to reach into his cheap, stained, bulging pants and share the task of servicing his ecstatic release. He was a sweet thing. Angry and helpless. We wanted to see that. We wanted to love that.

My blonde sister licked her freckled lips and laughed so hard at the thought of this, that her face folded into new and fantastic shapes. At twelve years old, Charlie was still tiny and somewhat pre-pubescent. She wore black jeans and black eye shadow and had developed a bad case of acne around her hairline due, in large part, to never washing. Every morning I watched her barely splash water on her pustules and then wipe it with one of our ragged protestant towels. I was a year and a half older, much larger and more ungainly. I washed carefully and chronically, but there wasn't that much difference in our spotted and stained complexions.

Like me, Nigel was almost full-grown at fourteen. He was easily six feet tall already. He had big feet and hands; his bones were long and hungry. When we walked home from school together, he'd detour into snow banks to fill his untied boots with muck and water. He'd truck down the street with his long legs splayed and his coat half off, shaking his fist and jeering at the cars that whipped by us in four lanes of traffic. With Nigel kicking his feet out sideways like he was shaking the dust off, we made our way past the Baptist church, the skating arena and the bucolic industrial parkland our parents had provided for us out of their commitment to the dream of the happy family.

Nigel's mother was mad, too. Charlie and I had no doubt of that. And although we were never invited to visit and find out with our own heavily made-up eyes, we did enjoy making phone calls that toyed with her trembling sanity. She'd answer the phone with a British accent as precise and formal as the carefully arranged knife and fork we longed to pick up and plunge into our father's heart during our tortured Sunday dinners. We'd inquire after Nigel in monosyllables. Nige? No. Do you wish to speak to my son, Nigel? (Popped bubbles and giggles in response.) Can I help you? Hey. Sure. Go get Nige. Would'ja? We could feel her indignation, feel her bottled up: fastidious and furious. A hushed and polite Nigel would come to the phone from somewhere on the other side of the formal divide. Yes. He'd see us later. Maybe. If he could get out of the house. Get away from *her*.

My younger sister and I knew how to make what we wanted with Nigel happen. Our older sister Martha had carefully and deliberately trained us. Martha would call us down to the basement, where her boyfriend lay prone and expectant on a scratchy tweed couch, and she'd share us with him. Charlie and I thought it was normal to practice on our older sister's boyfriends. She'd direct us in the art of seduction with an attention to detail that made it all seem so easy. There were techniques to be learned, and errors to be avoided.

Like the night Martha took Charlie to a pizza joint at the local plaza. There was a guy on the stage playing guitar. Do you like him? Martha leaned in close to Charlie and took Charlie's wrist in her tiny, pointed, carefully manicured hand. She looked into Charlie's face, and Charlie had a vague sense that she was slavering with interest. Do you like him? Sure, said Charlie. She didn't really know what to say, was always a little uneasy around Martha. I'll get him for you, Martha promised, and got the whole ball rolling.

Martha and Charlie hung around until the last set was done. Then Martha batted her eyes and offered to help the cute guy pack up his gear. They ended up in the front seat of his truck — with Charlie by the window. You can have my sister too, said Martha after a while, and Charlie ended up reaching in and finishing up the job — jerking her hand up and down till her arm ached.

Or the time Martha invited me on a drive with her boyfriend and one of his buddies. I sat in the backseat, in a cotton summer dress that made me think of the kind of lilac-studded spring evenings that must have been crammed into my unconscious, given my exposure to them. You can do whatever you like to her, Martha told the boy beside me, except fuck her. Then followed a series of long car rides and one-sided grope sessions. I even took the opportunity to memorize Elizabeth Barrett Browning's "How Do I Love Thee" for him — while I waited for them to come pick me up after school.

Nigel is easy. Charlie and I can get Nigel.

But then Nigel starts taking fits. The first time it happens we're just out front of the Baptist Church near our high school. The church has bright neon lights and messages written in black plastic lettering. No man comes to the father but by me. The wages of sin are death. Believe in the

Lord Jesus Christ and thou shalt be saved. Nigel is walking between us, and we both have one of his large hands in each of our hands. It's late afternoon. Early January. Dark and bleak — the way it always is in the suburbs — where the sky is low and loud, and the foliage weak and stunted. A car starts up beside us.

Suddenly Nigel starts gripping my hand and trembling. His hand starts jerking and tightening. His arms begin flailing, and it's not the old rage in geek form that we love so well. It's not the pointed and passionate rebellion that he wears in his whole lovely, gangly body. It's something different. Nigel falls and we bend over him, delirious with excitement. His body jerks and twitches. Nigel, we say. Nige! We're here, Nigel! Can you hear us? And Nigel is banging the frozen ground with the back of his head and digging his heels into the ice. Nigel! How we love him. How we dream of saving him. And now the gift of this. This absolute loss of control. This harvest of self-abandonment.

Nigel lies on the ground. Emptied. His eyes are closed. He looks as delicate as a woman, as vulnerable as a child. Our hearts are gloriously full. We bend over him, and give him our full attention. Nigel moans. He is weak, pale and needy. We are fierce and brave and ready to take him, except there are too many people around. He has landed on the edge of a parking lot near the skating arena. The place is too public for our intentions. He opens his eyes and sees us. We are angels with peeling lips framed in neon and the word of God. Ardent, attentive and enthusiastic. Accompanied by the sound of traffic and the smell of French fries.

The next time it happens, the site is more conducive to action. It's lunchtime, and we've left school to hang out at John's place nearby. John's house is fun. His parents work and they're never home during the day. In the freezer, John always has boxed and frozen burgers, pressed between waxed paper. They're greasy and delicious and we slap them into a Teflon pan and heat them till the edges are congealed and brown. We eat them slathered in mustard and ketchup, between slabs of Wonderbread. My sister and I can eat three of them at a time.

Nigel doesn't eat in front of us. He's too wired. He's too busy scuffing and spinning around on the linoleum in the kitchen, humming and singing to himself. I lick the ketchup from the edge of my mouth and watch him. He's always moving. I look at my sister and we both laugh at him.

John takes his girlfriend to his bedroom. The three of us move to the living room and turn on the T.V. Samantha Stevens is in trouble again. She looks like my sister. Nigel slumps heavily on the reclining chair and tries to watch, but he can't keep still. He pulls the knob and leans back. He leans forward and sits up again. He pulls the knob and leans back and the chair flies backwards. His big feet are in the air. His socks are stained and mismatched, and his big toe is sticking out of one of them. Charlie and I are too lazy to move. We sit on the couch and wait for him to get the chair back up again. Wonder why he doesn't just get off and do it that way.

It takes too long for him to respond. After a minute, we

notice that his feet are twitching in that tell-tale way. It's all we can see over the exposed action of the bottom of the chair. The chair starts jerking rhythmically: bumping and trembling.

Then we're by his side, maneuvering his spastic body off the chair and onto the carpet. Nigel. We're saying again. Nigel! — but not too loudly, we don't want John and his girlfriend in here. After a while the twitching stops and Nigel isn't moving. His eyelids are blue-veined and lovely. The silky hair on his upper lip moves me. His neck is long and exposed.

I kiss it and feel the pulse of his heart under my mouth. Nigel doesn't respond. Nigel, Charlie breathes into his ear. Nothing. But he's breathing. Helpless. Charlie runs her fingers though his hair and kisses him full on the mouth. I unbutton his shirt and stop to kiss his belly. It's as smooth as a child's. Charlie pokes me and I look up. We both look at a point slightly below my mouth, where the material of his pants is bulging. Charlie pulls at the zipper — delicately, to avoid waking him. I'm so excited, I can hardly breathe. My turn.

Nigel stirs and we both stop. We run into the kitchen, giggling. When Nigel joins us, we're eating peanut butter cookies and making a pot of tea.

Charlie and I decide we want to do acid. One Saturday morning, when our parents are strangely and suddenly absent for the weekend (where did they go? they have no friends), and Marcia seems to be in charge. One bright, cold spring morning, Charlie and I wake up and decide that the thing to do is acid.

We figured we could get a hold of it. Knew there were places where dealers hung out. People we'd heard about. People like Gordie Reynolds — a few years older than we were, hung out with a group of guys that were always in and out of prison. And why? Well — they probably sold acid, for one thing. They were shadowy comic book characters to us. Penciled in at the edges. Gaunt cross-thatched cheeks and loose jeans and cowboy boots.

We headed down to the mall first. It had been a plaza for years, and the winning attraction had always been a Simpsons store that jutted out from the center of the plaza and had a return policy my mother liked. In that Simpsons, I once had a strange and vivid encounter that seemed somehow indicative of something essentially flawed in my character. Something about me that was irritating in a primary way. I was with my mother — holding her hand? — and I looked up to see a woman, a stranger to me, trying to catch my eye. She seemed to be mimicking my expression, and in that mirror that was her, I saw the face of a gaping fool with bulging eyes and an open mouth. I closed my mouth, and she held my eyes long enough to communicate contempt for everything about me.

Now the plaza was a mall, with Simpsons in the center of it. Charlie and I went there. It was a long walk, beside four lanes of loud traffic, gleaming in the sun. We crossed the hydro field, curling against the sharp bright wind that always lived there. We passed the local sacred Indian burial ground. It was a small hill with a sign - kept neatly sodded and clipped by the municipal government and surrounded by sullen housing. When we reached the mall, we set ourselves up at a bench somewhere just outside Woolworths, and waited to bump into someone young and plausibly evil enough to get us some drugs. There were people at the counter inside Woolworths, but we knew they were just old people — eating pie and drinking coffee. One little girl sat alone near the window, with a big piece of cake and a glass of milk in front of her. Her mother was probably shopping, Charlie said. *Our* mother didn't shop at Woolworths — communicated a kind of disdain for Woolworths — but she'd never buy us a piece of cake there, either. Or fries and a coke — which would go down good right now. The lucky little girl watched us.

Charlie was doing a theme in black, as usual. Her adolescent body looked impossibly compact and slender in tight black jeans and a black sweater. She was wearing a funky little multi-coloured and crocheted vest and a faded blue jean jacket. Her bangs hung in her eyes and she liked them that way. Charlie had developed a technique of looking out from behind her hair, with her head cocked to one side. She'd look directly at you with the part of her eyes that still showed behind her greasy fringe, and let her mouth drop open while she felt around inside it with her tongue. It was an insolent affectation, and I thought it was brilliant. She was doing it right now. It made me feel very cool.

I wasn't in floods anymore. I had taken Denise's lesson to heart. Had learned to love Lee jeans — to thrill at my first pair — and to take new cords home and sew them up the in-seam to exaggerate the bell and make them hip-huggers. I'd taken the seam in so far on the pants that I was wearing that the crack of my bum showed when I sat down. Like it was supposed to. Just like the bottom of my pants were supposed to be chewed up from dragging on the ground and getting trod underfoot.

Suddenly Denise was standing in front of us, kicking at my boy's running shoes and saying hey. Charlie and I looked up. Charlie did her look. Denise was impressed.

"What are you guys doing?" she said. And she almost sounded vaguely deferential. As if she wanted to play with us or something.

"We're just hanging," I said, supporting Charlie's measured silence. "We're looking for some acid. Do you know where we could get acid?"

Now Denise was interested. "Acid?" She said. "I wouldn't mind doing that. I don't know where to get it. Somebody might come by here."

That's what we thought, too. And the three of us settled in to wait for the appearance of potential dealers, or friends of dealers, or people in the know or anybody that wanted to spend an early spring afternoon at a mall in Scarborough hanging around making a wee scene for everyone and looking for some drugs.

I was shy of Denise, but Charlie knew her tough younger brother and got along with him. Charlie boasted about how much we loved acid. Talked about some trips she'd had. None of it was true.

Denise talked about her boyfriend. How they were breaking up. How bloated she got on the pill. She watched people go by with a sad expression on her face. Denise looked tired.

Finally it was late afternoon, almost evening, and we'd hardly seen anybody we even knew. We decided to continue our search at the arena. The rumour was that Gordie Reynolds would come by there some time in the early evening with the goods.

The sun was going down and it was getting colder. I was stiffening with cold in my blazer — it was getting hard to move my hands — and Charlie kept turning to me and chattering her teeth on purpose. We found another bench outside the arena and waited, shivering on the wooden slats. We watched parents emerging with children, walking to their cars. They looked over at us disapprovingly.

Soon, across the parking lot, we saw them coming. Even from a distance, we could see that it was Gordie Reynolds, in a lumberjack shirt, carrying a large paper bag. His entourage was similarly attired and they were all striding across the field toward us. We got off the bench and waited beside it, as if the meeting was prearranged. As if Gordie Reynolds had agreed to meet us at this hour, this place.

Up close, Gordie's face was so hideously scarred by acne that the flesh looked intentionally gouged out. He had red hair and opaque blue eyes. When Gordie sat down on the bench, tossed his hair and looked straight at me, I felt as if I'd never seen anyone so evil and ugly. The guys positioned themselves around him, talking and leaning. Denise and Charlie and I said nothing. Gordie stuck his chin out and said,

"You want something? Dime bags? Angel dust? MDA?"

"Acid?" I asked, feeling like he wasn't real, like he was some sort of mythic and grotesque apparition. But the guy standing beside him looked cute.

"Sure," Gordie said, and reached into the bag and pulled out a piece of paper. It was stamped with three-eyed toads. "How many?" he asked, then tore off three bits of paper and took our money in exchange.

Denise, Charlie and I decided to go back to our place and take it. On the way, I suddenly heard someone calling my name.

"Sarah!"

We turned around to see Gordie Reynolds and his gang following us. "Sarah!" they called again, and my heart leaped and I forgot all about how much Gordie scared me. I was thrilled to think this gang of guys — years older than I was — had taken such an interest in me, that they had taken the time to learn my name and were now following me home like love-sick suitors.

We let them catch up with us. At home, Martha flipped out. The guys were out back, laughing loudly. Get those creeps away from here, she said. I was mildly surprised at her lack of interest in a group of older guys in jeans and leather jackets. Was she jealous?

Denise, Charlie and I each took a tab of the three-eyed toad. I turned to Charlie after we swallowed and said,

"Isn't it cool? We're doing LSD." Charlie suddenly cried out — "LSD! — I thought we were doing acid!"

Denise burst out laughing, "That's what acid is!"

Charlie's eyes widened. She followed me outside whispering, "But I don't wanna do LSD, Sarah."

Too late.

Outside, somehow, the sun was not yet down, and one of the guys had helped himself to the mug my father kept handy for dousing flames when he was barbequing.

"Here!" One of them said, extending the mug to me. It looked as if it was filled with beer. "Have a drink on us, Sarah!" They laughed.

"No thanks." I was too shy to take a drink.

They tossed it on the ground, laughing. One of them had pissed in it. I didn't know if it was funny or not. Denise seemed to be trying to catch the eye of a guy in the corner. She clearly liked him.

Charlie grabbed me. "I'm going," she said.

Where are you going?

"I'm gonna go find Nigel," she said. "I don't like these guys."

I didn't get it. These guys were way cooler than Nigel. These guys had five-o'clock shadows and loose-fitting jeans. These guys looked like they could beat somebody up if they needed to. Like they would know how to defend themselves. Not like me. These guys looked powerful — good people to have on your side.

One of these guys came up to me. He had dark eyes and a loose grin. "Hey!" he said. "You should try some of this shit too. It's MDA — it's amazing!" and he handed me a cap.

I took it, but I slipped it into my pocket for later. Behind him, Martha was standing in the screen door making rude gestures.

"I guess we can't stay here," I said. Denise was too enthralled by the whole crowd to ask why.

We headed back to the arena. Along the way, I started to get a surge of energy. I felt my stiff muscles loosen up. I felt almost athletic. Like I wanted to leap and run.

Soon the guys were setting off firecrackers in the parking lot, while I leapt up on cement lampposts, spun and marveled at my gracefulness. Never had Scarborough seemed so beautiful. The sky was a deep jewel blue, and our voices echoed like they were already memories. People came running out of the arena to catch us and we ran — me — me! Scrambling fearlessly over chain link fences, and laughing with pleasure. We ended up at a plaza surrounded by apartments. Denise and I held one another by the arms and spun. The tops of the buildings made kaleidoscopic designs on the night sky. The guys watched us, and talked to one another.

"Hey!" Mr. Loose Grin said, "We're gonna have a party. You two are especially invited. Wanna come?"

Of course we wanted to come. The air felt like silk on my arms. His face seemed to lift and shift and settle down again.

"Sarah!"

That was Nigel! Where was Nigel? Right beside me. Nigel!

"What are you doing?" he said.

Charlie was with him. She was standing over by the Mac's Milk store. She looked stuck in place. She leaned into the brick facing with a terrified expression on her face.

"I'm going to a party."

"With those guys? Don't go."

"Come on!" said Denise impatiently. But I didn't care how impatient Denise was. I was deliriously happy and drunk with sensations.

"Charlie needs you," said Nigel. "She's in trouble. Look at her."

I looked at Charlie — at the intensity of her position — and started laughing. I felt like I might never stop laughing, and that possibility created the edge of a new kind of fear inside me.

"Come with us," Nigel said and I decided to go.

Denise looked at Nigel. She looked him up and down. It seemed to me the pupils in her eyes had swollen to meet the edge of her irises. Her eyes were completely black.

The streetlights suddenly flashed on. A new drama was beginning.

"Come on!" said somebody from Gordie's gang. They were already walking down the street away from us.

"Come with us!" I said to Denise, brazen with the inventiveness of my new decision.

Denise looked at Nigel.

"I don't know," she said. "He looks pretty goofy."

"Fuck you." Said Nigel.

"Fuck you." Said Denise. "I'm going to the party."

And she left. Nigel looked at me.

"You're completely wrecked," he said.

"I know," I said — feeling a sharp pleasure rising inside me at his concern. It excited me so much; I wanted to start laughing again.

"I shouldn't have let her go."

"Charlie's over there!" Now I did start laughing.

"No. I mean that tough girl you were with just now," he said, "I should've talked her into staying."

Nigel walked over to a corner post and started banging his head against it. His action created reciprocating trails of light in the air. Even Charlie watched in fascination. When he turned to look at me, he'd gouged his forehead and it was bleeding. The blood strobed across his face; the stripes swelled and receded. Nigel was tribal. From Nigel's mouth came flaming words. Promises of redemption.

"Don't you know who those guys are? Don't you know what they'll do?"

I didn't.

"Do you even know where they're going? Maybe we can call the police or something."

I didn't. I could see the group of them in the distance. I couldn't tell which figure was Denise's. She was lost in the crowd. I walked over to check out Charlie.

"I don't like it," she said. "I just don't like it."

And she started to wail. Her face bent and broke into cubic dimensions. I saw Nigel swaying toward us. Going down on the pavement like a hacked tree. All of us. Head down, feet up — into the abyss. I thought it was beautiful.

I Know Angelo

My mother only ever sent me one postcard. It was of Nietzche and it had this joke: I think about you all the time, but the penicillin helps. I kept it for a long time and threw it out when I got pregnant. I realized it didn't mean a thing.

Angelo's in his leather jacket, his hips leaning over the restaurant counter. He's missing a tooth in front from rubbing coke on his gums. He flirts with the counter girl so she'll give him a little glass of bleach.

You think I don't know about Angelo. I know all about him. If you think I don't know about him, then you don't know about me.

Angelo asks for a job in every restaurant we walk into. Mostly there's never any work but they pour him free coffee for trying. I watch him walk past the picture of boats and turquoise blue beach scenes of Greece laminated with scotch tape on the wall, going down between the tables like he's on roller skates. He heads with his briefcase to the girls' bathroom at the back of the restaurant.

Most cowboys only smoke cigarettes between their toes nowadays. I only stopped using junk because I was pregnant. I get lonely waiting for Angelo to shoot up.

Angelo pulls on the plywood door of the girls' bathroom too hard. There's a poster of a belly dancer on the door. The picture is rolling up so that she looks like she's scratching her leg.

When we were kids in Virginia, my mother used to disappear into the bathroom for hours. We could hear her chewing on her toothbrush hard. If she came out with red lipstick on, we knew she was going out.

Looking out the restaurant window, the stars are plunked like pennies in the middle of the sky. I'm too scared to wish for anything.

I sat in the window eating a block of cheese with a knife. It was easy to spot my mother. She used to like to dance when a car passed playing music to make us laugh. She liked skinny black boots and black suit jackets. She would sew stars on the lapels. I used to think she looked like Abraham Lincoln.

My family used to pick cotton before the Civil War and then they picked cotton after the Civil War too.

The souvlaki tastes as good as cigarettes. Angelo's in the bathroom long enough that I know he's getting high, his pants falling down over his ass, trying to wake up a vein from under its comforter of bruises and scabs. He's the mad scientist of the modern age, re-inventing the China Town fire cracker.

I've been carrying this little Chekov book around with me. There's a Kleenex marking the third page, and when I try to read it there is the feeling those lucky pennies on the sidewalk are your eyelids. It makes me feel like Angelo and I are only just around the corner from being classy people. That out the corner of my eye, Angelo looks like he's wearing a suit. That out of the corner of my eye, he looks like the guy who landed Oscar Wilde in prison.

My sister would get nervous when my mother was gone. I would keep cleaning her glasses with a dirty cloth to make her happy. When the lens came out she started to cry. I wore the empty frames so that I couldn't see her out of the corner of my eye.

When Angelo is love-stricken, he will chew on my stockings. He will dance all over the mattress in an undershirt.

His wet hair in the morning feels like a cat's paw that's stepped in the milk bowl. Waking up, finding each other's toes under the blanket, was like finding noodles at the bottom of the sink. I got up in the morning and stood against the wall, breathing deeply. The wall was very thin and the neighbours were smoking pot. I would get high, guilt-free.

Angelo said from behind I looked like I could be in a magazine. Sometimes if I was naked, we'd get shy just looking at me.

The landlord said if we don't want our walls "flesh-coloured" then to stop smoking. Angelo hated the smell of pot. He threw his blue boots at the wall on either side of me like a knife thrower.

My father said Angelo and I will be what's left over after the nuclear bomb.

Angelo didn't like to be naked long in the morning. He was beautiful while he slept. Angelo had a red bruise on his shoulder where he claimed he was hit by an ambulance. There was an orangish ring around his nipple which sort of looked like a ring of dirt.

Angelo was raped by a drug dealer he owed three hundred dollars to. He tells everyone he was hit by an ambulance. Since then he was insecure about me looking at his body when he's not looking at it.

My sisters didn't say anything when I pulled our mattresses out into the living room and put them together. We found a string of Christmas lights in the closet and taped them to the ceiling. We hear them coming unstuck one by one at night. The dirty plates that are scattered all over the floor will catch them like raindrops.

Angelo has been my boyfriend since I was fourteen. I used to know everything that Angelo did. I used to be able to guess which street corner he would be on, flaunting his little hips like the Ace of Spades. We met in high school and learned everything there was to know about English class and stealing and prostitution and being in love together. We punched it in to our veins and scars and eyelids. We punched it into our brains.

Angelo punched me in the face because he thought I was holding out on him and I was. I was twenty years old and I went into the bathroom with a thirteen-year-old boy who wore a lampshade on his head. The thirteen-year-old put coke on my inner thigh and then snorted. It felt like all my pubic hair was falling out. He kept fondling my tit while counting out his change on the back of the toilet.

Me being the queen and Angelo being king, we used to have sex in front of this old lawyer for some extra money. That's the only time we had sex. We had to save up for then. We didn't have any sex left in our knees. We were like weak batteries: you turn off the walkman for a while hoping for one more rock and roll song even though it sounds all warped and slow. We would show up on the lawyer's balcony like monkeys trembling in our T-shirts. Every time the lawyer would open the door, Angelo would scream STICK EM UP and jump up and down, his fingers pointed like guns. That's how I got pregnant, from an old guy with his hand in his pants. Shuddling the chair to get a better look, a framed photo of Claudia Shiffer over his head.

And I remember exactly the moment I conceived.

My tights were all torn apart at the crotch. It felt like warm chicken soup. Angelo's underwear were rubbing against my ankles like string beans. His nipples were like pansies. He was taller than me so I kept being able to kiss them. His lips hung like toilet paper floating in the sink. His breath was like if you could buy morning in a can at the supermarket. I always said I love you a hundred times when we made love.

And according to the magazines I was still using heroin while I was almost perfectly sure I was pregnant.

All my clothes stank. My sister was mad at me for wearing my mother's black shirt with yellow orchids for pyjamas. I threw all my mother's clothes out the window. I even took off the shirt I was wearing. I put my thumbs over my nipples, watching the shirt fall down to the sidewalk like a gasp.

After we got up, Angelo left to go to the park with these yellow clog type shoes. They were almost high heels.

Under his T-shirt you could see tattoos of birds flying all over the place on his chest. They flew by like I blinked too much. There was a tattoo that said my name, CHLOE, on his arm but I never read it. I bit on his lip like a bite of an orange. He didn't look in my eyes when he was thinking about drugs. Angelo was wearing this red Che Guevera T-shirt. I think Che Guevara would've had Angelo shot.

I hated being alone in the apartment. I felt a chill every time Angelo left, playing the xylophone on me. The ends of my sleeves were wet from doing dishes.

There was phlegm from a stranger's cough on the ceiling.

Outside the window it seemed like there were crows even though there weren't any crows.

I went down the stairs with no socks. There was this shiver in my spine. Four months since my last hit and I still get that feeling that someone is hitting my note somewhere. The landlord gave me a bag of oranges on the way down the stairs and I had to carry them around all day. I couldn't eat oranges. I could only eat greasy food. Food that tasted like light reflected off the street, food that had been bundled in a dirty sweater to keep warm and fed to me from a spoon with Angelo's spit.

We were afraid to open the fridge because my sister saw a cockroach in it a few days before. I sang the Italian love song from *Lady and the Tramp* over spaghetti so it didn't seem like we were eating the same thing every night.

Waiting still for Angelo, I give in and order a Budweiser. It's like sunshine. I drink it with both hands wrapped around the bottle. These guys call to me from the back. I used to put these safety pins at the bottom of my skirt so that when I danced it looked like I was a flapper. I'd do anything to get attention.

Sometimes after he'd leave the apartment, I would follow Angelo to the park. My hair flying around me with this distant feeling, like it was going all the way to New York State.

Angelo has this way of standing when he figured out a way to get junk, standing like he was comfortable having staples in his toes. He didn't recognize me. I sat on a bench watching him. He opened a briefcase in front of him. A kid threw a quarter in. Angelo leaned over and pretended to spread a deck of cards on the ground. He played this game of solitaire with invisible cards. A drug dealer walked by, bent down, and took a curled bill from the corner of the briefcase and replaced it with a flap of dope.

Sometimes Angelo carries around a duffel bag with a glove and a baseball bat instead of a briefcase. He convinced the cops he's going to a baseball game. Angelo is one of those thieves who just smashes doors open with his boots. Angelo is one of those thieves that carries around a baseball bat in case he has to smash your head open. Angelo is one of those thieves who just doesn't give a fuck about anyone. He would kill your kid to be sure of his fix. I swear to God without any hesitation that he would.

When I walked back into the apartment, Angelo was already there. He was washing the dishes with orange rubber gloves. He stood there holding up the door frame like a halo. He was in an Iggy Pop mood. He was smiling and had the radio on loud. I was afraid he was going to start dancing. When he dances he knocks everything over. He was excited about the oranges. He put them into his shirt like tits. Then, just like that, he sank backwards into a chair on the nod and I was jealous of him. I wanted to be the stoned girl in a chair.

God didn't give me enough to get by on. Dope makes me live on what I don't have.

It was like lying in a doll house. There was only little furniture. The windows were made of thin plexiglass. You crawled into a miniature bed. Then one day maybe you wouldn't wake up. One day you would actually be a doll. And that was good, too.

I was in detox for three weeks. You know what the worse feeling was five times worse than morning sickness? The worse feeling in the world was a fetus kicking junk inside of you. To have it squirming and kicking and you think you hear it scream-ing: you fucking whore, you bitch mother, give me my fix, you ugly wench, filthy cocksucker, lesbian bitch, go suck some more dick and get me some junk.

But you get over it. It takes three years at least to stop thinking about it everyday.

The social worker came in and asked me a question about my mother. The ceiling was the colour of a fly's wing. I shrugged with my thumb kept stuck in my eye so I wouldn't cry. The social worker said it's normal for girls to have bad memories about their own childhood when they are pregnant.

There was no toilet paper left. We wiped our asses with rags and left them in the bathtub afraid of what to do next.

My mother hadn't come home for three weeks. We kept calling the phone number that gives you the time.

Angelo comes out of the girls' bathroom. His lips are gray. His polyester collars are like fancy goldfish tails. He keeps licking his thumb like he's about to smooth something down on my face, but he can't decide what. When he gets like this, he always wants to touch my belly. He goes for the missing button on my kimono.

I only ever wanted crazy love, the kind in a Van Morrison song I heard in the back of the Toyota eating candies and driving out from the circle of light at the 7/11 and into the wilderness. All the locks on the car doors were shut and the windows closed — like being in the most secure suitcase of the soul. My mom was frantic in the front seat pointing out where she saw a UFO the night before.

I love that. I love when Angelo gets soft and sweet on me. Soft like a Q-tip. Soft like the crazy in his head. I wake up out of a stupor and he's putting these petals in my hair with his thick stoned fingers.

I like that he makes me feel like a perfect curl of hair, like all my words are pastries lined up in the window at the bakery.

Angelo is the thing you leave out of love as you get older.

I want the baby to be like Angelo. He leans over to rub my belly and spills a shot glass of bleach on the floor and it sounds like rain on top of a car when you're kissing in it.

MICHAEL V. SMITH

What We Wanted

Barry Somer's body went from screaming round the pool, knocking on foreheads, swinging from the shower rail, and flinging boogers, to doing nothing at all, to disappearing, to dying. When he was eleven a dump truck flattened him against its grill and then the crumpled boy that was Barry Somer slipped under the truck and disappeared. That was when I looked away.

The crowd of neighbours who came out to help, or gawk, or bring their kids back into the house saw the smashed and tattered body that was Barry, but I didn't. I was the last to see Barry as Barry and not as a broken mash of whatever bones and skin and hair death leaves behind. And if I'm right, I was the last thing he saw too.

They can say what they want, but I wasn't haunted by Barry's death. That was something of a relief. It was the living Barry that woke me up with night sweats and had me vomiting two out of three meals. I never told them. In the twenty years since, I have never told another living thing.

We were boys together. When my mother wanted me to join a sports team to impress my father — I was a miserably underweight gangle of arms and legs — she claimed all I needed was exercise to grow meat on my ribs. The weight sounded appealing. I picked swimming because it was the only non-contact sport we could agree on. We bought a pair of baggy green swim trunks at K-Mart and reserved a place for me over the phone. I was moderately excited. I had visions of myself heftier, doing elaborate dives which I would choreograph in my head in slow motion. I would touch my nose with my feet. I'd be amazing.

My first day of lessons started after supper on a Tuesday. Mom decided to make something light so I wouldn't get cramps, but the cold cuts and salad irritated my dad. They bickered until I told them swimming lessons weren't worth going to if it only made them fight. My mom looked at the digital clock on the microwave and packed up our plates. "We're late," she said.

As she turned into the parking lot at the community centre, halfway through a cigarette, Mom sighed, "You could help me out a little here. Is your father doing all this for nothing?" She gestured at the brick wall ahead of us. I shrugged and opened the car door.

She took a slow drag on her cigarette. "Sometimes, I don't think you like us," she added, chipping at her nail polish.

Unsure what she meant, I smiled nicely, trying to convince us it was a joke, and closed the door. I can see she thought I was cruel. Perhaps I was. I didn't like them much. I didn't like their drinking and the scenes my mother made. I didn't like the way they could bellow at each other and, mid-sentence, how my mother could pick up the ringing telephone and sound sweet as heaven. My life felt small and cramped. We were neither financially comfortable nor well adjusted. I hated my body. I invented friends at school whom my mother asked to meet. I told threatening classmates I had an older, bigger brother who went to a school across town. I lived a lie to protect myself from my parents and another to save me from kids at recess.

Walking into the community centre with my swim trunks and towel in a plastic grocery bag, I saw three boys in ball caps goofing around. We'd signed me up for an all-boys group because Dad said it would be more competitive but, oddly, the swim instructor turned out to be a woman. Jenny was tall and lean, with unusually rough hands, and long chlorine-blonde hair around a tight little happy face. She was pretty enough, but more a failed movie version of a lifeguard than an actual bombshell.

My mother came in after me and filled out the forms, signed her cheque, and said she'd be back for me. "Have fun," she coached, tousling my hair, which she'd never done before, in a move designed to make me look the part of a sporty kid.

I had never seen a public indoor pool. Dad didn't swim, which made paying for an hour at an indoor pool an unnecessary luxury. Swimming either involved a trip to the river or a three block walk to the local park's gated and crowded cement pool open for the height of summer. As the door to the change room closed behind me, I knew again that I had fooled myself into thinking things could change. I was sick with fear at what the next eight weeks held in store for me. We were sixteen pre-pubescent boys who already seemed to be grouping off into cool and uncool, in a cement room, without windows, with a large shower area, a row of freshly-painted toilet stalls, and two sets of urinals, kid height and adult.

What I never realized until standing in that mess of boys was that we would all be taking our clothes off, unseen by the instructor. I was already trying to devise ways to get out of swimming. Jenny could be dangerously careless or the pool water could burn my skin. I considered faking an accident, only I was fearful I might drown for real.

Perhaps Barry noticed a look of dread on me right away. Perhaps he saw doubts across my face, but I didn't notice him when I came in. I have no idea where he was in the mix of boys pulling their shirts off. At that age, I tried not to look at boys. By comparison, my own skin felt softer, unconvincing, fake. I wasn't real like other kids were real. I didn't exist the way other boys made space for themselves in the world. It was and is a truth I stand by, that when boys take their clothes off, they *need* to be noticed and respected, which paradoxically makes them cruel. Watching them was both taboo and what they dared you to do.

I headed straight through the change room with barely a glance at anyone. I locked myself into a stall with a loud click of the deadbolt and slipped my trunks on.

When I came out, Barry Somer was waiting for me, holding up my pale blue briefs. He'd grabbed them from under the cubicle without my noticing. "Cute," he said, smiling. "They're like cotton candy."

He was a big kid, big in his hands and feet, with a thick

neck, which made him seem more muscled than he was. He had clean hair which looked freshly cut. From first sight, I knew he wasn't menacing, not mean, but restless. He was a nice attractive kid. It was just the two of us in the change room's white tiled bathroom area and he was smiling a killer smile at me.

"Where do you live? I'm across the street."

"On Carlisle."

"Which house?"

"It's yellow, why?"

He shrugged and handed me my underwear, no jokes, no teasing, no humiliation, which dropped my heart to the lower depths of my stomach. With that bit of generosity, he was capable of convincing me to do just about anything. The look on his face said he knew it, and he couldn't wait.

I took my flimsy briefs from him and tucked them into a leg of my pants and rolled them up. Next week, I'd bring a knapsack with a zipper to keep better hold on my stuff.

When my father asked me later that night, as he turned the ground for my mother's flower bed, how swimming went, I choked on my plan to get out of it.

"Great," I said.

"How many laps did you do?"

"We don't do laps."

He looked puzzled, not at me, but at the shovel sticking into the dirt. "What do you do?"

"We hold our breath. And dog-paddle. And the dead

man's float." I thought he knew all this. "We're just learning. It's a beginner's class."

"But you can swim," he said. He looked me in the eye with a wrinkled brow.

"You have to do the first class," I lied, authoritatively, "before you start doing laps."

"Oh. So you'll be doing laps when you're done?"

"Next week," I lied again. There seemed no point trying to explain the organization of levels and testing and badges. "We'll do lots of laps," I said and he went back to gardening.

Perhaps I'm more like my father than I care to admit. I don't like children. When they begin to talk in full sentences, when school comes into their lives and they associate with each other, their minds change. I'm convinced they warp, betrayed by the trust they placed in their parents. How could we not resent being abandoned to a room full of noisy, spoiled strangers, each wanting to be cute and loved and necessary at the expense of every other demanding kid in the room? How to retaliate? How do we lose our fear and begin to feel secure in our abandonment? We create roles for each other grounded in shame, guilt, humiliation, and fear. Those who invent the harshest situations for their peers are the ones who feel most secure.

Barry Somer had a talent for making himself feel better. Our first week there, he convinced a slim hairy kid, Arvid, to hand over his retainer case. Barry quickly slipped the retainer on his own teeth and sang a poor, but effective, rendition of *Happy Birfday*. The jokes weren't particularly clever, but they came from nowhere. It was his spontaneity that fascinated, which saw us waiting for the next prank at the same time as dreading his attention.

In the third lesson, Barry and I were paired up as floating partners. Jenny showed the group of us how we were to support each other under the lower back as we tried to relax, with our eyes closed, and float face up. While holding her whistle, Jenny explained, "Now the person standing will lower his arms when the floater says, 'Okay,' at which point the floater will be held on top of the water. It's real easy if you just relax."

My cousins had tried this trick with me a few times the previous summer. I wasn't expecting much.

"You ready?" Barry smiled at me. "You're first." His hand underwater absently toyed with the drawstring hanging out of his trunks.

Jenny walked towards us, stopping just to our left, checking to see if everyone was in place. "All set?" she asked, and blew her whistle.

As Barry extended his arms in front of him, I let my legs give way and was lifted into a cradled position next to his chest. He was warm. It wasn't what I expected. It wasn't scary, it wasn't nerve-wracking, it wasn't exciting. With Barry's arms under me I felt oddly safe. He was comfortable. I opened my eyes to see him looking at me, inches above my face.

"I got you," he said, so I closed them again, giving my

okay and trusting my body to do what it had to. Barry let me go. My skin felt cold in two lines across my back where his arms had been.

The water gurgled in my ears and lapped loosely at my temples as my hair swirled about my head. The thick smell of chlorine settled in my nose. My arms and legs felt both heavy and light. The more I relaxed muscles, the more I could feel my own weight held atop the water. If I needed him, Barry was there to catch me before I sank. With the dead man's float, you face down, like you've given up, but with my face to the ceiling, I felt hopeful, like I was waiting for something, like at any moment I might rise up out of the water and fly.

With a sudden bleat of Jenny's whistle, time was up. "Good!" she called. I stood, feeling a little disoriented, carrying my weight. "Now let's switch places. The rest of you float."

Barry punched my shoulder. "You did good. Don't drop me," he said, and jumped into my arms with a splash of water. He hitched his arms around my neck so that even if I let him go, I'd still be supporting us both, then he proceeded to bounce. "Am I heavy? Heavy? Can you hold me?"

"That's enough, Barry, get ready," Jenny said, the whistle between her teeth. As she traveled the width of the pool again to ensure we were all set up, Barry stretched himself out.

"Ahhh," he sighed then smiled at me. He was heavier in the water than I thought he'd be. I was wondering how heavy I had been and was secretly hoping he wouldn't float at all, when he whispered, "You wearing your blue underwear?"

I squinted at him, confused. "Not under my bathing suit."

"No, today. I want to know if you got them here today?"

"What for?" I asked.

"I want to try them on," he said as the whistle blew. He closed his eyes, stretched himself out and said, "Okay." I let him go and stepped back. He floated butt-heavy at first, then managed to relax into it more, though he took his breath in rapid gulps.

When the lesson came to a close, I headed for the change room. Barry was right behind me. Inside, I took my bag off the bench and walked into the bathroom area. Another kid, Stevie, with acne, changed in a stall too, which made me feel less like a freak, though Stevie raced to be the first kid in and out of the room. When I arrived each week, he was already in the pool, or waiting on the tiled deck, his swim trunks on and a towel wrapped around his shoulders.

Stevie was in the stall at the far end of the room when I walked in. I could hear him bumping around. I chose a stall mid-way, pushed the door open and entered. By the time I turned around, Barry was there. I just looked at him, my heart doing laps in my chest. "No," I said, barely even whispering.

He glanced from the doorway to the last stall where Stevie was still shuffling, and mouthed, "Come on," like he was about to get seriously caught, so I stepped back, letting Barry in.

As he pulled cotton boxers from his bag and held them out, he motioned with his free hand for me to give up my briefs. What was I supposed to do with the boxers? I wasn't putting on someone else's underwear. Barry bugged his eyes out, making a frustrated face, to hurry me up. Both of us were dripping wet. He was nearly standing on top of me, a towel around his neck and mine about my waist. If I couldn't talk to him, I didn't know how to get him out of the stall without giving him my briefs. And, yes, I wanted to see him do it; I wanted to see Barry Somer in my underwear.

I handed them over. Without hesitating, he dropped his swimsuit and stepped out of the legs. I caught sight of his dink, redder than mine, when he hunched over and slipped his first foot through the leg. I could smell the chlorine in his hair. He didn't bother to dry off.

We heard a metal door squeak open and Stevie pad by, in too much of a rush to notice the number of feet in our stall. Barry winked at me, grinning. "I like them," he said. I grimaced like I didn't know what he was talking about. He looked down at himself, packed into my underwear, with wet marks spotting the cloth. I was excited, and thankful to have the towel around my waist.

Motioning to the boxers in my hand he coaxed, "Put them on."

I frowned, shaking my head. For one thing, I had an erection. And we'd taken long enough changing as it was. My mother wasn't going to wait forever. Somewhat irrational though it may have been, I was terrified she'd see me.

"You gotta do it sometime," he said, and then with a click of the lock, he stepped out of the stall, snatched up his swim trunks, and added, "See ya next week." He toweled his hair, pushing the door closed in my face. A few seconds later, I heard him say as he entered the change room, "That was the longest dump of my life." Somebody laughed.

Meanwhile, I had Barry Somer's underwear in my hand and none of my own to put on. I was late. And felt freaked out. I stuffed his boxers in my bag, dried myself, and dressed, without underwear. I'd get a fresh pair when I got home.

Safely in my room, I closed the door, dropped the knapsack on my bed, and grabbed yesterday's briefs off the floor to put on. I'd no sooner picked up my pants again when there was a knock on my door and Dad came in.

"Your mother wants your wet things," he said. I held my pants in front of me. "You forgot to drop them in the tub."

"I'll bring them," I said.

"Just give it here, I already made the trip," he said, sounding like he wanted to be nice but was actually impatient. "Are they in here?" he asked. He took hold of my bag.

With that, Barry's gray cotton boxers left the safety of my bedroom. I whipped my pants on, visualizing my father holding up a foreign pair of boy's undies and asking me questions I couldn't answer. I had only been seconds behind him, but already Dad was in the bathroom with my mother. When I reached the door, he was just leaving.

The wet swim trunks dropped in the tub as I stepped around Dad. The towel was in Mom's hands, with the boxers lying plainly on top. "What's this?" she asked. She knew I only had briefs; she'd bought every pair I owned.

Dad turned around. I froze. Mom caught my terrified look and turned her back.

"Mom, I said I'll *do* it." I tried to sound thoughtfully exasperated.

"What's what?" Dad asked.

"His underwear's wet too, that's all." Mom hung them over the shower curtain rod, then threw the towel up too. She made a point of not looking at me.

"We were joking around in the change room," I said, trying to sound normal.

"And you got your clothes wet?" Dad asked.

I shrugged. "Boys were throwing water. I was getting dressed."

"Well, that's not such a big deal," he said. Then, as an afterthought, he asked, "How many laps did you do this week?"

I told him fifteen. Last week I'd said ten.

"Good," he said, and I followed him out. If Mom didn't

get me alone right then, I was hoping she'd never come back to ask.

The next week I missed class because my dad had to drive to Caledon to help a guy from work fix his refrigerator. My mom wouldn't take me on the bus, or let me go alone. I didn't think it was in my own best interests to debate; she hadn't confronted me about the boxers. I'd taken them down that night and hung them to dry on the door handle inside my closet, safely out of sight. For two weeks, they were stored between my mattress and box spring, except for the odd time when I took them out to look at. When the time came, I slipped the boxers inside my swim trunks and folded the whole thing over, just in case someone looked in my bag.

Though I insisted I could at least take the bus there, Mom was firmly determined to drive me. Since she'd decided to act like nothing was wrong, I had taken her lead, but the tension only made her petty.

Barry was waiting outside the community centre, doing his best to look nonchalant as he leaned against a concrete post, scratching a rock against the wall. Right away, Mom scowled. "Look at that kid. Be lucky you don't have his parents," she said, pulling our rusty Acadian up to the curb.

I jumped out immediately, before Barry could make any move towards me. "Bye, see ya later," I said cheerily to my mother, then slammed the car door and ran past Barry.

He followed me inside. Safely through the doors and

out of sight of my mother, I turned to Barry. "Do you have them?" He smiled, patting the side of his leg. "Give them to me," I ordered, thinking they were in his pocket.

Taking me by the wrist, he led us across the hall into the girl's change room, which was empty, and into one of their bathroom stalls. There were two rows of them, instead of a wall of urinals. It was a weird feeling, like being in a world gone wrong. "How are we going to get out?" I asked.

Barry giggled. "Through the door."

"What about Jenny? She's gonna change here."

"She's in the pool already."

My stomach was in knots. Barry was breathing heavy enough for me to feel his warm air against my skin. He stood inches away from me. The girl's stalls, painted light green, had an extra dispenser on the wall beside the toilet paper. I felt crowded. "I brought yours," I said. "Let's trade."

As I pulled my bag open, Barry undid the button on his jeans and unzipped them. "What are you doing?" I asked.

"I have them on."

For a second, I had the impression he'd worn them the whole two weeks, but then realized he must not have wanted to carry an extra pair with him, which I thought was smart, though I wasn't able to put his pair on, even with my parents out of the house. "Okay," I said. I turned toward the back of the stall to give him privacy. Though I wanted to see his dink again, I couldn't bring myself to look. There was some general shuffling. I could see him bend over in my peripheral vision and then he stood, silent. It occurred to me that now was the time to turn and hand him the boxers, giving me a chance to peek, but I couldn't bring myself to do it. My stomach roiled and burned in my belly. Taking his boxers, I held them out at my side, waiting. He didn't take them. There was a silence in the bathroom that made me crazy; only the low hum of the pool's filtering system traveled through the walls.

Then he touched me. He set a finger against my arm. I turned, with my heart pounding, afraid of what he might make me do. He was still in my briefs, with his pants on the floor beside him. "I like you," he said. There was an awkward smile on his face. As I stood there, unmoving, he played with his belly button. He was trying to explain something neither of us understood. "I think you're pretty," he continued. "My brother has a girlfriend and they make out. I kissed this girl on the bus once, with everyone watching. She gave me the tongue. She didn't really like me though. You have nice eyes. Sometimes my mother wears make up on her eyes, but my dad doesn't like it. Do you have a brother? Or a sister?"

I couldn't stop myself from sounding belligerent. "No," I snapped, unnerving him.

And he said again, "You're pretty," which made me angry. We were eleven — we knew we could lie to each other to get what we wanted, but I didn't want to be talked into kissing him. I couldn't kiss a boy voluntarily. *Was he stupid?* I wondered. *Could he be that stupid?* I hated him offering me this in such a way that I wasn't allowed to accept. I hated the way he was so desperate to convince. Had he only humiliated me in private, had he insisted then, with force, with threatening intent, we'd have both been happy.

With Barry's boxers out of my bedroom and my own underwear safely back in the dresser drawer, I felt like myself again, safe. The only threat Barry posed was what trouble he might cause each Tuesday night, and I intended to ignore him. I imagined how it would sting him, to see that I was uninterested. Done.

It was three days later, Friday afternoon. My mother had sent my dad to buy two trees to plant along the back fence because she wanted something to look at from their bedroom window. Dad wanted dogwood he'd seen advertised in the paper, but Mom said no. She heard the car pull up, the trunk door slam shut, but Dad didn't come in. She went to the window and called out, "What did you get?"

He said something that made her yell, "What the hell for?" and I heard him shout back, "They were on sale." That's when I figured I was better off at the park. I hung out on the monkey bars until some teenage girls showed up with their boyfriends trailing behind.

I was gone an hour. When I got back, Mom was at the sink rinsing a shirt she'd stained at lunch. "Your friend was here on his bike," she said, very matter-of-fact.

"Who?" I asked.

"That kid from swimming." Her tone said she wasn't

impressed; it was obvious to her who was sending his underwear home with her son. "I told him you were at the park. He's coming back."

"He's not my friend," I said sourly.

Mom gave the shirt a twist and wrung out a stream of water. "Then how does he know where you live? You shouldn't tell just anybody our address. It isn't safe."

I shrugged.

"We're having supper in an hour; he's got to be gone by then," she said, turning on the tap to end the discussion.

Anxious, I decided to wait on the front lawn. He wasn't coming in my house. I wouldn't even let him on the property. When he pulled up on his bike, I'd tell him he had to go home because my grandmother was sick, or I hated him, or my parents didn't like me hanging out with losers. I was busy devising the fastest way to get rid of him as my stomach lurched with anticipation. Barry Somer came to see me. *Me.*

At the end of the block, a bicycle came round the corner. There he was, Barry Somer, in his blue and green striped T-shirt and head phones stuck over his ears, biking down my street, passing along the sidewalk on the other side of the road. I called out to him, but he didn't hear me, so I waved. As he looked over, he grinned and my stomach clenched tighter.

Then, like careful planning, a dump truck turned the corner. Directly across from me, a moving van was parked on the road at the Kennedy's, blocking Barry's view of the street. And the thoughts ran through my head, the various feelings: this dump truck, that boy, this heartsickness, that bike, this hand of mine, that driver, that truck, that boy. I decided on impulse. If he made it across the road before the truck sped past, I would give in to what we wanted and be Barry's fair and hungry equal, or I could see it all go to pieces with one simple accident and never be plagued by Barry Somer again. I motioned him over.

For the split second of impact I froze, Barry and I both breathless. I didn't believe he'd be hit. I didn't believe it could happen until it did. For a second, he was a cartoon: arms splayed, his mouth a black spot, and one rubber leg swinging under the truck. The bike bent around the other leg.

Then, easily, Barry Somer was dead.

I bolted for the house just as my father raced out onto the porch. Behind me was the noise of squealing tires, the truck's horn and scraping metal. In my few seconds to the door, I tried to gauge by Dad's manner if he had witnessed me with Barry or just Barry getting hit. Remembering back, all I see is a man who would betray nothing. He was a grim stone-faced father, with hands that shook, racing to the road where a boy lay dead. I ran through the front door, into my room, and dove under the bed in a sweat.

From that day forward, I disappeared, I was free. My parents forgot me, what they wanted from me and what they wished I was. So I come forward now because I can, to tell you, I killed a boy. I live with that, with perhaps less difficulty than you might expect, because it has prepared me, hasn't it, for the way we love one another?

STUART ROSS

The Interview

My feet have touched more pavement than dirt. When I say pavement, I refer to everything that is not dirt. When I say dirt, I refer to everything that is not pavement. Actually, I must expand on this. When I say pavement, I include the floor of my father's car, I include the monkey bars in the park, I include the hardwood surface of my bedroom floor, I include the carpet in my aunt's living room and den. I also have to throw in escalators, linoleum, and the endless metal fields of my dreams. When I say dirt, I refer to water and to grass and to sand. I must include mud, which is a combination of two of the above elements. Also the emerging roots of old trees, the trunks of trees, and rocks. Rocks are very important. I've spent a bit of time on rocks and it was quality time. But I've spent more time on pavement. It feels so much more molecular. Like flesh. Which is something I haven't categorized yet, but I think maybe it's half dirt and half pavement.

*

Where had I gotten to? Oh, yeah. I'm eleven years old and Larry Stein is sitting on my chest with his hands pinning my arms down. I am lying on my back on pavement, and I'm trying to squirm my way out of this. A crowd begins to form around us, and I see Debbie Larker. She is puny and has dark hair, and her mother is missing several fingers. Surely I would someday marry her. I found this out — about her mother's fingers — when I went to her house to work on a geography project we were forced to do together. And now Debbie is watching me lie on my back under Larry Stein, so I have to try to act nonchalant, to appear in control. I have an idea and I put it into action. "Larry," I say, "you're such a homo. Get off of me." Larry's grip on my arms loosens a bit, and as the circulation returns to them, I can feel all the little pebbles that have become embedded in my elbows. I peer beyond Larry's shoulder, but I can no longer see Debbie among the spectators. "You're the homo," Larry says to me. "A double homo." I wiggle about a bit, try to rock from side to side, but I can't get out from under Larry, and when I try to reach up and shove him off, his fingers dig into my arms again. I have many loyal friends, and they are sprinkled through the crowd, joining in the growing chant, which deals with what a double homo I am.

*

When I lose my temper, I'm careful not to smash things. I would get in so much trouble, and also I might destroy something I'll later miss. So what I do is shove my furniture around. I have a bed, and this I shove diagonally across the room, knocking over a chair. I push my desk away from the wall, as well, and slide it in front of the door. This way, my brother can't get in and see me crying. My bookcase is attached to the wall, so I can't move it, but I take down great armloads of books and stack them on the floor. I'm careful, because I don't want to wreck their covers. I also pull my dresser out of the corner and turn it carefully on its side. When I'm done shoving everything around, I flop myself onto my bed and become like jelly. I sob and yell into my pillow, and it is my room. A room I have control over. I wiggle and wobble on my bed, until my tears have run dry and I have fallen asleep, into the world of endless metal fields.

*

I think we've reached my seventeenth year, or perhaps my thirty-fourth. Regardless, what happens is my self-esteem begins to mistakenly build and I can actually talk to people and occasionally look them in the eye. So an old man comes into the library where I'm working, and he asks if I play chess. I guess I look now like the type who plays chess. I look down at his fingers, and they are thin and bent in strange directions. I figure he must be good. I tell him I play, but not well. We agree to meet in the park beside the library later on, and he will bring his chessboard. We do this for years, every day playing chess for hours, so that I have to sneak in through my bedroom window so my parents don't get angry. (I must be seventeen.) The old man's name is Schaeffer, Mr. Schaeffer, and as we play, he tells me about his ailing wife, in his thick German accent. He loves her very much and his eyes water as he talks. His eyes are always watering. I wonder if when you get that old, everything just seems so sad. I become a stronger player with every game of chess. Mr. Schaeffer loans me books to study, by Znosko-Borovsky and Reuben Fine and Emanuel Lasker. I study the classic openings, learn about the strength of the measly pawn, go through the end games until I know them inside-out. But still, after three years, the score is six hundred and twelve games to zero. Since my self-esteem is so enormous, I feel I have a chance of catching up. It's only a matter of time. But before I have the opportunity, a strange thing happens. An old woman meets me in the park. She asks my name. I tell her. "Klaus is dead," she says. I look down at her gnarled fingers and say, "I didn't know his name was Klaus."

*

Can I go now? You can probably figure out the rest of my life based on what I've just told you. It follows a predictable pattern, with few surprises. I will leave you hair samples and nail clippings, which might be some help as well. If you have any questions, you can call me. Besides, I'm late now. I have to pick up my mother's belongings.

Smiling, Waving

"I regret the abortion. Oh, boy. I regret it a lot. I look at myself in the mirror and I just want to jump off a cliff. I'm too fragile. I'm not saying it's not the right decision for you. You have your master's degree and everything. But me, I just want to blow my head off. Why did I abort? I'll never know."

The mother's walking through a parking lot with her daughter. The mother keeps clearing her throat as she talks. At one point, closer to the car, she grabs the daughter's hand. Then she lets go. Flings it away.

The mother was pregnant last year. The daughter is pregnant right now. The mother did not mean to get pregnant. She has been pregnant a lot. Once it was pleasant. Now it is not.

The mother pats her hair down. It's windy. Street signs bend and twang.

Her bald spot shows. It shines like a dime in the car windows she's walking past.

"Maybe I'm just hungry," says the mother. "Maybe I don't regret it. Are you hungry? Do you want to split something, or do you want your own? Whichever. I can afford it."

The daughter teeters a little. The mother looks at her with concern. She knows what it's like to be knocked up in high heels. Things will be better when they've had lunch. They will laugh and hold hands. They will guess about the waitress's face: harelip or bar fight?

A fat young couple skips between mother and daughter. The mother thinks: It's so nice when the retarded find people to date.

The mother met a man at the doctor's office. His head was right where she stares when there's nothing to file. She tried hard not to stare at him. Picked at the stains on her lab coat. Called her own phone number, told the dial tone to come in for a follow-up.

His hair, what there was left of it. Wispy like a baby's. She wanted to pet it. Even eat it. When a woman came in to make an appointment with the other doctor, the good one, she said: "He's not hair all week."

His folder was the thickest in the office. Yes, yes they did it in the bathroom and he kept pressing on the hole in his throat to say "bust the balls." But the post-it she stuck on the back of his folder, blank and pink, is what makes her look back and think, "interesting day."

The mother studies the daughter. Short, straight, bright red hair. Much brighter than when she was born. It was mud colour then.

And her chubby cheeks, pink from the wind. Long neck, kinked forward. A bad burn mark along her collarbone.

Who burned her? Who burned her little girl? Was it that awful boyfriend she lives with, the one who got her pregnant but still smokes Camels and makes her smoke Camels too, even though she's pregnant and never smoked before she was?

The mother hopes he gets lung cancer.

The mother has seen lung cancer, first hand, at the office.

And AIDS.

And models with breast lumps.

And all the rest of it.

The mother throws back her head and picks up the pace. Forgets that her daughter is pregnant and short-legged. Starts to skip.

A big, deep voice across the parking lot calls out the mother's name. She turns around.

A man, by the hot dog cart, by the metal bench, by the bra store. He has golden hair. Honey bees circle him. He is naked. From where she stands, far away, the mother can still see that his nipples are brown and round like rare, old coins.

He is waving. His arm makes a big arc over his head. Smiling. Waving. She is smiling and waving back. Drops her purse to make the big arm arc bigger.

The mother is made to think of all the happy times in her life.

The first time she was pregnant.

The second and third times.

The time she kicked a mugger in the balls and he fell backward and said "what. the. fuck." and how each word was a sharp gasp.

And now this naked man waving.

Her arm starts aching. She drops it to her side. Pink plastic bracelets clink back in line. She turns to wink at her daughter. With one eye shut, she can only see half of her daughter. The half with the head, on the ground. She decides to open her other eye.

Her daughter has no legs. She stops at the stomach. There is no blood. Her legs are gone.

The mother bends down. Hovers over daughter's face. Daughter isn't dead. Daughter says "Hi."

The mother runs, screaming. Toward the naked man. Naked man bucks backward, starts to run.

"Help! Help! Help! Help! Help!"

The mother can't keep up. She stops to catch her breath. Leans against a fur store window. They have a half-off sale.

Walking back to her daughter, her face is in the sunset. The ambulance has come. A Black lady is holding her little girl's dead head. The mother stops, stares at the sun. She walks back, sun-blind, to where the sale was, the one the naked man ran past.

House Contents and the Big Wild World

I've got this problem. Well, let's just say this thing, this thing that I inherited. I'm terrified of going outside — I feel my heart travel up my esophagus and into my head whenever I'm out there. I saw it happen to my mother. When I was a toddler, we'd be making our way to the park and she would start to slow down and repeat: "We're going to the park, to the park, just a nice little walk to the park. Everything will be fine." The park was the parkette behind the subdivision down the street, but more often than not we wouldn't make it that far. She'd start shaking the stroller, telling me it was time to get out and walk, and then she'd tip me onto the pavement and put the stroller over her head. She'd say: "It's o.k. we just have to go home now. Little Sue, just take Mommy's hand now and walk us home. Come on now honey, be a good girl now."

I was used to it. I'd given up moaning that I wanted to play in the sandbox because as soon as I started wailing she'd start wailing even louder. She'd be there on the sidewalk screaming through the striped canvas: "*Suuuuusan! Take me! Home! Now!*"

That nosy Lillith who was always spying from behind her curtains would squawk from her front porch: "You just be a good girl now Sue, and take your mother's hand. She's just having another one of those fits. Just turn her around and lead her home."

When we got home, Mom would close her eyes and climb the stairs like that until she reached the bedroom where she'd pull the blanket off her bed and crawl through the clothes hanging in the closet and sit back there on all the pointy toes of her high heels. She needed to sit there for about an hour or so and then she'd be all right.

I thought I was all right. The wider and wilder the world the better, I used to say. I used to do crazy things: road trips with my girlfriends, even hitch-hiked through Europe as a teenager and the way I met my husband, well, there's a story. I didn't exactly run off with the three-eyed man from the circus, but pretty close. He was a trucker, making his way from Florida to Maine with a truckload of oranges and he stopped at the Howard Johnson's where I was waitressing one summer. We got to chatting and I said how I'd never been to Maine and he told me he was stopping there for a while to do some fishing and I said: "Well, how about taking me with you? I've got a month and half before college starts again." We settled it right then and there over the third free re-fill.

Needless to say, we ended up marrying and moving to Phoenix. I never did go back to college. Time went on and there we were doing pretty well for ourselves, Lore was working at the Caterpillar plant in Wallaceberg and I was being a mom, looking after our two year old, but then, out of the blue, I was reminded. Like a big déjà vu but way way worse because I could feel myself tipping Lucinda out of the stroller. For Christ's sake she was only a baby and there she was on the sidewalk howling her head off and the neighbours all came rushing out and they were screaming at me: "What happened? Whaddya do to her?" and all I could do was lie down on the pavement like a cat and cover my ears.

Next thing I knew I was in an ambulance being, shunted off to the General and Lucinda was bawling there beside me in the arms of some strange lady who lives on our street who was looking at me like I was a freak from hell. Oh God, it was awful. And then at the hospital when they had checked us both out and nothing appeared to be bruised or broken they started talking to me real slow and asking me if I knew where babies came from, and what I was planning on making for dinner, and whether there was anyone I felt was trying to harm me or whether I heard people telling me to do things.

They called Lore at the plant and he came on down looking worried as hell. I was trying to tell him that everything was all right and I was gripping the back of his neck real hard when the doctor asked if he could see him privately. We said no. I mean, we both said no.

And so the doctor said fine, and asked Lore: "Is there any evidence of mental illness in her family?"

"Jesus no!" I shouted. "Why won't you listen to me when I tell you that it was just all the sun and I was really tired and Lucinda was fussing and I just felt all dizzy like I needed to take a rest!"

"Well, your mother..." started Lore, and looked at the

doctor who was nodding like a vulture, "she was about two hot dogs short of a family barbecue."

"Could you explain exactly what you mean by that?" asked the doctor, and Lore said, "Well, Mary just used to freak as soon as she got outdoors. I mean, I think she didn't feel right unless there were four solid walls around her."

The doctor asked me if I was agoraphobic. I told him I didn't have any problem at all with spiders; that I wasn't squeamish about bugs like most women.

"Fine," he said. "But how do you feel when you leave your home; how do you feel when you're in the middle of a crowd of people?"

I wished he hadn't asked me that because then I got it in my head that I was going to have a fit if I ever got into a crowd of people. I got so scared that I was going crazy, so scared that if I went outside my head would start spinning and I would start shaking and I'd just have to lie down and hug the pavement.

Lore was so good with me though. He'd say: "Hon, this'll all pass. Just take your time. You stay in the house as long as you need to. We'll get Bucky's mom to take Lucinda to nursery school. You just work on relaxing."

I tried all sorts of relaxation techniques which the social worker recommended — breathing and visualization exercises where I'd imagine being outdoors and being my chipper old self, meditation and yoga, but geez, after about six months of all this I was getting stir crazy, really restless and so goddamn lonely.

I started ordering in food in the middle of the day, pizzas and Chinese, just so someone would come to the door and I could have a little human contact. Lore would come home and say "Jesus Suze, I'm really sick of cold pizza for dinner," but I couldn't help it. He was starting to get angry at me, wasting all this money on food we didn't need, so I thought I better find a way of coping which would bring us in some money. I decided to have a house contents sale. Seemed right to me.

I placed an ad in the local paper that read "Everything must go" — I thought that was catchy and exciting and would be sure to draw in a crowd of people.

Lore was working the weekend shift at the plant which meant he wouldn't be around all Saturday or Sunday and that's when I get loneliest. I'd be hearing all those summer noises, burgers sizzling on barbecues and sprinklers going, and even Lucinda splashing around in the neighbour's pool, and here I was trapped inside alone all weekend. Well, this weekend was different. I had a great time greeting people at the door and bringing them in. Giving them a cup of coffee and telling them to make themselves at home. A whole swarm of people, the whole day long asking me questions and taking tours of the house and me making them happy saying: "You've got a real bargain there. I'll let you take it off my hands for fifty bucks — that's a tenth of the original price." Everyone was happy and by Sunday afternoon I'd made over $3,000. I'd sold everything except three knives and forks and Lucinda's little bed.

But by Sunday evening the emptiness of the place was ringing in my ears. I scrubbed all the floors to distract myself but Lucinda was having a bird because the TV was gone. I defrosted some pizza for dinner and Lucinda and I were sitting there on the floor and she was picking the pepperoni off my pizza when Lore walked in. His face looked like it was about to cave in. I brushed crumbs away from my mouth and looked up at him as sweetly as I could and said: "I thought we'd try redecorating."

"But what was wrong with the furniture we had?" he asked, incredulous.

"Oh, come on Lore," I said. "You said that the suite reminded you too much of your parents, and you've been saying for months that the springs are coming through on the Lazy-Boy.

"Yeah, but the television? And the air conditioner? The air conditioner was brand new! Are you out of your mind? What were you thinking?"

"Oh, Lore," I tried pleading, but he didn't want to hear anymore. He was standing by the window and I was staring up at his back and he was saying, "Susan, I can't handle this. I can't handle you anymore. I just can't handle it. Maybe you should go and stay with your sister for a few days."

It was awful. I thought I was going to die. But Lore took me back. He came and picked me up in the station wagon about three weeks later and as we were driving home he said: "They're gonna have to be a few changes round here," he said, and I sat silent, grateful and nodding.

The first thing I noticed was that he had replaced the furniture with all sorts of cheap white mela-something-crap. The stuff that comes out of a kit from Scandinavia. The second thing I noticed was that it was all bolted to the floor. I mean you couldn't even move the chairs around, they were permanently arranged for a party of four to sit at arms' length from one another. But I didn't say a word. I know when to keep my mouth shut. I may be smart, but I'm not stupid.

Things have been going along pretty smoothly for a while, mostly because I am on my best behaviour and trying to keep my mouth shut. But I'm starting to feel pretty awful again. Lonely and restless. I keep thinking about placing another ad in the paper. Lore doesn't know it yet, but I'm pretty handy with a screwdriver.

EILEEN MYLES

Excerpt from Cool For You

In North Building, they used those pale green, yellow, light almost grey-blue bowls — plastic ones that the government buys and distributes everywhere in America so that everyone is aware of institutional eating. The clank of it. The metal soup spoon clucks at the bowl. The people who never go outside eat the only thing that keeps them alive and sometimes they just starve for days. Not eating was not considered a negative behaviour, and residents were often either out and out pigs or skinny starving — *sticks.* Angry waving sticks by the window.

Huge vats of watery oatmeal would be rolled in every day at 12:15. Usually my own stomach would be growling and I'd hear the bluster and smell the stink in the halls. It was food. Watery oatmeal. It reminded me of a sweater. A Xerox of a sweater you're handed when you need to get warm. It wasn't even tweedy this oatmeal. It was blue grey brown. It was beige, it was grey. It picked up the plastic lights from the side of the bowl. It shimmered like the big metal tubs it came in. Where do they keep the Kennedy girl, I wondered each morning. Where's the milk, George? I asked on the first day.

The milk's in it, George's eyes twinkled. George Barlow. A wonderful man. We had long conversations in the clothing room. We'd be figuring out the boy's outfits early in the day. Grab some pants, a pair of socks. George had this twinkle in his eye and a slightly moist look around his lips. He was incredibly old. 36. He had been at Fernald all his life. He said they had decided he was a little stupid when he started school and they sent him here and nobody minded and nobody found out. You're family, I inquired. He gestured at himself innocently. I didn't know any better. I just figured I was stupid, too.

After the big shakeup in the sixties, he said, they noticed that I knew what was going on. If anyone asked me anything I'd tell them. Usually they didn't ask. They assumed I was dumb. One of the attendants a few years back began to teach me to read. It's not so hard. I didn't know that was what they were doing. The letters. His eyes twinkled like he meant the letters were doing something. Oh yeah, I said. That.

I'll probably get out of here, he said, looking around. He smokes a pipe, George. And he eats the food. Where's the milk, George? The milk's in it, he told me. Mixed in. It's easier. They don't mind, he assures. I saw a big fat man in overalls pouring it down. He sat in a huge high chair. With the bowl to his lips, looking. Eyeing his friends.

No sugar, I asked George. It's in the coffee, he gleamed. Lifting a see-through plastic cup of coffee and pouring some onto Peter's cereal. Thanks George, Peter slurred. Some mornings I wanted their oatmeal but I had already been there too long. I mean you could try the oatmeal in your first week when you didn't know anything yet, you could get away with tasting it, being dumb.

I wanted it. I only seriously considered having it when another attendant was in the room because if I was alone with them and I had a bowl of it, I would be one of it. If I had it when George was there it would be like being one of them even though he could talk about it. Once in a while I would have half a cup of their coffee in one of the plastic cups. "See-through" but really you couldn't because they were so old.

They had been washed by big machines, again and again, tall plastic cups that had lived their lives in institutions so now instead of being see-through they were "scratch." That was their color. With ridges for a safety grip. The coffee was beige, sand-colored, grey. It was blue-grey coffee, tan. Flavored with milk, watered down, not much, not real milk. Probably government surplus powdered milk, probably that. So it was grey, like endless land. I drank a half a cup of the stuff. They looked at me, disgusted, whoever I was working with, but they'd done it, too, we'd all done it one morning or another, drank their coffee as if it were ours.

Is there a recipe book for everyone? In America, when it comes down to that: here's something for everyone, a book or a cup of coffee, a bowl of oatmeal, that not you or I or anyone we know would ever want to eat, but food that anyone would eat when they had finally been determined to be at that position where they would eat anyone's food. I don't mean eating from the dumpster. I mean the mechanical lunches you got in school. Those vegetables no one wanted because you could see they had been prepared for anyone. Extra food. To think you might end up eating it one day, looking around, the day you forgot who you were.

DEREK MCCORMACK

The Elf

"Sloppy," the manager said. "Look at the smudges." He crumpled my sheet.

I dipped my pen. Wrote: *Things are jolly here at the North Pole.*

The guy at the next desk slipped me a rubber. "I'm Blake," he said.

"'Nautty?'" the manager said. "It's spelled n-a-u-g-h-t-y." He crumpled my sheet. "Are you s-t-u-p-i-d?"

Kids sent lists. Dear Santa. I had to send letters back: *I hope you've been a nice boy and not bad.*

"Don't let him get to you," Blake said, rolling over in his chair. "He thinks he's such a tough guy."

A horse is sure a big wish. Are you sure you don't want a doggie?

"Do we sell doggies?" the manager said. He picked up the Christmas wish book. Threw it at me. "If you can't do the job," he said, "I'll find someone who can."

I started over. *A horse sure is a big wish. Wouldn't you rather have a Steiff horse doll, item 8044, $4.95? Or a cast-iron horse and buggy, item 9652, $8.95?*

"It took me time to catch on," Blake said. "There are tricks."

A Visit from St. Nicholas. A Christmas Carol. The Selfish Giant. Blake gave me books. "Go through those," he said. "If you find yourself in a jam, lift a line or two."

'Twas the night before Christmas, I wrote. *And what to your wondering eyes will appear? A mahogany chessboard with bakelite queens.*

The manager picked it up. Handed it back. "Whaddya want?" he said. "A pat on the head?"

Blake winked.

Chutes shut. Dust covers on addressographs. The manager swept through the mail room, killing lights. "Wrap it up," he said, exiting.

Blake blotted a letter. Spritzed it with peppermint perfume. He dropped it in the Out bag. The bag was brimming. "Done?" he said.

My hand a charley horse.

He grabbed it. He pulled back my fingers. They cracked. "My first Christmas," he said, "I thought my arm would fall off."

He kneaded my palm. His thumbs rubbed my lines. "Truth is," he said, "I'm glad you started working here. It was kind of lonely. Not talking to anyone all day."

His hands slick with sweat. "It's worse around Christmas," he said. "Being on your own. You know?"

"I've got something for you," I said.

"Ink blots," the psychiatrist said. He dropped cards on the desk. "Ten in total. I made them by squirting ink on a piece of paper and folding it in half. You probably played this game when you were a tot — it's called blotto."

"Am I in trouble?" Blake said.

"When I give you a card," the psychiatrist said, "please hold it in both hands like this. Tell me what you see there, what it means to you. There are no right or wrong answers."

Blake picked up a card. "Can I pick it up?"

"As you wish," the psychiatrist said.

"I don't know," Blake said, a husk in his throat. "Nothing. A mask. Is that right?"

"Whatever you say," the psychiatrist said.

"I can't tell," Blake said. He picked up the next card. "Two men, maybe. Or a fountain."

A ballerina. Smoke. A judge's wig. A beautiful gown. A Christmas tree with globes.

The psychiatrist glanced sidelong at the mirror.

"Jesus," the manager said. He was standing behind the two-way. "How'd you know?"

I shrugged. "He tried to make me go fairy, too."

He clamped my shoulder. "You did good, kid."

I thanked him. I could smell his talc. His aftershave. He was beautiful. Blue eyes. Blue shaven. Lips pink as nipples.

He said: "I'm sending you to Happyland."

I blew up a pencil balloon. With my finger I poked in the knot. I made a twist for the head. Double end-tied the nipple. The nipple was a nose.

"What is it?" said a little girl.

I called it a reindeer. I made penguins, rabbits, bees. Poodles floating over their leashes.

Call Me Collect/My Sister is In Love Again

"They're beautiful," I told him.

My friend Morrow is showing me his collection of little black dresses and smart brown handbags. They're not the only things he collects, but they're the most prominent. He's got the dresses all lined up in his closet. They're all variations on a theme, minorly different, but each one its own piece.

"Do you ever try them on?" I ask him.

"Oh no," he says. "I don't think they'd fit me. And I like to just see them as beautiful things."

To him, they're like art. The way you might buy a painting, he buys dresses and handbags. He has a special shelf along one wall where the bags are arrayed.

My friend had a friend who used to buy all the different Nike shoes. He'd buy one pair to wear, and one pair to keep. The whole line. It was insane how much he spent on shoes, but I supposed it was the same impulse. He'd stack them in his room. I never inquired as to whether he got them in all the sizes or not. I guess you have to draw the line somewhere.

The reason I'm thinking about collections these days is because the other night my friend Em asked me if I collected anything, and I was hard-pressed. One of the convictions I'd developed at an early age was that interesting people collect interesting things.

"I collect books," I told her. Then thought harder. "I collect impressions. I mean, when I write, I'm collecting the people I meet, the things we talk about, what we saw, did, you know."

Em collects zines. My mom collects those plates with nice pictures on them that you're not supposed to eat off. I think they're gross, but she seems to like them. And I don't have to live with them, so I look the other way. My dad likes to collect tools, and make variations on birdhouses. I used to date this girl who told me the story of a friend she had who used to collect kids' lost shoes in the summer, and their lost mitts and toques in the winter. She herself always took a polaroid of every new person who stepped into her room. She pinned them all up on the wall, like the Devil character in that movie Highway 61.

Once, I asked my friend Marla what she collected. Marla is really quite normal. And she cultivates that. She's very domestic. She has this vision of a well-stocked household. She doesn't like Martha Stewart but she likes her products. The IKEA catalogue is like porn to her. She jokes that she's going to have her own cooking show one day - but it's not such a joke. I can see her running the cookbook department of a major publishing firm one day.

"Do you want to see?" Marla smiled, impishly. "It's in there," she said, pointing at a set of drawers.

"Whoa," I said. "It's in there?"

"Yah," Marla nodded.

"There's a lot of there, there." I told her. It looked like she could hide a body in there.

"Go ahead."

I walked over to the drawers and slid it out. What I see are jars. Lots of jars. All kinds. It looked like years of Saturday afternoon garage sale scouring.

"You collect jars?" It was less of a question and more of a statement. Most people collect things in jars. Marla collected jars. In some small way, it was beyond my comprehension.

My Sister is In Love Again

My sister Beth visited Montreal about a month ago, just before school started again, and we hung out for awhile on St. Laurent. My sister's really cool, the kind of person I'd like to hang out with anyway — even if we weren't related. This time she tells me she's in love with Holden Caulfield. I'm laughing because she's *always* in love with someone. Every time I see her she's in love.

"I thought you were in love with the Strokes," I say.

"Well — Holden Caulfield is this year's Strokes," she replies.

"I thought that was the White Stripes."

"They're a close second," she laughs, stopping to light a cigarette.

"I mean," she says, inhaling, then blowing smoke

circles. "I know he's not a real person. But if he was — I'd totally date him."

The thing she likes most about him is that he talks tough, but he's completely soft inside. He's so fucked-up, and doesn't know anything, about himself, about the people he hangs out with. He's living a life of complete ambiguity. "He doesn't know what he wants to be when he grows up, any more than I do." Beth digs her port-wine red copy of *The Catcher and the Rye* out of her bag. It's a copy she stole from school. I'm trying to imagine the thousands of copies that must go missing every year from schools across the country. They must fill gyms. She's trying to find this passage she really likes but can't locate it. Her bookmark is about three-quarters of the way through. "I'm reading it for the third time," she tells me.

We stop by the ice cream place beside the headstone carver's and I get some chocolate and ginger ice cream from the beautifully androgynous scooper. "You know, of course," I tell her, "J.D. Salinger is this reclusive old guy who always had a thing for young girls. I mean — not age-inappropriate ones, but just a lot younger." Eating orange sherbet, Beth mumbles, "I don't care. He can be a dirty old man if he wants to. He's forgiven. I mean, he wrote *Catcher*. He's kind of earned it."

"I wonder if he was like Holden Caulfield when he was younger," I muse. "I mean, he would have had to be — if he could write the character. Maybe he was channeling a younger version of himself. Maybe Holden Caulfield's going to grow up to be this hermit writer stashing away years of manuscripts."

"If Holden Caulfield was a dirty old man, I'd be his dirty old woman," my sister proclaims. I laugh. The hot summer sun is melting her sherbet level with the lip of her cup and it's looking more like orange soup. I'd already given up on catching all the runnels of chocolate streaming down the sides of my cone, and my hand was a chocolatey mess. "I have to find a bathroom," I tell Beth.

"Who would you want for a dirty old woman?" she asks me, as we look for an eatery that's not going to hassle us too much for using their bathroom. I give this some thought. Finally I answer, "I think the girl version of Holden Caulfield is the Claire Danes character in *My So-Called Life*. If she were real I'd date her. But I think I'd have to get in line."

"*And* be more of an asshole," my sister added. "Which shouldn't be too hard for you," She quipped. "That chick always went for complete jerks." Beth tossed her sherbet cup into an overflowing trash bin.

"Sexy jerks," she conceded, "But still jerks."

MARLENE ZIOBROWSKI

Garbage

I don't know when you started, but I do remember the first time I noticed. You came home with a chip bag affixed to your chest, just below your breast bone. I didn't see it until we were getting undressed for bed.

It caught my eye: Smart Food. Its bold yellow and black looked good against your pale skin. I think I told you so, and now of course I wonder if that only encouraged you. I touched it, ran my fingers around its edges, crinkling the plastic. This seemed to give you pleasure and so I didn't pull away. You sighed as I drew the back of my hand across the bag, as I felt the texture, strange under my fingernails.

I'd like to think that I was only responding to your signal for more, but I must admit: I was also curious. How did it attach to your skin? What made it stay on? I slid my hand over it, fingers overlapping onto your flesh, and pressed my palm flat. I could feel your heart beating. The metallic coated material gave a tinny edge to the rhythm: *phapp-thapt phapp-thapt phapp-thapt*.

In that gesture I felt so close to you. It had been a while since you had responded definitively to my touch. I could feel your weight leaning against my palm. This is the excuse I give myself, even now.

I caressed you and you sighed again. My one arm

holding you against me to free up my other hand to explore where plastic met flesh, I was unable to resist. I slipped a fingernail beneath the bottom jagged edge. So slowly, gently, I twisted to slide my finger under.

No glue. Just cool dry skin and chip bag.

I remembered that skin.

I remembered how you used to want me to touch you.

I wanted you.

I pressed in, up.

Your eyes grew wide. "Yes," you said. I distinctly recall: you said "yes." I pressed and imagined my tongue tracing finger's path, taste of your skin juxtaposed to the sweet and nothing taste of plastic. I felt the slick of sweat pooling on shiny silver, dissolving into your flesh as later I might lie by you, curled against your dreaming and I'd follow you. But as I worked one whole pinky under the edge you screamed.

I slid my finger out.

Plastic folded to skin, pushing out air, refusing.

But the fuse couldn't have been permanent, because a week later the Smart Food bag was gone, replaced by a scrap of a family-sized pack of Doritos. The violent orange didn't suit your complexion so well, but I didn't tell you this then. The aesthetic, I told myself, is such a subjective category.

In time, more often than not, only patches of your skin showed through. The type of trash you collected shifted from compact and malleable to brittle, bulky and heavy. Some nights sleeping I'd bump against you, heat-seeking, and end up with a coke can or empty beer bottle wedged against my kidneys. Once, sitting in a movie theatre, I leaned to kiss you. You turned suddenly and some large metal object attached to your head whacked me in the face. I watched the rest of the movie with my nose humming the way it does when it's thinking of swelling up.

The funny part (and I can say this now) was the way in which you insisted nothing was wrong. You sat through that movie and others like it, afterward asking me where I'd got the bruise. I'd ask you: "Hey, what's happening? What is this ... accumulation of trash?" And you'd reply with that fabulous non sequitur of yours I've learned to loathe: "No." Pretty much that. You'd say "no," as if "no" was supposed to tell me something. But sometimes you'd elaborate: "I'll tell you later."

And then later, I'd ask you: "Is it later now?" and you'd say something like: "What? Oh this? I'm sure I've told you about it before. It's a new coat. I needed a new winter coat anyway. Do you like it?"

And I'd think: "Oh."

As in: "Oh, o.k.: kind of retro but could work... in some circles... maybe... I dunno...."

And feeling foolish for my lack of faith, I'd wrap my thoughts around the idea of your new coat, your new Look. I'd itemize the insulating properties of chip bags, bread wrappers and balled-up newspaper, contrasting these R-factors to that of spun cotton, wool and hemp. I'd do rough calculations on backs of envelopes of how much extra room our new house (the house you still insisted you wanted to buy with me) would need to allow you to move freely and not knock the furniture in passing. I'd take out videos from the public library on recycling and urban culture. I'd sit up late in the kitchen after you were in bed, reading about fashion trends that merged with eco-reclaiming projects and new construction materials technology, all in the hope of getting in touch with what I was missing. I worked very hard to believe you. I am a dedicated worker.

Once, after one of my more skeptical days, I asked if you could take your "coat" off at night. I knew you could hear the quotation marks, but I was too tired to care. I said: "We can use a heavier blanket if you're cold." I showed you the blanket I'd made, just the right woolen thickness for our two bodies to sleep close and not overheat. You laughed at me. Clearly I was being absurd.

I knew then that if I didn't laugh back, you'd become sullen. I laughed back. I didn't want to spoil the mood. I put away the blanket.

Out of our apartment, I began to look at other people with a different eye. In the line at the bank machine people were subtle but I could see...something. Was that a brightly coloured cuff link on the handsome woman in front of me? Or did I just see a taco wrapper poke out her sleeve? And the graying, nattily-dressed man at the check-out: wasn't that a scrap of glossy fashion magazine showing below his trouser cuff? And the sweet, flirting, young thing at the convenience store: that could have been a tattoo on her shoulder blade, but it kind of reminded me of a chocolate bar wrapper, too. I observed that we were not alone, you and I.

But when you started with the duct tape, I knew my exercises in belief were not helping me. Not nearly enough. More was at stake than my apparently archaic fashion-sense. Especially when you started leaving bits of duct tape face-up on furniture so I'd end up with patches of it stuck to my ass or back of my arm. The first few times this happened, I peeled the tape from my skin and told myself you meant well, that you were encouraging me to join in. I told myself you were being gentle with my attachment handicap. And after that the tape wasn't such a big deal, once I learned the trick of rubbing it with an ice cube then pulling with a sudden snap. And isopropyl alcohol worked wonders at getting the residue off. And hair grows again, I figured.

Then, once while you were away, I left a big piece on the back of my thigh. Just to see what the appeal was. The first few days were o.k., but it got pretty itchy. By the third day I was scratching and drawing blood speckles.

"Enough," I thought, and tried to peel it away.

It wouldn't budge: not with ice cubes, not drenched with alcohol. After soaking in a hot bath I managed to yank it off. The rash soon faded where the tape had been, but over the next few hours it came up again around the residue. By afternoon, it had spread down my leg to my knee, up onto my butt and around and across my belly, leaving a perfect rectangle of white in a curving field of red splotched welts. It wouldn't fade, no matter how many antihistamine tablets I took.

You were away for two more excruciating days, but then you came home. Even before you had unpacked you noticed my glowing white rectangle offset by red rash. Fascinated, you wanted to stroke it. I have to admit: your sudden and unexpected attention surprised me and I said: "sure" and positioned myself so you could comfortably reach.

But the rash itched and your fingers tickled. In reflex, I brushed your hand away when you touched one of the more sensitive bits. I didn't mean for you to stop, but you glowered at me and stepped back.

While I stared, trying not to cry, you pulled a swatch of tape off your arm. I thought, hoped, maybe you were taking it off to give to me, since you must have figured that I needed the adhesive more than you did. I was afraid. It was bright blue, my favourite colour (but I wonder if you knew this). One-handed, you deftly covered your mouth with the tape. Then I must have asked you aloud how you'd be able to talk, because you peeled back one corner and mumbled that you could eat well enough through a straw. I had enough sense not to insist just then that I wasn't going to be putting anyone's food in a blender.

I spent that night in my upstairs study. Before I could fall asleep, though, I had to scribble about how I wasn't going to blend anyone's food, no way. Not me.

I tried to leave. "Just for a while," I said, which was true enough. A few weeks later I came back and you had bought more duct tape. Rolls of it stacked up the stairwell, down the hall. Red, blue, green, silver, black. I came into the bedroom to pack some things. You were on the bed. At least, I think it was you. I wanted to shake you, see if you were alive under all of that tape and garbage. Covered head to foot, now seamless. I tried to touch you, to say I was leaving. You moved your arm. I like to think it was a wave goodbye, but maybe you were afraid that I'd pull a strip off and were shoving my hand away.

Hating The Librarian

"Won't be serving your type here," yells Mr. Mayhew, right into my face. "No heathens in my business!"

He strides toward me, backing me out of his butcher shop. Mr. Mayhew squints past his big veiny nose and I scramble away. I trip on the stoop and fall to the sidewalk. A few locals catch the whiff of drama and hover nearby, shaking their heads and clucking after me. I brush the dust from my hand-me-down pants and stand stiffly. I look down at my oversized work boots, down where the polish has rubbed away and down at the ugly old laces, broken and retied in knots. I curse them.

"No more meaty bones for Effie," I think as I stumble away. "No more dripping raw meat smell." Instead, she will mournfully work her way through a large bag of kibble and we will eat extra potatoes.

Dad and me.

I will not go into the butcher shop and I will not even go near the butcher shop! Still shaken, I cross the street and buy a fresh loaf at the bakery where no eyes meet mine, no voice calls hello. Crowds part for me at the corner store so I don't have to line up when I pay for our wilty soup vegetables in coin.

And the whole time I hear those flickering whispers

that sear me on my way through town. I walk quickly with my head down until my path is blocked by two sets of pretty, sandaled feet.

"Watch where you're going!"

"Yeah. Out of our way, Freak."

I look up at Lindsey and Tracey from my grade seven class. They wear matching sundresses ordered from the Sears Spring and Summer catalogue. One in pink, one lilac. Tracey grabs the shopping bag out of my hand and swings it in front of me. Lindsey laughs and pushes me hard and the two run off shrieking, dumping the groceries on the ground. I gather up my things, our supper, and try to put them back into the torn bag. The bread is dirty at one end and a cigarette butt sticks to it. I brush it off and then run, before the tears come.

I run down the street and don't stop until I hit the worn path leading through the field to our house. I am safe in the tall grass under the big sky with the early summer sun. I stand and let the water fall, and curse my sister Angie for leaving me in this lonely, mean place.

Angie and the librarian, peeling out of here on the two-lane highway. Into the middle of nowhere. I suppose they'll just keep driving until they pass the nowhereness and end up Somewhere. A gas station. A city. Or maybe they'll stop and lay down in the millions of miles of corn and sunflower fields. Embrace in the middle of those leafy stalks. Count June bugs, and twist their fingers together, the way they did right before they climbed into the librarian's car and drove away.

Before the librarian it was Angie and me.

Angie walking with me to my school and then over to the high school for her classes. Angie and me doing the shopping, chopping the vegetables, rolling out pie crusts and tucking in those slivers of apples coated in cinnamon sugar. Humming to the radio and our hands never still. Last summer we picked fruit from bushes and trees, bent low over beans and tomatoes until we ached with the weight. Then the long days of canning in the steamy kitchen. I remember the rows of pretty jars, filled and wiped and neatly labeled to keep us fed through the winter.

I worry I won't know how to do it just right. That I'm not strong enough to lift those heavy bushels alone, or stir over the stove with the long wooden paddle.

I am hating the librarian.

With those ugly suits and thick glasses. And underneath it all, a clear complexion and bright eye that Angie noticed. I never understood why she lingered at the sign out desk, why we had to always stop by to pick up books she didn't have time to read. Poetry! The librarian's own poems, to make matters worse. Why Angie smiled and flushed and started keeping secrets from me.

Then I remember all those fingers knotting into each other before they left.

Angie's and her's.

And the look in Angie's eyes and how her happiness gave her a holy shadow she never had before. And the way they seemed to belong, standing tall and good.

Nothing at all like the dirty words people threw at

them. Neighbours who had gladly eaten at our table. Angie's table. And patted her shoulder and wondered at her quiet strength holding us all together after our mother died.

"Look after Dad," she said to me that day. And, "It won't always be this way. I promise." Did she even know how it would be? Did she think she could protect us by leaving? Or did she fly, not caring that the snare set for her was what held us now between its hungry jaws?

I spit the tinny taste of hate out of my mouth.

After all, it's not like she wanted to. The message was clear. They hissed it on the telephone and hurled it onto the porch. They sprayed it on the Ford pick-up and shattered the front window with it.

"Get out before you wind up burned in your beds. Tied to a fender. Dragged out of town!" Even if Angie disowned the librarian she had no chance for a new life here. Not like the neighbours with their heartbreaks and lost loves, sifting through the chatter to start over fresh. I take some deep breaths. I stand tall and good in the grass. I start walking again through the field with even steps, cradling the bruised groceries in my arms.

In the kitchen I chop an onion and set it dancing in the hot pan. I wash sweet carrots and new potatoes in their fragile skins. I stir some flour in and watch it thicken, sticking to the onion pieces. Then I slowly add the vegetable stock kept in the fridge from yesterday. The big leafy spinach feels good in my hand and I remember to save it until the end, to just drop it in the hot soup so it stays a bright green colour, the way Angie taught me. I turn on the radio and hum along while I work. Effie croons with me and noses the counter edge for scraps.

When we sit down, I notice the lines on my father's face. His hair is wispy and hanging the wrong way. Away from the part that is starting to thin. He is a big man but in that chair, silent and bent over his soup, I feel his grief eating him up.

"Our circle is shrinking," I think. "Me, Dad and Effie. Our little circle of three."

The telephone rings two short blasts. For the neighbours, not us. I wish it was Angie but she would never call in ammunition to the switchboard operator or the neighbours on our party line.

Dad scrapes back his chair. "You done good. A right nice supper for an old man like me." I smile at him even though it hurts my face. His big farmers' hands carry the bowls over to the sink and rinse them in water I boiled on the stove. He fumbles with the dish cloth and the little container of soap.

"I'll do them, Dad," I say.

"Naw. Look to your school work. I'll be out back a while yet."

Effie wags and follows him out the door and I am alone in the kitchen. I can't bring myself to open the heavy book with all those mathematical problems. Just looking at the cover brings back the long day of insults at school.

The Virgin Mary wall clock ticks loudly, steadily, from across the room. We look at each other. Her arms are open wide and her sacred thorny heart glows in the growing dusk. She belonged to our mother and I like to think they looked the same. Quiet, peaceful brows, straight noses and a sad look to the eyes. Now I think she looks a bit like Angie, too.

"Mother, Mary and Angie, I wish you were here with me or me with you."

I sit at the table with the checkered cloth and try to conjure them.

"Mother, Mary and Angie, come back to me now. I need you." The steady ticking answers me. It beats in time with my pulse and the more I concentrate, the more I can smell the lilac perfume from my mother's hair, washed and combed and curled on a Saturday night. I can hear the quick bounce of her shoes on the floor, dancing with a younger version of my dad in his good clean shirt. He twirls her round the wood stove with his hand on her tiny waist and they slow to a close waltz. Angie's voice fills the room, laughing then singing a song about love. She sings and we watch my parents sway and turn, smiling right into each other.

The door clicks.

Dad and Effie hesitate. We look to one another and then to the fading figures still turning between us. Dancing Dad in the good shirt vanishes first. Then Angie like the morning mist. Mom leaves an icy kiss on my cheek and little ones, longer ones, on Dad. She smiles up into him and is gone, almost before he knows that what he saw is true. He stumbles into the kitchen with wet eyes and shaky hands. I help him to his chair and hug him to me. He squeezes me back so tight I can feel his heart thumping, thumping in time with mine.

"How be I put on the kettle and make us some tea, " I say into his broad shoulder finally.

He traces the skin that her lips brushed against. "Thank you, Daughter."

Effie and Dad and me sit in the kitchen. We take slow hot sips from our chipped cups and keep time to the waltz with our feet.

We are humming that old song about love.

María

Usually I tell people I never had a friend who was female until I was in high school. That's my excuse for not having messed around with girls when I was a kid, like every other woman I know, lesbian or otherwise. But that's not entirely true. There was one.

She invited me to her party. María Santiago, who shared a desk with me seven hours a day. María Santiago, with Mexican fudge, sunflower seeds, and stories. I'd listen to her whenever she wanted, which was mostly while Mrs. Magili was teaching, and I got in a lot of trouble for it, but I didn't care. Besides, Mrs. Magili was just jealous cuz she couldn't hear too. María was her favourite student. No matter how many times tables I learned, I couldn't compete with María's big brown-green eyes and her long brown braid. My mom had given up on mine a long time ago. I always got it dirty or tangly and she worked too much to spend time fixin' it. But María's was perfect, all shiny, tied tight back behind her. She even let me touch it sometimes during reading hour. That's when she'd whisper the fairy tale stories she liked best to me, and tell me to kiss her hand cuz she was a princess, and I would. She'd always say that I could be the princess the next time, but it never happened and really I didn't care.

She pulled the invitation out of her spelling book and

handed it to me right in the middle of class. It was a little square envelope, bright yellow with my name in her writing. *For Alex*. I opened it to Hello Kitty asking me if I'd come to her party. I started planning her present right then. It would have to be perfect.

I made my mom take me to Funky Monkey's T-shirt shop. I walked through each row touching and smelling the stacks of soft T-shirts. I loved the way new cotton smelled, like my great aunt's roasted almonds, even though I'm sure it's just some combination of factory chemicals. But in the store, I let myself be tricked until my mom told me to stop it cuz it looked weird.

I picked out a real nice pink T-shirt and had pretty purple flowers pressed on. The steam machine pushed the two together and the big man behind it warned me not to touch her shirt for ten minutes. I snuck my hand in the box anyway and the purple burned me just for a second and then warmed my fingers. It cost a lot but I promised my mom I'd do anything if she'd help me buy it. María would look beautiful in this and everyone at the party would like me. I'd get invited over more and her friends would be nicer to me. I was sure of it.

María's house was on the street on the other side of the freeway. I went there a lot because it was part of my paper route, but my mom didn't like it. It was long and narrow and a lot of the cholos lived there. My mom thought they were part of a gang, but they weren't. They dressed up and drank beers in the yard, but they never did nothin'. No-body ever did nothin' in my city.

Her house was pale pink stucco with three short steps in front. I walked up. I knocked on the heavy metal screen that you need a key to get into. Under my arm I had my present wrapped in the Sunday comics with a big white bow on top. In a few seconds, the door had a husky voice.

"Mija, hay un gringuito a la puerta and he's got a present with him. I told you to only invite girls."

My toes moved into each other. I waited. There was no face yet. Finally María's little voice came through the screen holes.

"Mami, that's Alex. She is a girl. I swear it." The metal opened and she grabbed my hand and pulled so fast I hardly got a good look at her big lacy yellow dress.

The house flooded me with garlic and onions and chicken. The air was warm and wet with them in my nose. María took the present from me and put it down with a bunch more in a room with beds in it. She said all the shiny boxes were for her, but she couldn't open them till later. Then she pulled out a little box from under the bed, filled with all the marbles I'd ever given her. She had a better collection than me. I didn't care, I was just happy thinking about them sitting right there under where she slept every night.

"Come on," she said and then we went to a big room of flower furniture with plastic on top that kept it brand new forever. Five other girls were there. All the friends she was with when she was not with me. I knew their names. They knew mine.

They told María to come sit with them and she ran from me. I was still standing in the middle of the room. I kept walking and sat down on a big rug in front of them, because it seemed like I should. Yvette, the long dark tall one in the middle, said Salvador, who was in grade five, liked María. And I was happy for her because she had told me twenty times before how cute he was.

Her mom came in the middle of the story and asked me if I wanted a soda and I said yeah and then I said yeah again a couple seconds later because she was still looking at me and forgot to listen. Then she went back into the kitchen. That was when Yvette said it wasn't fair because they had to play all those games before they got sodas. I said I'm sorry, I didn't know that, and I'd play the game too.

"Okay," she told me, "But you have to sit at the other end of the room first, so we can decide what to play." I looked at María and she nodded that I should go. But she always did everything Yvette wanted, and like a fool, I went.

I stood next to an orange tile kitchen with big pots all over. Her mom handed me a bubbly styrofoam cup and I drank and bit patterns into it while they talked.

The game started with a blindfold. María's fingers touched my neck softly when she tied it on. I giggled when all these hands pushed me into circles. I kept giggling until I heard the sound around me stop with a big thud. In my nose, the garlic turned into dust.

Maybe I was only in there two minutes. I have no idea. I just remember pounding and muffled laughing and crying. And then, their big ugly smiles when the door opened. They couldn't stop joking about it the whole day and the whole rest of the year at school. They would all just burst into gross laughs at any moment. Then they'd tell the other kids at school how red my face looked, all puffy with tears. How I looked like I thought I was going to die. Imagine that, dying in a little closet. How stupid, they'd say, then they'd laugh some more.

I don't know if it was because I looked white, or because I got good grades, or because I looked like a boy or what. It didn't matter. All I knew was that when grade four started and we had different homerooms, María wouldn't say a word to me. I couldn't talk to her at recess or go to her house or anything. She never told me why. She never answered me when I'd catch up with her. I even wrote letters. I'd drop them off on her front doorstep during my paper route. I know she got them.

Hi María,

You ran real good at P.E. I saw you. You coulda beat Cristina if she hadn't cut you off. I told Tony that too.

Your best friend,

María,

I got mad today cuz David told me I don't look like a girl and boys will never like me. I hate him. Remember when we stuck gum in his book. That was cool.

                              Your best friend,

Dear María,

I saw you in the shirt I gave you today. I heard that Sal said you looked pretty in it. I swear it. Real Pretty!! That's what he said. I'll tell you how I found out. Call me please.

                    288-0786

María,

Don't tell, but me and John John ripped off all this great candy at the liquor store. The owner didn't even see us come in. You want some. I got a whole bunch.

Dear María,

Did I do something wrong? Is it cuza that test? I didn't know the answer. I'da let you cheat. I swear it. Please tell me what's wrong. I miss you.

                              Your best friend,

When I think about it, she never spent time outside class with me anyway. She never had lunch with me or talked to me when Yvette or Cynthia were around, her other best friends. It was enough that she came alive at our desk, when she made me more important than anything else. I suppose that's why I was so happy when I got the invitation. I thought everybody else would finally see how much she liked me. How I was the *real* best friend.

But she laughed with them.

The Stairs

Exhausted, I had just stepped off the bus, having been on tour for months. The band had actually pushed me awake and off the fucking bus, right in front of my door. Now I was slam-stepping up the stairs towards my third floor apartment. I had half a bottle of beer in my pocket, a suitcase in one hand and a guitar in the other. As I hit the second floor to start my final assent, there it fucking was. A vagina — sitting on the stairs.

I stopped dead.

Not, I realized, because I was afraid. After all, I had a vagina, my girlfriend had one and I had spent a lot of my life at close quarters with many a vagina. What made me stop dead in my tracks was the turmoil in my thoughts. Like an adding machine, my brain began screaming out the numbers and types of intoxicating substances I had consumed over the last few months. One of those magic pills or powders had to be the reason for this twat sitting on the stairs in front of me. I am using the word twat as an added description for Miss Vagina, this was one tough looking vagina, I'll tell you. Picture a Miss Potato Head, with a vagina for the head, pierced and wearing motorcycle boots on these toothpick-like legs, along with a leather vest and some weird custom made sunglasses (how else would they stay on, if they were not custom made?).

Then, believe it or not, the damn thing pulled out a cigarette, offered me one, and lit the fucking thing. Now, I have seen a vagina blow smoke before, this is not a new thing for me. The vagina blowing smoke *that* was attached to a stripper who put the cigarette to those special V lips, and right in front of my eyes took a drag and expelled the smoke. To finish the stripper story, she would then offer the cigarette to a customer who was instructed to put it in his or her mouth and stand perfectly still. You guessed it. She pulled out this huge bull whip and sent that smoke flying across the room. This was the first time, however, I had ever seen a vagina in leather purposely light up. As the twat took a deep drag of the cigarette and blew a white cloud of smoke in my general direction, it began speaking to me in its sputtery, airy way.

"You live upstairs?" it asks.

I can't believe I'm fucking answering.

"Yes."

"It seems like a nice building," Miss Vagina or Miss Pussy or Miss whatever the fuck at this point, says to me. Now a thought rushes through my mind. I start to hyperventilate into a panic attack. Suppose this "nice building" kind of talk from Miss Vagina was a prelude to it moving into the building, into my building. I don't know why it freaked me, just a knee jerk reaction, I guess. I mean, it's not as though I fit in as your normal everyday apartment dweller either, and there are people who live here that look at my girlfriend and I with disdain or fear. So in spite of my common sense, I'm ashamed to say that the pure fear of something, or someone, freakier than me and outside my huge mental catalogue of freakiness, caused me to react badly. In response to Miss Vagina's statement, "Seems like a nice building," I replied, very sure of myself, "I don't know, the building's got its problems."

"Oh really?" comes the reply in a way that sends shivers down my spine. It had the sound of, the air of, "I know the owners and I'll be sure to tell them you said that." Fuck, Fuck, *Fuck*, what have I done? What was I doing talking to a sputtering vagina smoking on my, and I say it again *my* fucking stairway? Suddenly the stairway dweller bounces up onto its feet using those amazingly spindly legs and heads down the stairs towards the door. I can hear the clomp, clomp of the boots as they hit each stair and hear the door screech open and slam shut. At this point I am tempted to follow the leather-clad vagina and do some weird detective work, but my brain and body has had enough over the last few months and certainly the last few minutes.

I was so tired my eyes began watering. I was standing on the stairway, steps from home, staring down the stairwell. Starting back up towards the apartment I began rationalizing the encounter with the vagina; by the time I reached my door I was laughing at what the mind can do to you under different experiences and substances. I unlocked the door, stepped into the room with my happily barking dog running between my legs over and over again. I dropped everything on the floor and finished the beer in my pocket, heading to the bedroom. My girlfriend, with a very sleepy voice says "Hi honey, welcome home," I said to her, "How are you, man, I missed you really bad."

"Me too hon, love you."

"Love you too, baby, see you in the morning, " I say, as I fall into a deep, exhausted sleep.

I woke next morning to the wonderful smell of breakfast being made, a nearly daily ritual in our house for ten years. I stumble from bedroom to bathroom to kitchen and sit down at the table.

"Morning honey," we both say at the same time. I continue with "You would not believe how tired I was last night. I thought I saw a vagina dressed in leather sitting and smoking on the stairway."

"Oh, you met Valerie," she says.

I trip to my feet speechless, trying to say "Are you fucking crazy, a talking, smoking leather-wearing vagina and with the name *Valerie*?" The words won't leave my completely dried up mouth. Struggling to get my breath and speak, I look out the window. I see Valerie the Vagina on her scooter, with a smoke dangling from her mouth pulling up to our building.

MARIKO TAMAKI

Hump

On your best days, the world should be loud and
technicolour, nonsensical but cool, like the text in the Ko-
rean greeting card I bought in Chinatown for my cousin.

Happy sun fun today for you!
You are birthday boy you are glory in a word!

Neon pink letters that likely meant nothing to the people in the country where they were produced. Exuberation
without any specific meaning. Because when you don't know
the language it's just the sounds and the feeling, a foreign
experience spelled out with vowel sounds and exclamation
marks.

It's 6:30 a.m., a crisp sunny morning in Sunnybrook
Park, the only time a city this populated feels squeaky and
new, right out of the cellophane. I'm standing in a baseball
field, on the line you would normally cross rounding second to third, my hands stretched up above my head. Just
breathing the air feels intense, like freezie-breath minus the
cuts in the corners of your mouth. Everything looks like the
sharp and overly-defined background of a video game,
too blue and too green. For as long as I'm awake at this
hour I can maintain the high that goes with a feeling of

accomplishment, eyes wide letting in the light, pupils rapidly adjusting.

I'm supposed to be pretending to be a tree, surrounded by other Torontonians, also pretending to be trees, but I'm actually pretending that I'm reaching to touch the morning-blue sky. I'm imagining this is actually possible and making it my goal for the day. Carl, long like the sunrise shadows of the maples behind him, stands on the pitcher's mound, droning out instructions to the crowd standing in scattered rows in front of him.

"Okay now, so, we're like trees, and we can, like, feel the wind through our fingers.... And now I think we're going to bring our fingers down, you know, take your time, just like fall...."

Like, you know, take your time.

Everyone takes a deep breath, not because we're told to but because it feels like the right time to do so. Bending down I can smell the dewy grass *squitching* beneath my feet.

Carl.

In regular life, Carl is my coffee guy, puppy brown eyes and a gentle voice, somewhat under-developed looking but sweet in a way that compensates for it. Carl works at the Bean, an arty coffee house in downtown Toronto that sometimes holds poetry readings and political meetings, although it really shouldn't because they have no room. The only thing I really know about Carl is that Carl is a self-righteous vegan with a severe distaste for all things dairy. If you ask him for cream for your coffee he'll warily point to a table several feet away, a table he never touches. Before I met Carl I never knew that cream, white and smooth, could feel dirty. Now whenever I drink cream it takes like old butter, wrong.

Being in the park, stretching and pretending to be nature is part of Carl's alternative master plan, also known as HUMP. HUMP happens every Tuesday and Thursday morning at six, weather permitting.

I've been coming here for three weeks.

The idea behind HUMP, according to Carl, is not so much exercise as physical expression, the willingness to let your body do things that feel good, like stretching and being outside, rolling around in the dirt, being a tree. Art. It's all about energy, according to Carl, the energy in the earth, the energy in our bodies working together. Movement. Movement equals power.

Humans

Use

Movement for

Power

Free yoga organized and led by a man whom I suspect doesn't really know much about yoga.

Not that I mind.

If this was Bridget Jones' diary I would probably be doing this either to lose weight or get over a boyfriend. Fortunately for me it's not and I'm not. I hate that book.

I've given myself a bunch of reasons for coming here, a lot of which have to do with the fact that this is outside and I'm almost never outside and I probably should be. Carpet is not grass. Then there are my thighs which, while comfortably plump, are also pulled so tight they squeak when I walk. *Stress.* Sometimes when I walk my ass and hamstring are so tight and sore that I actually have to grab my ass to relieve the pain. It's because I pinch my bum together when I'm nervous. You could bounce a dime off my hindquarters when I'm nervous, but there's a price to pay for that.

Mary-in-accounting has a stone of stress that lives in her left buttcheek. Like George Costanza's wallet, it keeps her permanently tilted to the right when she types. She looks like that old V8 commercial about people being unbalanced because they don't have enough veggies in their system.

I talked to my doctor about it and she told me I need to relax. Get some exercise, she said.

I tried going to proper aerobics but proper aerobics and me are not really compatible. Susie, my aerobics instructor, was very pushy. She kept telling us to get our knees up, very weird. She spent the entire hour blowing this whistle dangerously close to my ear.

Deafness is not the quickest route to stress free bliss, I don't care what the YMCA tells you.

I like this much better. Carl is anything but pushy.

Carl is too content and stoned to be pushy.

I bet if you saw me in the park right now, curled up in a ball on my side pretending to be a rock, my nose pressed to my knees, you'd think I was crazy. I am not so worried about that because when I was sixteen years old I was crazy. Several days after my sixteenth birthday, my parents put me on medication because I was sad all the time and hid like a dust bunny in the corner of my room, avoiding all human contact. The meds made me happy but they also made me run. It was like speed coursing through my veins, white light blasting out of my ass and propelling me forward. I ran like I was a cat on fire. I ran in my oxfords and boxer shorts because I didn't have any proper running clothes. It wasn't long before I realized I couldn't stop. I started pulling muscles and straining my ankles. Eventually, three weeks after I became the fattest kid on the track and field team, my parents took me off the meds.

And I stopped running.

There are all different kinds of crazy.

For the second half of HUMP we dust the dirt off our track pants and gather in a circle. Carl starts us off clapping and stomping. Clap clap clap clap — stomp stomp. After a couple rounds, pairs enter the circle and "socially interact" using body movement.

This is probably the loosest and strangest part of the morning, if only because you're actually touching strangers, something you rarely do in Toronto unless you happen to lose your balance in the subway. Unlike Fight Club, HUMP has a no-hurting rule. No hair pulling. No hitting. There are those who break the rules but it's few and far between, as I understand it. Last week I wrestled this girl with really long white dreads. It was probably my least pleasing HUMP thus far. She kept pinching me while I was pinned down. Fortunately she's not here today.

Instead, I end up wrestling a fuzzy guy in cut-off-track shorts and a March of Dimes T-shirt with a face like a teddy bear. We clap hands onto each others' shoulders and spin around, taking turns pushing and being pushed. I dig my toes into the dirt and use all my strength to get him to move. I'm sure he's humouring me, it's like pushing a Buick. He smells like cedar.

Eventually, after several back and forths, he pushes me away and does several long kicks over my head. I squat down to the ground, noticing suddenly that, as he kicks, I get a bit of a view.

At the end of our fight, fuzzy man extends a paw to me. I accept it and he pulls me into him, wrapping his wooly arms around my torso and squeezing me tight, pushing my face into his T-shirt. Eventually he lets go and everyone claps as I return to my spot and two other people enter the ring.

My girlfriend says the thing she finds most amazing about this chosen activity is how little I think about it. I have vague notions but I'm not really into explaining this and, if I were called upon to do so, I might not even be able to do so. As I take my place in the circle I feel squeezed but strangely energized, like somewhere inside me, under my lungs and beneath my heart, there's a soft buzz of electricity.

After we've wrestled for a while, Carl gets us to lie down on the ground and stretch out, to practice breathing and letting the air into our lungs. I've heard some people say that when they're lying down they can hear the earth hum. Sometimes, if I listen really closely, I can hear something that sounds like traffic.

On the way home I pass the Tai Chi class that practices a good distance away from us so as not to be associated with our strange movements. I'm growing fonder and fonder of Tai Chi. It might end up being the next step in my morning activity; I'll bet they have some place to go if it rains. Tai Chi looks like a bunch of people all slowly pushing an elephant.

Everyone has the same look of quiet concentration on their faces, like they're in a library instead of a park. As they move in synch to point themselves west, a flock of seagulls erupts behind them, almost unnoticed.

Off in the distance Carl walks his path home, surrounded by a small group of wrestling types. Every time I come here there's a few more that leave with him to help him open up the shop and drink milk-free lattés. Today one of them holds his hand.

Three months from now I'll find out that Carl has abandoned HUMP to start another group that will eventually move into a commune and grow apples. I'll hear this through rumour. Once or twice I'll come to the park and it will be empty except for joggers.

I'll wonder if being in Carl's new group involves sleeping with him. Then I'll take up Tai Chi.

EMILY SCHULTZ

The Mothers

1.

THE FIRST THING I LEARNED BOTH BACKWARDS
AND FORWARDS WAS THE LORD'S PRAYER.

At Mary Marlies' house in her mother's basement, we
held our own youth group. Her mother supervised us in a
sense. Everyone got a chair and one would be marked on
its underside with a cross. Like a birthday party's X, whoever had the lucky chair would get a prize, a bible picture
postcard of the misty Virgin Mary or Baby Jesus. And we
would sing, "Jesus Loves Me," "Little ones to Him belong,
we are weak, but He is strong..." and say the Lord's Prayer.
But in Mary's bathroom after the meeting, Amy Simpson
would swing her legs while she peed; it took a long time
for her to get the pee going sometimes and Mary would
pretend the bathtub ledge was a tightrope, teetering along
while we sang quietly, "Jason loves me, this I know..."
after Jason Pinto in our class, with reasons that changed
depending on whether he had stolen our hats at recess or
tagged us in the gym. Then, abruptly, sometimes mid-verse,
Mary would jump down and say earnestly as a seven-year-
old can, "Stop it!" as if she couldn't bear the blasphemy, as
if the whole thing had been mine and Amy's idea.

"Group" was mainly Mary's project though. More than

her mother's, and it became very important that we be there every Monday. At school in the morning, she would begin by making promises, allusions to "Oh, what will the prize be today?" and that it was something special, very special, maybe a glow-in-the-dark Jesus nightlight that plugged in and everything. When it turned out to be another postcard, Amy and I fumed secretly in the bathroom without Mary, me running the taps to make her pee, and she saying, "If you learned the Lord's Prayer backwards and forwards, isn't that kind of like the opposite? Putting it in reverse?" Right then we set about learning the prayer word for word entirely backwards, the way boys in our class said their older brothers played their albums in reverse to hear messages from the dead. Whenever Mary promised an extra special prize for Group, Amy and I would look at each other and silently mouth the last line backwards from all the way across the classroom, our secret curse on Mary: *Nem-ha, reve dna reve rof. Yrolg eht dna rewop eht.*

So of course, it's no wonder when she finally caught on, she promised to fill my pillowcase with spider eggs. She said they would hatch out while I was sleeping and crawl all over me and eat me alive. I started having nightmares and wouldn't go to bed. My mother decided to put an end to my religious education after that.

2.
ALL MOTHERS' ANGELS HAUNT THEM.

Later, Mary Marlies' mother became a bona fide leader at the church for a group called "Keepers," which I guess meant keeping the faith or keeping the light, although it always seemed sort of a shady name to me, like keeping secrets or something. I never went, but it was basically their church's equivalent of Brownies. All through elementary school Mary Marlies gave out Christmas cards with the Virgin Mother and the little baby Jesus after the rest of us had given out cards depicting Santa and Rudolph in ridiculous situations, or better yet, opted to give out candy or nothing at all.

"Don't you think it's creepy?" Amy asked me in grade five, just after the holidays, as I was helping her and her mom un-decorate. She pulled the cards down off the wall.

"Amy..." her mother warned, "Christmas is about more than a new pair of leg warmers." Or some reference to some other now outdated garment or game that Amy had recently received.

"I know," Amy nodded, over her shoulder mouthing to me, *nem-ha reve dna reve rof.* "It's just that they've got all those pictures and figurines through the whole house, and the bathtub Madonna with spotlights, and it's all about Jesus loves the little children, and Mrs. Marlies can't stand Mary or her sisters."

"Amy!" her mother warned. "She's got four kids, she's got her hands full, that's all. Of course, she's not that bright, they're not the best-off family in town, but they manage." Mrs. Simpson spoke in that low, all-knowing mother voice. That judge-not-lest-ye-be-judged voice. It didn't sound a whole lot like she was disagreeing with Amy, but as if she had to qualify the statement in case there was a God who was listening who might damn us for picking on those who were less fortunate. She packed the ornaments carefully into the white plastic tray. "God is in all of us," Mrs. Simpson said, wrapping the tree-top angel in layers of white tissue paper. "Even on our bad days, we carry Him deep down inside." When she put it like that, I couldn't help but imagine God as a half-formed child, yellowish and illuminated, swimming in a sac of red fluid like the foetus in the anti-abortion literature that I'd seen.

Like most of the families in our neighbourhood, the Simpsons were occasional Catholics, dutiful but reserved. Amy rolled her eyes discreetly, and began to sorting the cards into keepsakes and throwaways. Mother Mary was first into throwaway.

I knew what Amy was getting at. Life at the Marlies house held a hauntedness. Their daily rituals were as far from grace as we could imagine at that time in our lives. There was never any milk in the fridge, and we didn't ask for snacks when we went there. Mary was so thin that if you punchbuggied her arm, no matter how friendly a tap, she would bruise clear through to the other side, almost as if there was no blood in her. The basement was full of dolls with their eyes penned out, and everything smelled faintly of pee. Despair was like a flickering spectre kneeling on their living room floor in front of the television — she could be seen when the daylight reached a certain patch of the carpet if the channel was changed at just that moment. A blue and gold hologram Jesus in a gilt-looking plastic frame hung in the alcove beside the front door, and in every room He carried His cross. "Don't go down in our basement alone. The stairs will open up and you'll fall into Hell," Mary had once told us solemnly. "I mean it. There's ghosts down there."

Mrs. Marlies spent her days lounging in the house watching soap operas in a long black sheer bathrobe with her hair in tight pink foam curlers. Several times when we'd come home after school with Mary we'd caught her that way, 3:30 in the afternoon and still not dressed. She'd jump up immediately, point at the vacuum sitting in the middle of the room, and croon, "Mary, give me a hand. I started to do the rugs but I think I put my back out. I was just taking a rest to see if the pain would go away." We'd look embarrassed that her mother was still in her housecoat and visibly half-naked. Mary would stall. And after about three minutes Mrs. Marlies would yell, "You stupid brats! You never lift a finger to help me! Your father's going to be home in an hour and there's going to be all hell if this goddamn house isn't clean, Mary!"

At 4:30 Mary's father would come home and regardless of whether the carpet had been cleaned or not, it would be, "This place looks like a shithouse! Mary, what are all your friends doing here? Who said you could have them over? What are you doing playing with that? You're in the middle of the floor, taking up the whole room." He'd make a lousy demonstration of pretending to swerve around Mary, nearly always managing to step on her hand on the way past. "Well, get out of the *fucking* way, then," he'd say as she yelped. The word carried more weight than a backhand.

Mary's teenage sister, Josephine, would come into the doorway, lean her whip-thin arm on her hip and watch as we quickly detached from the scene. The younger sisters, Sarah and Ruth, popped their heads from the bedrooms down the hall, stood picking noses, then scuttled out of sight like cockroaches. Mrs. Marlies would send us home as politely as possible under the circumstances. She had to get supper ready, and then drive over to exercise class or the church.

Even then, I had this image of Mrs. Marlies waking up next to her husband and praying that she'd never married him, never had any kids, never had any reason to pray.

My first exposure to sex was at the Marlies house. It was Mary's birthday and we couldn't very well get out of it because they'd rented a VCR for the evening. So we were part obligated, and part tempted. About two hours after we'd bedded down on the living room floor, and pssted and giggled and done all of that, Mary fell asleep, and then everyone else followed suit. Except for me and Amy. She was sharing my blankets and we were quietly taking turns drawing words on each other's backs with our fingers: *Jason-L-Janie* and *Jason-L-Amy.* Mr. Marlies came out of the bedroom, and the hall light came on. He walked into the dining room that stood between the hall and the den, where we were.

"Eddie?" Mrs. Marlies called from the far end of the house, a hushed urgency in her voice that even at that age I somehow knew not to mistake for desire. "Come back to bed."

He stood in the double doorway with his hands on his hips. He was wearing a pair of blue briefs exactly like the kind my dad had, except he filled them out more. "Who's still awake?" he said. He said it, he didn't whisper, almost as if he was bidding anyone who was asleep to wake up. I felt Amy freeze behind me, and I lay still, not even daring to shut my eyes. "Who wants to play hide-and-seek with me?"

I didn't know what he meant, but I knew what he meant. Amy's fingernails bit into my bicep. He was looking at her, what he could see of her, her blonde curls on the pillow. She was the pretty one, the girly one, and we both knew it. She squeezed until I could feel the circulation cut off and I knew if he came to take her, he'd have to tear her off me first.

He turned and walked away. "Don't let the bed bugs bite," he said gruffly over his shoulder with a bit of a snicker.

Amy and I didn't say a word. Then or ever. She pulled the blanket over our heads and I turned over and faced her. I pulled her face down into my chest and held her around the shoulders. She curled her knees up to her stomach and tucked her feet between my thighs. They were ice cold and I didn't fall asleep until the digital clock on the VCR said 5:15.

I dreamed of a centipede with one hundred feet, and on each foot an inside out sock. He was curled up on my pillow when I opened my eyes. "Wh-wh-wh-what are you looking at?" he said in a voice like the caterpillar in *Alice In Wonderland*. He slid off my pillow and charged into my mouth. I jolted awake. Old threats never die; I still hated bugs.

Amy's hair had fallen on my face, and her fingers were crushed palm up underneath me digging into my ribs. The light fell through the rust-brown sheer drapes and the beige carpet looked like it'd been stained with blood in blotchy flower-shaped patches. Mary was sitting up already picking at an old scab on her elbow.

"I don't feel good," I told her. I got up and went to the bathroom, made a big production of flushing the toilet several times and running the water. Amy and I were ten years old. We'd watched *Sixteen Candles* and made it through the night. When I came out, I went straight to the phone and called my mother to come get us.

Sheila Shepherd's mother didn't have the God-fixation but their house was just as creepy when we went there. Mrs. Shepherd worked nights at the factory and was obsessed with dogs. She had a ten-year-old Scottie named Jonas, which strangely, was Sheila's older brother's name. It might have made sense if the dog had been named by Jonas himself, but it wasn't. Mrs. Shepherd named it. Both of the kids hated the dog. The boy Jonas used to fill the dog's water dish with Sprite, root beer, or beer, hoping that the dog would get gas and their mother would decide it was too stinky to have around the house. But the dog merely belched and lapped up more. Sheila used to steal the blue ribbons off it and keep them in her desk at school. One day she pulled them out and counted them in front of us on lunch hour.

"This is how much my mother loves the dog," she said. "Three-hundred and fifty-seven, three hundred and fifty-eight, three hundred and fifty-nine ribbons in the past ten months."

We were impressed. It was a lot of love, obviously, to keep replacing ribbons when they went missing, as if there was a never-ending supply. We liked dogs, frankly, and almost understood Sheila's mother's obsession more than we did Sheila's.

The problem for Sheila was that she never saw her mother. Hadn't seen her, in fact, in the ten months that she had been taking the dog's ribbons. Her mother had switched shifts, working opposite hours from her father. She now worked from three in the afternoon until midnight. Sometimes, Sheila said, she stayed up and saw her father off to work, and then she could see her mother for a few minutes. But other times, she would lie half-awake, overhearing her mother talking to Jonas, the Scottie, in the kitchen, opening the refrigerator to get him milk or treats. Or she would hear her inviting him into bed with her, brushing his fur, she'd cluck and fuss, and make cutesy noises in his ears. Once, Sheila said, she asked her mother if she could iron her clothes and lay them out for her for the morning. "You're ten years old, Sheila," her mother apparently replied. "You're not a baby." Jonas, the second Jonas, was her perpetual child.

When we went for Sheila's birthday party, we saw the walls full of professional photographs of Jonas. Jonas with a ball, Jonas with his bows, Jonas with his trainer and Mrs. Shepherd. Over the couch where our parents had hung our school photos, Mrs. Shepherd had only Jonas. On the fridge there were three pictures of the family. A baby picture of Sheila's brother, a baby picture of Sheila, a picture of Sheila at nine months crawling across the floor towards a startled Jonas.

Jonas sat in Mrs. Shepherd's lap at the table. He was wearing a fresh blue ribbon. When we sang "Happy Birthday dear Sheila," Mrs. Shepherd manipulated Jonas' paws to wave at her, "Happy Birthday says Jonas," Mrs. Shepherd intonated loudly over top of all of us. Mr. Shepherd snorted, went to the fridge and got out a bottle of Blue. He didn't seem the type to put up with it, and it was obvious that he adored Sheila. He kissed her, and he teased us, and he'd bought her the Michael Jackson album and silky red jacket with the name of the nearest roller-skating rink emblazoned across the back in gold letters. Mrs. Shepherd gave her a hand-knitted cardigan with pictures of dogs on the pockets and the back.

Sheila on-purpose/by-accident left it in the gym at school and it got thrown into the Lost and Found box in the office until a third-grade girl, a kid from the geared-to-income housing, wound up claiming it later that spring. When Sheila saw her with it, she followed the girl home from school, beat her up, and took the sweater and hung it in her own closet never to be worn again.

Jonas was put to sleep the next year. Mrs. Shepherd didn't get another dog until Sheila left home at fourteen to move in with her boyfriend who was out of school and worked at the Shell station. I would see Mrs. Shepherd out on walks with the Shih Tzu, which she'd adorned with red ribbons, and called Sheila.

3.

UNCONDITIONAL LOVE IS ONLY POSSIBLE IN
SOMEONE ELSE'S SITUATION.

By the time we'd all hit thirteen, we were ready to do some serious mother-swapping. It had become obvious to each of us that our mothers had certain idiosyncrasies that we were fated to inherit.

All of the stereotypical teenage traits, we saw emerging not in us, but in our mothers. It was as if they were growing larger in front of our eyes, their bodies became bulbous and sexual, bizarre and foreign. Their voices seemed to change.

Suddenly, we were aware of them in ways we had never been; how they laughed, the voices they used on the telephone, their atrocious taste in music, the frequency with which they shaved their legs, their clothing choices to our functions and their fussiness over what we deemed age-appropriate clothing for ourselves. Our awareness was acute; when they walked into rooms, we could *smell* them.

If any sense was going to come out of this, we knew it was up to us. Our mothers were hopeless. Their wills were out of control and it was our job to lay down the law. For the sake of our individual houses as well as our united social well-being.

For some girls in my class at school, there was an intense courting of guilt, and sexual exploration was the main means to exceed parental expectation: the reward/punishment of new attentions — shame, shame and extra Sunday servings of shame. The rest of us used unspoken, unwritten codes of silence regarding these matters, including outright avoidance, while still carrying an abstract sense of duty to the family, primarily to maintain a certain level of attractiveness without high-heeled boots or excessive eyeliner.

But even at the time, we knew that these were only the basics to surviving our parents. The contradictory morals in our individual houses were as different and unnoticed as wallpaper. We knew the patterns without looking, had traced them in boredom during our younger years, then stopped seeing them, in fact, forgot they were even there...until our friends came by and began hanging about our houses while our parents were out, commenting on everything from the refrigerator contents to the bedroom closets. Everything was suddenly about what we had or didn't have. Frozen pizza or canned Alfaghetti, no-name products or brand labels, board games or video games, pads or tampons. And none of it, not any, had to do with our fathers. Everything was our mother's faults.

Almost as much as we categorized each other, we categorized each other's mothers. Mrs. Marlies was a sulky pushover who let Mr. Marlies tramp over everything. Mrs.

Shepherd...well, we never went to the Shepherds' by that point. Mrs. Simpson was the cool mom who was willing to drive us places and let us meet up with boys, never failing to remind us of our feminine power and, of course, the best way to maintain power (abstinence). And my mother, Mrs. Blasé, who was just liberal enough to be passable among my friends, but still too firm to be a favourite, and just never quite, well, Mrs. Simpson.

To me, Mrs. Simpson was the small town version of sophisticated. She was in the process of divorcing, and though money was tight, Mrs. Simpson still had subscriptions to magazines like *Cosmopolitan, Chatelaine*, and okay, also the less elegant but ever popular *Woman's Day*. She dieted and had disco dresses stashed in the back of her closet. She was the first mom I knew with the guts to go ultra-short with her hair and ultra-heavy with her make-up. She was a fashion-plate for the mid-80s — her bangs blonde-silver spikes, and her blush like racing stripes. Mrs. Simpson never complained about the divorce even when she and Amy moved into a one-bedroom duplex apartment and had to share a room. Instead she would say, "Well, we just have to think of *our future* now," as if without Mr. Simpson, she and Amy had become a couple. She consumed cigarettes like candy and talked about all those big topics like God and Love in the same breath. Issues we skirted in my house. She was at once a woman of frivolity and of great strength.

If there is unconditional love in this world — something the talk shows were fond of discussing at the time, though they never came to this conclusion — it undoubtedly occurs only between girls and their friends' mothers. And only for a very brief and beautiful period of time. Through all of grade seven, I wanted to live at the Simpsons', and by some unfathomable twist, Amy wanted to live at my house. She said her mother was an old cheese doodle, and at least mine was reasonable.

Is it a terrible thing for a daughter to say? I never loved my mother the way I loved Mrs. Simpson.

All the horror movies at that time were about bad mothers. Or whores, of course, who never go out of fashion, at least not in the movies. But bad mothers were really in. I'm not sure it occurred to us that there could be bad daughters.

I spent every weekend at Amy's house, and didn't realize what it was doing to my mother until I called one afternoon to say I wouldn't be home for supper. My mother wouldn't talk to me. She'd made roast beef. I didn't find out this reason until later. She just handed the phone to my father. I could hear her crying in the background. I'd never heard my mother cry before.

My dad didn't say anything for a minute. Then he said the same thing I'd always heard my friend's mothers say about their husbands. "Your mother works hard. So that you will have things." He didn't sound angry, but point of fact. "Come home."

The sad thing is, that wasn't the moment I knew I

couldn't live at the Simpsons' forever. I didn't figure that out for another half a year.

Amy and I were in grade eight. We were hanging out under The Bridge with some kids from the school on the other side of town. We weren't supposed to be hanging out with them, and especially weren't supposed to be under The Bridge. The Bridge was one of three, we said to each other, and when our parents said, "Don't hang out under The Bridge," we decided they must have meant one of the other two. Especially since this particular bridge was the closest to our neighbourhood, we said to ourselves, it could therefore not be as bad as the other two. Still, we knew, that not even This Bridge should we be under.

But we were under it. A couple of guys were drinking beer from cans, but we weren't. We had gone so Amy could meet The Boy I Was Secretly In Love With. In fact, Amy had just gotten her first French kiss from The Boy I Was Secretly In Love With, and she was standing around inhaling air like it was in short supply. Since she seemed to be having a hard time recovering her lung capacity after he'd put his tongue in her mouth, The Boy decided it might help if she took a drag off his cigarette. Which she was doing just as we heard her mother's voice.

"Oh shit," I said.

Amy jabbed the cigarette at me, and she would have looked completely innocent if she hadn't started coughing just as her mother's wooden-soled sandals came clanking down the metal stairs onto the grate beside us.

"Amy," her mother said in that voice mothers use when you know they'd rather slap you than speak to you. There was a long, shocked pause. "Let's go," she said finally, with only a glance at the cigarette I was holding amateurishly between my index finger and thumb.

Amy didn't say anything, just started up the stairs ahead of her mother towards the car in the lot. I took a step forward to follow, assuming I was going to get it too. But my adopted mother continued without another look at me. "I'm taking Amy home," she said over her shoulder, and I listened to the clank clank clank as she climbed the bridge stairs with her back to me.

I realized as soon as she was gone that I was still näively holding Amy and The Boy's cigarette.

"Wanna finish it with me?" he asked with a smirk that implied he might have meant more than the cigarette.

I looked at the long hair and the pair of tight white jeans that had first drawn my attention. Somehow they didn't seem so attractive anymore. "No thanks," I said and gave the cigarette back, and left.

I thought that when I got home my parents might already know where we'd been. But Mrs. Simpson hadn't called. I was disappointed. Amy told me at school the next day that her mom didn't feel it was her business. I lived at their house three days out of seven, but I wasn't her *business*.

It was only then that I wished I'd stayed and finished things with The Boy.

4.

SOMETIMES STRANGER THINGS ARE BORN.

The first babies began a couple of years later. Friends from grade school like Mary and Sheila, and acquaintances we'd made in high school. Their bellies swelled up and we watched them transform from a distance. Become round and awkward. While people tried to say nice things about growing up quickly, taking responsibility for one's action (we seemed to be living in the anti-abortion capital of Canada), and having that motherly glow, we saw only ugly blue sweatshirts and old pink genie pants. In a juvenile way, pregnancy was like a proof of purchase. Though you could cut it out from the box and mail it in for a prize, we were old enough to understand that a) if the box was still full the cereal would go stale, and b) such prizes never have value. Why other girls our age couldn't see this, we never knew.

In the span of a summer our world was suddenly divided into two camps: girls who did, and girls who didn't.

Amy was still in my camp, but she kept sneaking over to the other camp when I wasn't around. She told me wild stories of The Gorgeous Guy she was seeing, and how she let him put his hand up her shirt. And then her shorts. And then, and then.

"I thought we should use *something*," she kept confiding. "But I can't go to the doctor. I heard that unless you're sixteen, you need your mother's permission to get The Pill."

"But you have to use something!" I said emphatically.

"You want to buy condoms for me? My aunt works at the drugstore, and it's not like she doesn't know who he is!"

"Oh my God. How many times without a...?" I gestured vaguely with my hand as if my tongue had turned to rubber and I couldn't flap out the word.

"You sound like my mother," she said. Then she wiped her hand across her face and admitted, "Five times, but he pulled out."

"Five times! What are you going to do?"

"Pray." There was not a trace of sarcasm.

In grade eleven, Amy started bussing to the Catholic high school, which was somehow considered "cooler" in spite of the lower availability of birth control information. Either prayer actually worked for her as a method, or she convinced someone else to buy condoms for The Guy. Or, by that point, he had his driver's license, and took her to some other doctor's office or some other pharmacy. Or maybe he was replaced by some other Gorgeous Guy who would.

The pain was like something living, chewing on my womb for breakfast. My stomach was in knots. I could only clutch at it, untuck my shirt to hide the undone top of my jeans, which otherwise formed a tight band across the aching. I had a spare for second period, and would slouch down across a couple of chairs in the cafeteria while my friends played a lusty round of Go Fish, wherein each card held the secret significance of some Guy or Other who the players might have crushes on.

Love was non-stop entertainment. Everything indicated a fuck: pop tabs pulled all the way off in one rip, cars on the highway with one headlight out, apple stems twisted to the alphabet song and snapping off on the letter of the right boy's name. I was seventeen years old, and I had graduated to the other camp. *Jason loves me this I know...*except that Jason Pinto had become a dealer and a burnout. The Guy's name was actually John, in *this* case and I didn't know if he loved me, even though he told me he did, several times. More important, I had grown truly tired of belonging to Camp Virgin. He was a fun guy, and though not altogether gorgeous, I was certain I was not the first girl with whom he had acquiesced. I liked him. Whether I loved him was not the issue at hand and in the hour between school's out and the five o'clock whistle when his parent's came home he was too hurried and excited to ask for declarations.

The condom had not been stored in his wallet for months on end, had been checked for punctures, had been kept away from heat sources, sharp objects such as keys, jewelry and fingernails. We'd both read all instructions, probably several times, at home locked in our separate bedrooms or bathrooms, months in advance of the day we might each find someone who would want to use one. It was the same way I had started reading the tampon instructions from my mother's box in the bathroom cupboard the day I turned twelve, even though it would be another year and a half before I had any use for them. But the condom was not 100% effective, and we knew this before we used it.

The thing inside me was not a baby. It was a disease. One the doctors called Chlamydia, as they worked at getting it out. In this case, tongs were not necessary. A prescription would do.

My primary doctor was a woman my mother's age, and I might have been grateful for a female doctor if she hadn't resembled Nurse Ratched. I had just watched the movie in conjunction with reading *One Flew Over the Cuckoo's Nest* for my grade twelve English independent study project. I could tell right away that the doctor had a low opinion of me, because she asked me the same questions twice as if she thought I hadn't told her the truth the first time.

There is nothing as definite as the sound of rubber gloves snapping on wrists for striking fear into a teenage girl. The sound of the wheels squeaking on the chair as it rolled into place. The heat of the light at the end of the table turned upon the most private part of you. Nothing as frightening except the pseudo-sermon that comes after clothes have been put back on.

Until then, I had hoped to avoid pregnancy at all costs. Now, so far as Ratched could discern, my ovaries were still intact and my fallopian tubes hadn't been damaged, much. That little word caught on my ear, and the fog closed in.

"Of more concern to me..." Ratched said, folding her hands in her lap in a way that bothered me immensely since it indicated that there was more to come when I was already quite ready to flee the facility"...is that you understand that the people to whom these things happen tend to face problems again...unless they take precautions."

What I wanted to say was, "Submit Exhibit A for evidence." To have the door swing open, and a uniformed marshal come forth with a manila envelope. In it, the sodden condom from that afternoon several months before.

What I said was, "Yes, I understand perfectly."

My mother was waiting for me in the parking lot. "Who did you see this time?" she asked, when I climbed up into the truck. She was wearing a flannel jacket of my father's, the cuffs rolled back. Her hands were like brown leather mitts on the wheel. Her face, suddenly filled with diverging lines, was heavier around the eyes and mouth than I had ever noticed before. She had grown with me. Her tousled honey hair was whitening as the snow fell behind her outside the fogged window in the milky mid-afternoon winter light. She was getting older as I watched.

When I told her, she said, "Oh! I like that doctor! I saw her once. I liked going to a woman gyno. She's very progressive and very good!"

My mother had been very nice about all of it. Nicer than any other mother would have been, I thought. She nodded her head, and asked only the questions she needed the answers to. So this time, I didn't contradict her. I nodded when what I wanted was to curl into a foetal position and cry. My mother started the engine and waited for me to fasten my seat belt like always. I did. With a cold metallic click, it slid into place, and caught. She was still my mother; I was not a mother. But something had irreversibly changed.

5.

IMAGINE THE MOTHERS GATHERED IN ONE ROOM.

Imagine them, as I did at that moment. Imagine them as a group, a cross-section of society, a clear colour photograph in a text book: a semicircle of women of all backgrounds, all family situations, all incomes. A demographic, from the clothes they wear to the things they carry. The flat yet feminine shoes, the handbags full of bandages and peppermints, the blazers, sweaters, or sweatshirts. Imagine them young. Imagine them old. Imagine yourself among them. Imagine yourself absent.

Imagine them, as in a dream, the crazy shapes they make against the light source you cannot quite identity. The secrets they might tell, leaning into one another, big-bellied, big-breasted, pear-shaped or as yet unformed. Their voices low, murmuring of blood, pain, patience.

Imagine The Mothers gathered together, murmuring, murmuring...

Imagine one mother. The image of a mother. The Madonna. The virgin mother. A pale blue and blonde postcard with hands clasped. Imagine the light behind her. How singular of virtue. Shining and praying. How alone she seems, how lonely.

Impulse Control

Jesus, that was a crazy time. I fucked around all over the place that year. Well, it wasn't really a year, but it felt like more.

That was my year with couples, too, and you know, scoring with two guys at once adds up fast. With a couple, everything seems like more, like when you sleep in the middle, and at first, there's so much skin you can't believe it, and then you start feeling really, really trapped.

It's not like I have a thing for couples, because I don't. You'd think a couple would have no space left for me anyway, but that's not what kept happening. What kept happening was just enough space.

Couples are easier that way. They have everything they need already, right?

So they're more relaxed about it. They don't want to get to know me. They don't care. I'm just dessert. They're already full, but hankering for a little something to top them up.

All they wanna know is a little something exciting from my past, like I used to be in the marines, or I'm actually straight, stuff like that. Guys love that shit. And a couple is just two guys who bring out the worst in each other.

Those guys, Jed and Peter? Jed was gone, the condom

broke and he went to — whatever, and while he was gone Peter called him Larry or Jerry or something.

That's the thing with couples. You never know their real names, because you're not supposed to come back to haunt them. So when I talk about guys, I'm not really sure who they are. There's lots of Peters, that's for sure. Peter and Michael. Bernie and Peter. Peter and Patrick. The two Peters, Peter R. and Peter C., that has to be their real names, just made up the initial.

Now with Jed and Peter, Jed was a cop and Peter was a lion tamer...that's another thing about couples. You never met so many cops. You could sleep around for years and meet maybe one cop. Two, maybe three construction workers. I mean real construction workers. Not faux-finishers. And you'd definitely never meet a lion tamer. Maybe in Vegas. I heard there were gay lion tamers in Vegas. I don't mean the lions were gay.

You start dating couples and it's fantasy land. Like marching straight into "Homo Depot" where the fags are all doing a big makeover, renovating their images and their scenes. Working some serious fag magic. Poof! I'm a cop. Poof! I'm a football coach. Poof! I'm an Olympic athlete. Used to be. Anyways. Poof! Whatever, so butch it hurts. And when they claim to be butch — you know what he wants. I mean they're still looking for the man. He wants to be over-powered. You know that right away. He'll be hurt if you don't at least try. The butch thing, really, is just a come on.

There's this thing with couples. You'd think they wouldn't be sex starved. I mean, what are they doing with each other? As soon as another guy's in the picture it's a race to get done in record time. Like it had been a while. Something had been a while. I figure it has to do with being in a relationship and still needing to feel attractive. If a man fucks you, that means you're attractive. If another man fucks you, that means you're still attractive. So with couples like that — there's always an opening for another man.

It's like playing a game, really, isn't it, and making the world go round. Fuck-and-run, like an accident almost, a hit-and-run gay accident, and the couple are the bumpers and I'm bouncing between them, scoring off each one, leaving them happy, but most of all, leaving.

That's why this other thing was right out of the blue. This stalking thing. I mean, that's just so not who I am. I am so totally not into that. And it's not like they were the greatest fuck in the world, either, because they most definitely were not.

I've never been charged before. Well, just that once, but it was all such a mistake everything was thrown out. It was never stalking in the first place. I mean, what's a few phone calls? And dropping by to visit — what's wrong with that? I knew they were home, too, the rats, I could hear the porn — *Marine Maneuvers* — we'd watched it together, you like that big cock, don't you private, oh yeah, the two of them acting out most of the roles, me, basically a cock in camouflage. That was like, the week before. Now they can't even come to the door. That's the bullshit part. If they had come to the door, it wouldn't be stalking — it'd be visiting. Hello!

At first I thought they couldn't hear me. I mean, I was outside and I could hear their porn. It was loud. That's why I started kicking a little harder. They don't answer the door, and that turns me into a stalker. One day I'm loose in their bedroom, the barracks they called it, I'm the drill sergeant and we're in the barracks watching videos, monkey see monkey do, and then boom, coupla days later, they won't even answer the fucking door.

Instead, the police drive up to take me away.

Jesus, is it just me or are cops getting younger? These two boys looked like it was the hallowe'en dance at high school and they went dressed as cops, you know, cute as sin, but so bland somehow I couldn't tell them apart — there was just two of them. I hate that. With two guys, you want them to be different. I sat there with the boy-cops back at the station thinking, what's going on? Am I too pissed off to find you guys hot or what? You could tell I was upset because I didn't even think about jumping them. It was weird. Young guys, great uniforms, but they had nothing going but this blank kinda politeness, although stern, very stern, you know, polite in that severe kinda way that makes you wanna puke. Please let me tell you exactly what is going to happen blah blah blah. They went on and on, spelling out exactly how fast and how bad this would turn out for me, if I didn't smarten the hell up. One of them actually yelled, and I had to agree, yeah, I should smarten up.

During the lull I looked from one boy-cop to the other,

147

both staring at me, I mean extended eye contact, and suddenly I had to remind myself that these guys were not some professional gay couple with a perfectly-detailed interrogation room in their condo. I was a little wasted, okay, did I mention that? Just a little twisted, and short-haired guys in uniform send my mind off into loops, and many of these loops start up or end up at that uniform bar, the Big Mess Hall, where the men are all dressed the same — the same as some other men. The Big Mess Hall is a uniform bar where the men are all dressed the same and the rules are all different.

So here I am in this little room with the two cops. One cop left and the other one, I don't know, it was like he swam into focus? Maybe it was just his smile. He was leaning with his shoulder to the wall and he smiled at me. He smiled and I smiled and the room lifted, like when someone you hate walks out. It was like seeing him for the first time. Even his eyes smiled. The cop pushed himself off the wall and started pacing in the small room, tugging at his uniform like it didn't fit anymore.

He stopped in front of me. "You can't keep this up," he said.

"I can try," I said.

I reached for his crotch, and felt the weight of his balls and the hot swelling. He pushed my hand away. "Forget those guys," he said. "Go find a man who treats you like you deserve."

The cop went back to the wall and was standing there, his hands crossed over his crotch, when his partner returned with coffee.

Now, I knew this wasn't a couple doing a scene. I knew that much. It's not like what they say is true, 'cause it isn't. I know when to keep my hands to myself.

When that doctor said I didn't have any impulse control, he was so wrong. I should have stood up right there and said, oh yeah, well doctor, how come I haven't already spit in your face, slapped you silly and jumped up and down on your head? I've got lots of impulse control, you stupid fuck.

I didn't listen to another word that doctor said.

I've got lots of impulse control. I've got good impulse control. What I have trouble with, what keeps getting me into trouble — is bad impulse control. The thing is, I never spend much time figuring it out. I'm more, like, sure, whatever. And when I do think about it, it always seems like it's the bad impulses that get me in trouble.

I can't explain it. The same things aren't always the same, you know?

So how am I supposed to know how things are gonna turn out? Like that bar I was talking about. All the guys in uniform? You see a man you like, you have an impulse to grab his crotch, and you do, and you get a blow job.

That's a good impulse.

You grab another crotch, you get arrested. That's a bad impulse.

That's what I'm talking about. That's what fucks a guy up. That's what makes this whole impulse control thing ridiculous right from the start.

Gink, origin of

"Gink" is what they said in place of a name Gink had before they made that up. It started with these kids I knew at the beginning of junior high. They were boys and there was no use in disagreeing with that at the time. In Dartmouth, your typical outcast suburban boys were still mainly a danger to themselves. Narrowly obsessed with *The Uncanny X-Men* or *The Lord of the Rings* or with a girl who couldn't be named.

It's a cliché but we played dungeon and dragons. They were just starting to make movies about kids going crazy from playing it, worshipping the devil and killing people. Obsessed is a fair way to see it: we played before school, at lunch, and after classes into the night; we didn't notice much outside of the games we thought we made up. I was practicing for subcultures I'd end up thinking I was making up. I don't know what they were doing, though Jimmy honest-to-god wanted to be prime minister some day and in the meanwhile thought Joe Clark would save Canada.

You don't really know when you're in love with someone you know at that age, only when you are in love with someone you don't. I could see that Jimmy was in love with Joe Clark, not just the idea of being him, being leader of the Progressive Conservative party, but with him. I can see the attraction. Joe was soft spoken, stuttering, and indecisive, like Jimmy, and maybe even well meaning, not a bad dad for a country, though not someone I would vote for. I think Jimmy connected with the way Joe got kicked around in the newspapers, with his struggle for respect. Respect was Jimmy's thing, though he wasn't any good at it.

More than I was as it turns out and that's how I upset everything; also being in love with the leader of our little group. Or thinking we had a secret understanding like in *Stand by Me* or that Herman Hesse novel, *Demian*. One night sleeping over at Ray's house, I whispered from the top bunk that the others — our friends Jimmy and Bug — were his slaves, and that I wanted us to do without them. We had been friends first, right? Since grade six. Why bother with them? And what did he have to say to that?

I didn't think there was anything faggoty about it, between Ray and I, and it didn't occur to me to think that it was about my maybe wanting to be a girl. Maybe if I hadn't been driven out that would have become something. Something even more disastrous. He was good looking, in a skinny blonde girl way, and I can see now how he would have been good to kiss. At the time though it was just us being confidential and superior. Two too-smart boys who read the same books and understood one another. Very homo, in retrospect. I dreamt of him asking forgiveness for years after he'd stopped coming after me.

I don't know what made me think I could get away with saying what I said. It had been one of those perfect days. We were hanging out after school, gaming maybe, not with dice or anything, just talking it. We were in the backyard at Bug's house; it might have been the last time we did that, though I think we did make up later on, maybe a year later, for a week or two. We might have been gaming — it's hard to remember anything from that year, or from anything before fifteen. Anyway, it was like a TV movie about the '60s: "Where were you when JFK was shot?" only with Ronald Reagan or the Pope, whichever one wasn't shot on my birthday. Both times I was so happy. It happened just like this.

We were sitting at the picnic table doing nothing much at all. The radio was sitting in the kitchen window and we couldn't really hear it, except to know that music was playing and then that cut out, and there was a newscaster speaking. Bug's mother was in the kitchen doing something and then she kind of shrieked and we all stopped our game and looked at Bug. After a second he gave a shrug and got up and stood there, looking kind of helpless. Ray got up then, and flashed us a little smirk — which is just what he was like — and then they went into the house to see what was wrong.

A minute or two later Ray came out alone, grinning. "So, what's going on?" I asked. His face half split, he said, "The President," or was it the Pope? "was just shot." I don't know why but I cracked up immediately and then both of us were howling our guts out. After a few minutes, I managed to ask, "Is he dead?"

"Dunno," and then we were laughing again, out of control.

When I finally came back enough to myself enough to remember Jimmy, I turned to him to make a joke. He looked so stricken that I didn't, instead I just turned back to Ray who arched an eyebrow and smirking again, said, "She's bawling inside."

"Mrs. Forché?"

"Both of them." His contempt lit up his face and I felt this perfect accord between us. I knew he felt it too and that I could trust him perfectly.

It was the next Saturday morning at Ray's when the big secret came out. He'd told Bug and Jimmy before I got there and they wanted to fuck with me, which only made sense really. I wanted to take Ray away from them, and I'd called them cocksuckers and slaves behind their backs.

When I showed up they were all sitting at the picnic table in Ray's backyard and they gave me these sickly smiles, and Jimmy made some high-pitched roadrunner noises. *Meep meep.* He was always doing that. He looked like the roadrunner with long bird-like bones and his white flesh hanging loose and unmuscled where it emerged from invariably matching adidas shorts and T-shirts. But the crest of hair above his pointy beak face was black not red. Or they didn't quite know how to get down to it. It must have been too much of a shock though, to get right to it, maybe because we'd been friends for almost two years. Ray said, "Let's go in and play D&D." So we went in but maybe they wanted to draw out the moment because he didn't get the game and nobody said anything about it. Instead we sat around in Ray's basement listening to "alternative music" from channel 13, the college station from Halifax. It was a weird thing for us to do because none of us paid that much attention to music except Ray, and he just listened to his older brother's banger stuff, Blue Oyster Cult, Black Sabbath, Pink Floyd.

The Monks' song with the lyrics, *"Nice legs, shame about her face"* finished and there were more sicko grins when Bug started it.

"You make me want to throw up." As if to prove his point he threw a snotty piece of Kleenex at me.

I didn't get it. I thought Bug was just being an idiot — I didn't realize he was just the edge of their mean. "What?"

Then he said, "You make me want to throw up. You're the faggot." His face was already puffed and red from the effort of being forceful.

I turned to Jimmy and Ray, "What's wrong with Bugger?" Hoping to turn whatever was going on against him — how dense could I be? — still not getting it.

I couldn't read Ray's face; there was something concentrated there, waiting, eager. He stayed quiet though, letting the others get their own back first. Jimmy was less restrained, "Watch who you're calling bugger, bugger! Bugger!" Which didn't make sense but now I knew he was on Bug's side, especially when he started to giggle in that hiccupping way of his. I was looking at him, so I didn't see Bug get up and reach over to punch me in the head.

I don't think it hurt much. Bug was just this baggy tracksuit kind of kid, with a white boy's 'fro. Not yet really fat, but his whole body was pouty. If he were a girl he would have had big tits. He kind of did.

I turned around to hit him, thinking I could probably take him and maybe Jimmy too, if I had to. And that if it got bad Ray would step in and we'd beat the hell out of Bugger and Jimmy. We'd had this conversation once, about who was the more powerful god, Thor or Herakles, and his family was German, which was pretty much the same thing as Norse and my father's family came from Lebanon, which isn't far from where the city of Troy was in the time of the ancient Greeks. Even though he was wrong about Thor being stronger the Herakles, I figured the two of us as being pretty much invincible. Instead he said, "Gink, get out of my house."

I didn't think I heard him right and I didn't know who he meant, and at the moment I was also distracted because from the television I was hearing Lou Reed's "Walk on the Wild Side" for the first time. So for a few seconds, a few minutes even, I think I just stood there while the three of them stared.

"Holly came from Miami, FLA.
Hitchhiked her way across the USA,
Plucked her eyebrows on the way,
Shaved her legs and then he was a she
She says, hey babe,
Take a walk on the wild side.
She said, hey honey,
Take a walk on the wild side."

It took one of them figuring it out and that's more or less how it happened.

They were talking among themselves, saying what a freak I was, and as I realized Ray meant me, I wondered what a gink was, what the word meant.

155

As if in answer, Jimmy started braying like a donkey or a harpy, "That's you Gink, that's you. Come on Gink, take a walk on the wild side. Come on! Gink. Gink. Gink." Both Ray and Bug got really flushed, and joined Jimmy's chant, "Gink. Gink. Gink." And started to walk toward me.

I still didn't really know what was happening and I thought if I could just talk to Ray alone I could make things make sense. There was this acid feeling in my stomach and then they'd pinned me, which was good I guess because I felt like I could just fall down. "Ray, what —

They were surprisingly restrained; each one of them only punched me once or twice, while the other two took turns holding my arms. Bug spit in my face.

"Come on gink, take a walk on the wild side!" was the last thing any of them said to me that day. Jimmy, hiccupping, his giggles turned to a raunchy cough as I made my way upstairs.

In the kitchen the TV was turned to the Flintstones so I changed the channel to 13, to catch the end of the song. It was already over and the news was on. I sat on a stool for a few minutes, until I heard the guys on the stairs. Leaving, I was thinking of what I'd say to Ray next time I saw him, about how he'd agreed with me about Bugger and Jimmy when it was just the two of us lying in the dark talking. And how everything would be fine again after we talked, maybe at school on Monday.

But by then I had a new name at school and that was the next two years.

Slut Kiss Girl

a brief note on early 90's nostalgia

There are no Google entries for people who OD'd in 1991 in a little shit town nobody knows. Before the idea we could make a living at this. Now there are awards for being freaks, but back then, we just rotted.

the birth of queercore according to hot chica

Ian Sayre was the king of the local punks, but I didn't realize that when I wrangled going to Doherty High for a day in an attempt to escape year eight of my ten-year sentence of being the scholarship kid at the local private school. He just seemed magic. Ian was a pretty boy with black ringlets and cheekbones, with the charm that comes with always being on yellowjackets. He'd fucked all the boys and girls in town without condoms and was looking for somebody who was left. He bragged about being a runaway and a hustler, how his mom was a sergeant at Fort Devins, a leatherdyke with pierced tits who'd only been with a man the time she made him. Said his dad was full blood, Cherokee, I think, one of the nations that do actually exist but which white boys pull out of their asses to sound mythic. This was the decade that my dad was sticking to the story that we were "Portuguese" or, alternatively, "from the British Commonwealth," so we fit right in.

1991 was the birth of queercore and Worcester had its own half-assed version. Worcester was a genuinely blue-collar punk town. The kind of town everyone moans about when they live there, reading MRR and cursing their luck that they weren't born in the East Bay. The ones that make it out look back wistfully on all those broke-ass nights driving cars in-between the runways of the local airport and watching the planes take off. It was all about people's porches, all the kids crammed into an old beaten up car. If you were a freak, you were in. Mostly.

Worcester's little circle of faggots and dykes were Ian, his friend Jay, Roach, Vicki, J.D., Abby and Megan. Jay was one of those skinhead kids about whom everybody said, "But he's a really nice guy, we've tried talking to him but those are his opinions, and who's to say what's right and wrong, anyway?"

Jay: "Look, man, when those Puerto Rican kids laugh at me and call me stupid cause I'm white, that's racism. When I call them stupid cause they *are* stupid everybody gets on my case." Poor boy. Aryan Youth Front was a big recruiter in my town. Polish and Irish kids whose parents said they were middle class because they owned their shitty houses but all the mills had closed down and moved south, it must have looked like a turkey dinner with all the trimmings to them. Roach was his little brother, this little fifteen-year-old crusty kid, kind of the Beaver of the family, the kid who kept doing things like taking a whole 24 pack of Vivarin when no one could find speed that week and running around the block twenty times.

Abby was fat, had one of those ape-drape haircuts with bleached tips that were cool on fledgling queer girls in 1991, carried a Guatemalan bag, that awkward mix of any available subculture found in kids to whom any subculture is rare. I'd looked at her first day of grade eleven and thought, *there's one*, and sidled up to her. I was assistant editor of the stupid school newspaper to add to the collection of "activities" to be put on my college applications; my great idea was interviewing her anonymously about being queer. She was all cool and enthusiastic about it, we both were, it was for The Cause, but as we did the interview we were both very quiet and terrified. The chief editor ran it as "Interview with a Bancroft Bisexual," a very big deal at the time. Vicki was a Clorox blond crew cut, short short hair and boy-suits from the Salvation Army. They were lovers and that is the only thing I know about it.

J.D. was older, had gone to Mass Art and dropped out like everybody did, all the poor artsy kids who went to that cheap, state-run art school. Then he'd gone to Orlando to draw pictures at *Disneyworld* and gotten fired for being queer; apparently Walt had left a stern law that real fairies weren't to be allowed. He was positive at twenty-four and in love with Ian, enacting that wounded beautiful fucked up young boy fag thing on him. There was controversy in the town over whether Ian had given it to him, as it was well known that Ian had hustled all the times he ran away. Megan, who was an older loud punk rock big dyke at twenty-four with her own car and big sloppy shag, who would pick up stranded kids and good-naturedly drive them home. Never had a girlfriend, sketched and smoked Marlboro Reds on her porch.

Vicki and Ian had a weight loss contest one time, and whoever lost less had to go up to the biggest, ugliest jock in the school and ask him out to the prom. Ian lost. I wrote letters to people I met at art camp, filled out scholarship forms, practiced my smile, my performance of beautiful exceptional unusual different for the admissions offices. I couldn't go bad, there was ten years of work and sacrifice involved in getting me out of here. How come Christian Slater made it look so easy in *Pump up the Volume*? The one time I tried to tie sheets around my desk and climb down the hedges to get to the all-night party it took two hours to even open the window because my mother said "What's that, Leah?" every time the window creaked. The bushes were arbor vitae and bended, it was hopeless. I didn't make it back to the all-night party.

The night of the all-night party at Ian's, when his mom was out on maneuvers, I'd had my mom drop me off early because it was too far to walk and there were no bus routes there. My dad was on year two of lack of work and the insurance rates were so high in Massachusetts that they couldn't afford to let me get my license. As I neared the doors in my slutty outfit, chatting on about the "spaghetti dinner some kids were putting together," my mom grabbed me with a look of terror and started crying, "Just use a condom Leah! Please!" Rollins Band was blasting as I opened the door. *"It could be your mama or it could be you! Drive-by shooting..."* and all the boys were bouncing on that recliner in a pile of ass-grabbing. Ian grabbed me and pulled me on top and I wriggled on top of his boner. I grinned. He kissed me. "We're doing a power bake in my room, come up.

I was desperately horny, needed to be fucked, but I knew none of the boys I met were any good. I knew they'd refuse to eat me out or come in five minutes, I'd read Marge Piercey and *The New Our Bodies Ourselves.* I wanted Carol Queen's boyfriend. I wanted the copy of *Macho Sluts* I'd stolen from the pile of books at my job putting anti-shoplifting tags on books in the basement of Worcester's only independent bookstore, $4.25 an hour but all the books you could steal from the pile deemed "not appropriate for a family bookstore," that included all the Re/Search books, lots of Burroughs and, of course, Pat.

I stayed up late writing letters to K. She'd write me back in her tiny black script. She was working her way through the pile of coke in her closet. The cops had pulled her over when she was in the dealer boy's car and she'd shoved the vials up her twat. One day her parents came home and found her naked shaking all over on top of her bed and taken her to the emergency room. *I told her many lies and they finally let me go.* She'd miscarried Greg's baby, the kid who'd gone away to school, tested positive and shot himself at the kitchen table with the result on the countertop in front of him. Bled into the toilet. I kept writing her to go to a doctor, Planned Parenthood, anything. Social worker kid. *Why? It's just my body.*

We met at art camp. Both on scholarship. I was hanging out in some kid's room and she was there looking through a telescope. Pretty, pretty. That kind of angel princess girl, soft beige hair, shorts, hoodie, but perfect. We went back to her room and started talking about suicide, but for real. There's this medley of all my favourite Jane's Addiction hits in my head as I remember looking at her, and she seemed like most of the songs embodied. We were going to go to a Jane's concert, seduce Perry, get knocked up and then move into a house and be lovers. I added the last part. I could see the squat in San Francisco with the purple women's anarchy sign on the door.

Let's get a van and run away. I'll bring my camera.
I walk from school to my job at the bank wearing an ankle length woolen skirt with stockings and garter belts underneath.

I loved her and there were good reasons why we never touched.

Worcester love song

Nobody's really rich in Wormtown, the ones who think they are own used car lots and outlet mall stores, but damn, they're doing better than most of the town. Norton's blew over my school, the world's largest manufacturer of ceramic abrasive tile. Every year another teacher got breast cancer or alopecia, and we got used to watching their hair drop out bit by bit during class. Worcester is the only place I've ever heard of where working class folks try to afford bottled water and it's thirty-nine cents a gallon, just for us. The second girl I kissed was from Leominster, one town over, known for the uranium in the ground water. She found out she had cervical cancer at thirty during the mandatory pelvic for egg donation, her first health care in ten years. All downtown was abandoned, Funland the toy store that'd gone bust with the big rotting clown murals, Union Station, big back when working class cities had trains, department stores and strollable downtowns, you'd drive by and see lots of skinny trees growing up through the roof of this Greco-Roman beauty.

When I was sixteen I was all winding down the empty streets wearing a.... I don't even know how to describe it. Gauze? With gold lamé over the top? One of those gauzy gothy numbers purchased at a dusty store with purple drapes and silver jewelry that is in the bigger of the smaller shittier cities and looks at the time like a bastion of alternative culture. Colours like mango, turquoise, berry, magenta and all that other hipster shit had not yet been discovered, The Gap was still worn by preps, and shopping in Worcester county on my mom's budget was all about spending a couple of hours at Urban Outfitters in Boston when we went for one of our big monthly trips to imbibe culture. Bookstores and people who were different. While staring wistfully at the colours, my mom would sniff at how fucking overpriced it was and how bad the stitching was, she could stitch better. The next day we went back to combing Marshalls and TJ Maxxx and Filene's Basement trying to find something good. This explains why at sixteen I had basically two outfits: the aforementioned black gauzy number, and a black leotard and one foot-length black gauzy skirt with one of those cord waistbands with a little bell on the end. I had not cut my hair since 1985 because there was noone in Worcester who could cut long curly hair right; my mom's hairdresser still used mousse and hairspray and kept pestering me to go back to bangs. Took me three years to grow them out and they hang in front of my chin.

I would go for a walk by myself. I wasn't allowed to close my door or walk off the street because people might rape me. She'd come by every half hour and open the door "just to see what you're doing." I had heard there were families where it was fairly normal for sixteen-year-old girls to go off on their own sometimes, unsupervised, but that must have been another planet.

Worcester is wide and has no public transit. The buses come once an hour. Walking in a real city gets you to many different places within fifteen minutes. Walking fifteen minutes in Worcester will get you three streets over and a few hundred more triple-deckers passing by your eyes. It would take hours of trudging to get anywhere and what you passed wasn't especially interesting, down Pleasant ten minutes until the first store, then another half hour until anything, down to Park with the Iandolli's supermarket and Elm Park, down Institute that had little three shops not-even-hipster, more like "collegiate" strip, cause it was next to Worcester Polytechnic Institute. That was where the aforementioned gothy shop was, and RoMo, this weirdly misplaced hipster boutique that sold Docs and lots of other things even the tiny middle class of Worcester couldn't afford, and then a diner, the Friendly's, and then more empty roads leading to the expressways that cut through the town, cut it into east and west end.

Downtown was half eight-story high-rises with all the windows bombed out and half a parking lot. The city council kept voting for more parking, as if that was the problem. Back in her day, my mother told me, Worcester was the big city for Central Massachusetts. She was cosmopolitan for living there instead of in Webster, the town where she'd grown up, a bachelor girl with her own apartment and all. There had been department stores, three of them, bookstores and restaurants, but then in 1981 city council decided to bulldoze it and replace it with a big mall. For a while the Galleria was the place to be, a place of wonder, big jukebox-shaped ceiling, and so many stores and a fountain with coloured lights and rocks. By the time I was walking past it all the stores except maybe six had closed and the bangas from the east end had carved up the parking lot into turf-level D-12, level B-6. There was a rain weeping on Common with Nation of Islam guys selling *The Final Call*, the newspaper office, the abortion clinic and the adult bookstore. There was a beautiful library behind the mall, in a squat cement building with two birch trees out front, limp flyers in a tray by the check-in and kids sitting on the steps with pocket knives, and like every bookworm girl in every story that's where I ended up. It was my city, and I had all the neighbourhoods of the library memorized, all the different places you could find lesbian separatist literature and self-published books about the women's peace camps that the one dyke librarian in Worcester I never met had ordered three copies of each and placed in the stacks.

The sign by the highway that said, "Every great city has at least one great college; Worcester has ten" and then a list of schools like Becker Junior College. There was also the "Worcester, Paris of the 90s" slogan they tried for a while. There was a little pocket of cool by the tracks. The Greyhound station, Easy Pieces the vintage clothing store, a music instrument shop. But nothing cool like in MRR. Just me, in my black trenchcoat, walking by myself. Not in a scene, not a punk girl. Then I would go home and sleep. I had every single piece of every single street memorized. I knew every single thing there was to do.

Nobody was ever on the street but me. Everybody drove. Nobody talked to each other. I still don't know how to nod and smile at people on my block. If anybody had picked me up and dragged me, nobody would see, nobody would do anything. When I walked, boys would drive by and scream, "Hey mamacita, fuck me hot chica!" They were mistaking me for something. "You're beautiful, you're just not the kind of beautiful they know about around here," my mom would say, brushing her hair furiously. Only they

166

do, mom, and it's called Puerto Rican. I knew what I looked like, even if she didn't.

But it was at least a real place, not a fake place. Real places were places like New York. Real places were like this city, where the chains and suburban developments hadn't penetrated. The buildings were old but real. But it wasn't a real place because nothing important happened there. To be a freak who was a real person, you had to leave here and go to a city, one of the other kinds of real places.

"So, would you have oral sex with me?" Jay asked. Almost proper. Sure, what the fuck, if you'll go down on me. I put on my Jane's Addiction T-shirt with the naked people squirming on it and went out. I showed up at his mother's house, just off my street for once, and knocked on the front door. Jay's mom opened the door. She was insanely like a mom from the 50's, almost like a grandma with her apple cheeks, tight gray poodle curls, and apron. I couldn't believe it. "Well, so nice to meet you Leah, I always like meeting Jason's friends." Her son loomed behind her, all bald six foot six of him. "Enough ma, hey we'll be in the back." I almost liked the asshole. He was fun to hang around with in that big dumb guy plus sidekick way, where you're the sidekick.

On the back steps, he said "So."

"So." Trying to look nonchalant, I bent over, pulled the buttons of his 501s open and started sucking. His cock was huge and wasn't moving. I tried all kinds of stuff I'd read about. I pulled away and asked demurely, "Is this okay? Is there anything else I could be doing?" tried for tantalizing.

"Oh yeah, yeah." I was smirking as I had my mouth around his cock. The Puerto-Rican looking girl sucking the cock of the queer skinhead. Ha fucking ha. After ten minutes with no results I pulled away. "Hey, sorry, do you mind if I... my jaw's getting sore." "Oh yeah, it's okay." He was too tired to go down on me. We clapped each other on the back and I went home. I didn't think anything of it.

The next day in school Ian showed up at lunch. They'd had a bet. "Leah, they're saying you made biscuits out of your menstrual blood and ate them." Slutty but ugly, too. We stayed down by the yellow lockers in the basement that day. That was the end of that. I wrote more letters to D.J. Filled out applications. Waited for New York, the closest city my mother would let me apply to schools at. Sarah Schulman's Lower East Side, a whole city full of folks with kinky hair and light brown skin. Up all night. I can go walking anytime, anyplace there.

dirty river

There are no Google entries for the girl who changes her name and gets away. Nothing to track down, unlisted phone number, different name on all the books. I don't know if I'm the only one still alive from that moment.

Sometimes when I close my eyes I see the streets I have memorized. Not even when I close my eyes: when I'm talking on the phone or brushing my teeth, sitting in a staff meeting, one of those ordinary moments the entire day is made up of, at the same time as I'm doing all that shit I'm seeing those streets. Park Avenue, Chandeler Street, with rows of rotting stores and the Honey Farms where I clerked the midnight shift, North High's parking lot, the bridge over the Main South creek. The same thing for eighteen years. Got away, not going back, got to a real place, then another. But this is the *real* real place, tattooed on the inside of my brain. The place where I come from.

Graves Street Junior Public

I remember kindergarten. My mom was third from the left in a row of moms sitting along the wall. They were gone as soon as we started exploring the room and playing.

Later we finger painted. I completely covered my paper with red paint, smeared my palms right to the edges. As I pulled my fingertips through the wet paint, the oatmeal paper beneath was revealed, creating the image of a lion in a cage. One of the boys across from me looked up. "My birthday was in May," he said, "I'm five."

"I'm five too," I said, holding up my five red fingers. "My birthday was in April," I added, smiling at him.

The girl next to me turned in my direction. "That's my *name!*" she said frowning. "Your birthday can't *be* April." She gaped at me, her mouth open then closing into a pout.

"I know my birthday is in April," I insisted. "That's the month Martin Luther King was *ass-inated*." I said this, expecting it will settle the matter.

April's eyes narrowed, "That's my *name!*" she shrieked as she lunged forward, grabbed my painting and tore it into pulpy shreds. Mrs. Ford separated us. I was given a new seat far from April. I had a new sheet of paper and shared the yellow paint with Nick. I began painting again; when I finished, it was a large yellow fish. After snack-time and a nap, we got to choose whatever we wanted to play with. I chose the bucket of blocks. I'm going to build a tower, I said. I sat cross-legged beside the bucket and worked. Multi-coloured blocks formed its base and many levels as my tower rose above my head. Nick stood watching.

"Are you a nigger?" he asked. Without waiting for my answer, he nudged his foot forward and toppled my tower. With the sound of the 'n' word I know I'm supposed to ignore him. My mom explained many times that Dr. King, who looked down from the picture on the kitchen wall, taught us to turn the other cheek.

I remained seated, gathered up my blocks and rebuilt. Nick was watching; maybe Dr. King was watching too. I didn't look up; I continued placing blocks, but before it reached its full height he nudged the base with his foot again and toppled my tower.

I began building my tower again. "Nigger blocks, nigger blocks," Nick said under his breath. My ears and face felt hot. I was about to place another block, but Nick kicked my tower over with such force that the blocks hit my face and filled my lap. He laughed. I clenched my teeth and stood. Blocks dropped from my lap onto the floor; my legs felt weak. I squeezed hard on the one block I still had in my hand. I looked him straight in the eye. "I'm Black," I said, swinging my right arm and crushing my block fist into his face. Mrs. Ford's intervention saved him from further blows. She sent me to the principal's office.

In the office, Mr. Carey wanted to know what I did to make him call me that. I don't know, so he called my mom because she hasn't signed the paper allowing him to give me the strap. I don't like Kindergarten. Mr. Carey called a spanking 'the strap' and you had to hold out your hands while he gave it to you across your palms. At home, a spanking was a spanking and it landed on whatever part my mom could get a hold of.

On the phone with my mom, Mr. Carey mostly listened. He held the receiver with his shoulder while he wrote. Her voice blared out when he stopped writing and pressed the receiver to his chest "...until I arrive" I heard her say. Mr. Carey pressed the receiver hard. "Sit and wait outside," he said, almost in a whisper.

I waited in the outer office, but I couldn't sit still. I kept thinking about the strap. I went into the hall and began counting the Elmer the Safety Elephant Awards. Graves Street School had won the safety award ten times; Elmer the Safety Elephant's flag flew just below the Canadian flag outside. There are ten plaques. Elmer smiled down from each of them.

I was walking heal-toe, heal-toe along the silver lines that separate the floor tiles when our car pulled up out front. My mom hurried in past me and into Mr. Carey's office. She closed the door after her. I couldn't hear what she was saying, but it sounded like I was in trouble. When she came out, I looked up at Elmer; his trunk held high. I waited for her to say or do something. She looked at me for a moment. "Go get in the car with Grandma," she said coolly. She followed me outside but we didn't go home.

Instead she drove up Lundy's Lane to the Dairy Queen, where we only went after the dentist. She didn't say anything about Kindergarten and I got to have a banana split.

I had finished my split by the time we drove silently down Lundy's Lane, down Victoria and turned onto Huron Street. I sat cradling the empty dish, pressing the plastic spoon to my nose with my tongue as we pulled into the driveway. My mom put the car in park, stretched her arm across the back of the front seat and looked at me. "That boy didn't hit you first," she said. "If you ever hit someone before they hit you first, I'll hit you so hard you won't land until the middle of next week." I put my tongue back in my mouth and let the plastic spoon drop into the dish. My mom wet a napkin with her spit and wiped something off my face. I didn't squirm away. There are some things you need to sit still for.

DEBRA ANDERSON

Passing Tammy

Being with Tammy was like running down the up escalator or peeing outdoors where you might get caught. With Tammy I smoked my first cigarette. We were in junior high and snuck away from school during lunch. Tammy clenched a pack of Dunhill's in her fist, ripped off the cellophane and threw it in the air. I didn't want to wreck our moment, so I didn't complain. I just watched the wrapping flicker and reflect light back at me, like the soapy bubbles I used to blow in my backyard.

Tammy wanted to light up right in front of the strip mall, but I had an aunt who lived nearby. What if she pulled up and saw me? Even though Tammy screeched "Chicken" and "Baby" the whole way, I managed to drag her to a side street. She boldly lit her cigarette, taking fierce drags and puckering her mouth like a really tight bum hole. When she'd stiffly remove the cigarette out of her mouth after a drag, it would make a loud popping noise. Then she would exhale in a noisy, breathy stream.

I furtively lit mine and tried to inhale. Like holding my mouth to an exhaust pipe. The heater on the end dangled a hot, threatening poker. I coughed a lot and spit big juicy ones on the pavement, nervously watching the street for my aunt. This was difficult, as I didn't know exactly what her car looked like.

After the first one, we each smoked another and Tammy tried to teach me to inhale it properly. But she didn't quite know how either. She just pretended she did. It was cold out, my fingers were getting raw and pink, especially around the knuckles. I couldn't tell where the smoke I exhaled finished and my hot breath began. So I just kept exhaling and exhaling. And peeking at the red brick house we stood in front of, to see if anyone was watching us.

"Don't be a fuckwad. Relax. Your aunt isn't going to see you. And if she did, she'd probably laugh at how stupid you're smoking. Do it like me. Breathe the smoke in like this," Tammy lectured as she huffed back a puff. Her eyeballs bulged.

I didn't see the difference between how Tammy was smoking and how I was, except for the eyeball thing, which happened to Tammy sometimes when she'd get excited anyhow.

When my cigarette was done, I could still taste it, my taste buds prickly goosebumps charred raw. All the way back to school, I spit along the sidewalk, hoping to get the taste out of my mouth.

"Cut it out," Tammy barked.

But I couldn't stop. Mini rorschach test explosions splattered against the concrete. I wanted it out of me.

In English class I smiled when I remembered what I had done over lunch. I still hadn't had sex, but I knew what it was like to smoke a cigarette. It was like when I finally got my period, or bought my first bra. And again, no one but me noticed the difference. By the time I got home for supper, I couldn't smell the smoke on me anymore and neither did my mom. I was safe.

It didn't occur to me that Tammy was dangerous. At least not at first. Tammy was the kind of friend you had who was just naturally extremely cool and you kinda hoped it would somehow rub off on you. She wore a biker jacket and Doc Martin Creepers with shiny buckles when all the other girls wore boring and babyish white Keds sneakers. Tammy knew things I didn't. I think her two older sisters had at some point shown her the 'right' places to shop downtown. But even if they hadn't, Tammy would know where to go anyways, unlike me who only ever shopped at Yorkdale Mall or "Dorkdale Mall" as some called it. Correction: Tammy called it that.

She was the one who lead me up the creaky, sticky Queen Street stairs to the Black Market my first time. The used clothing store smelled of urine, the inside of an old milk thermos, and that stale Kraft Dinner smell that wafts through the halls of my Bubie's apartment building. Tammy knew how to shop. We made wish lists together. Tammy was a lot richer than me, so she usually bought everything on her wish list and then made another. But what Tammy knew best was music. She listened to bands I'd never heard of. The Clash, The Sex Pistols, The Cramps, P.I.L., The Jesus and Mary Chain, The Cure, The Ramones. I had just barely stopped tuning into my parent's Easy Listening Station and settled into an indifferent groove with a chart-busting a.m. station. Before I met Tammy, I hadn't cared much about music one way or the other.

But Tammy was a fanatic. The walls in her room were covered in posters and flags from the headshops she'd introduced me to. They were sleazy places covered in posters of burly guys on bikes, rock bands and naked women. Places that made me feel as if I was being squeezed behind the fridge, my face mashed into that unrecognizable grit that never gets cleaned away.

I'd watch her buy cheap T-shirts with Sid Vicious on them from plywood bins. I bought one once with Johnny Rotten gaping crazily.

One time I tranced out, letting my eyes follow the swirls of the oily fingerprints on the glass, I was really grateful to be there, in a weird, creepy headshop that I never even knew existed before Tammy took me there, with a gross man behind the counter leering slightly at us. I was really glad to be hanging out with Tammy, so tough and hard in her leather jacket, shopping bags clutched in her fists rather than just holding them with her fingers through the holes in the plastic like everyone else. I wanted to be like her so badly. I actually thought I might soon, 'cause here I was with her instead of at home in my room reading or watching a video with my mom or fighting with my brother or something equally geeky. And I did feel happy, like something was changing, like something *had* changed, and then Tammy punched my arm, *kapow*, hard with her free hand. The force of it jerked her body back. I heard all her shopping bags rub against each other in that slick plastic wuffling noise. Then she started to cackle so loudly everyone in the store looked at us. But for once I didn't really care.

"Hey space cadet, you're it!" she screeched in her high-pitched, Tammy way and then laughed for about five seconds before she ran out of the store, again taking me by surprise. She always took me by surprise. Tammy charged down the thin, wood-paneled staircase to ground level and Yonge Street.

Smiling weakly, I rubbed my arm where she had punched me. Heat emanated like an asteroid had landed where she had hit my bicep. I could hear Tammy's feet thumping on the stairs. The shopkeeper stared at me. I pretended for a second I was Tammy, and I glared right back at him. It was up to me whether to follow her. And I did, of course.

Tammy's energy was a race car careening off the track, straight at you. By the time you realized you had to leap out of her way, there was nowhere left to go.

It was a Saturday, early evening, and the sun was setting. The walk through the maze of streets from the bus stop to Tammy's house was long and cold. My nose hairs were frozen, but my ears were okay under my hat. Tammy was too cool for things like winter hats. Her hair hung in wild straggly curls, like when you untwist a rope and what's left is all kinky.

"So which goofball do you like? Tell me," Tammy ordered.

"No one," I answered in what I hoped sounded truthful and blasé.

"Bullshit. I know you have a crush on someone, Reena, and you're gonna tell me."

"I don't like anyone. Really."

"Fuck you. You just don't want to say who because he doesn't like you anyways. Look!" Tammy shrieked urgently and grabbed my arm, applying pinching pressure around my forearm while pointing at a huge house we were passing with her free arm. The house looked new and had big windows and an orange basketball net mounted on a wood pole in the driveway.

"That's Jacob Zaidelberg's house. He went to my public school, and he was the biggest jerk-off! He still is a dipshit," she explained.

Every school has one or two guys in each grade who all the girls like. Jacob was that charismatic guy. It humiliated me that I had a crush on him. I liked to think of myself as more original than most. Jacob was arrogant and would never like me, only popular girls. But something about his long eyelashes, dark eyes and curly brown hair caught me. He moved really well in gym class, but I was never lucky enough to be in the right spot in line to be placed in his group for square-dancing. I ended up in the groups that Jacob and his friends would make fun of.

So I kept my shameful crush tucked close under my tongue, like the fact that one of my breasts didn't seem to be growing as fast as the other. But then there was Tammy, sand-blasting off my sweater to expose my secret to everyone. It was like she said Jacob was a jackass just to show me she knew who I liked, whether I'd tell her or not.

"It's cold. Let's get a cab the rest of the way home," she snarled. But I didn't have any money left. I'd spent it all

179

downtown, on a pair of used jeans and a Clash T-shirt from a headshop.

"Nah. We're almost there, Tammy. Let's just keep walking."

Tammy roared, "You bitch. You cheapskate bitch. You want my ears to fall off? You fucking cheapskate cunt!" She kept screaming, her words bouncing like a slapshot hockey puck, ricocheting off all those cookie-cutter rich houses. The ridiculous thing was we were walking on deserted suburban side streets the whole time. Not a payphone or cab in sight. Not even a car drove by.

I should have left then. But I didn't. I walked behind Tammy, feeling like a bitch cheapskate. Stared at the snow under my feet. I couldn't leave Tammy. I had said I would go to her house for a sleepover. Angie and Darlene were coming over later, too. It was kind of a big deal: Tammy's parents and sisters were away. So I kept walking. And by the time we got there I felt empty. Hungry too.

But when she started to cook I didn't want any. I couldn't eat. Not with her laughing at me like she was delivering punches. Not with her eyes small and hard and glossy, chin thrust outwards, attitude surging to form a mean, protective igloo she hid inside of and would only duck out of to threaten anyone who came too close. At the other side of the kitchen I could still feel the energy she radiated as she cooked. It was as if she wasn't Tammy, but someone I'd never met before, someone older and distant. A different species.

Tammy danced in front of the burners. Occasionally she

shoved the big shrimp in the frying pan. She danced a speedy jig, although there was no music playing and she wasn't plugged into her walkman (though she almost never went anywhere without it). She stared through the spot I occupied, not registering. Her chuckles jangled up my vertebrae like xylophone keys dinged in succession.

Then, as if she held a secret remote control inside her that changed the channel if she squeezed a certain muscle, or had a certain triggering thought, she saw me again in front of her. She opened her mouth and a noise leaked out, rusty door hinge creak creak creaking, massaging her throat.

"I'm only gonna eat the little shrimpy legs! These little legs are the best part and the rest of the shrimp is garbage. You can't make me eat the whole shrimp, ha ha, you can try but I will only eat the legs," she babbled.

"I don't really care what you eat."

Tammy threw her head back like a wolf and laughed. It sounded more like a human howl. I wished her mother were home. I wished Angie and Darlene were there, even though they weren't coming for another half hour.

"See? This is a delicacy. Watch me," she commanded.

I watched Tammy rip off the little legs of the shrimp and stuff them in her mouth, butter gushing down her chin and shining on her fingers.

"Mmmmm. So good," she moaned. "And this," Tammy announced, picking up the meat of the shrimp, "tastes like shit." She pitched the shrimp into the garbage can across the room.

I felt queasy, hearing leg shells crackle against her doggy

teeth, and watching her greasy lips fight to keep the legs inside as she spoke, while methodically throwing fat shrimp into the trash. Most of it hit the white wall just above the garbage can and then fell in. The marks they left made splattered yellow moon crescents.

Angie and Darlene arrived after I'd excused myself to hide in the washroom. I'd been in there for fifteen minutes when I heard the doorbell ring. It was safe to come out again. Tammy had already taken their coats and shoved them into the foyer.

"Get downstairs. We'll hang out in the basement and be bad asses tonight!" Tammy exclaimed.

We filed down the spiral stairs into the rec room. The rest of Tammy's house was spiffy and modern, but the basement was stuffed with leftover furniture from other decades in various shades of orange, brown and rust. Tammy ignored the nubby sofas and crashed to the floor, in front of a medley of miniature liquor bottles. We followed suit and joined her on the floor, sitting in a circle with the alcohol as our centrepiece.

"Uh, Tammy, where'd you get this?" I asked.

"Don't be a drag, Reena. Quit worrying. It's just from my parent's liquor cabinet." Tammy dismissively waved at me and then started cracking open the bottles. Wouldn't her parents remember what had been open and what had been sealed? Tammy poured airplane mini-bottles of red wine into big, clear beer steins and passed us each one. My glass smelled like rancid grapes. I tried to drink my first drink ever of alcohol. Tammy gulped hers down fast and poured another. Angie and Darlene drank up quick, too. But my glass didn't seem to be going anywhere. It tasted horrible.

Then everyone was giggling. Tammy sounded like a warped tape, slow and out of focus. Then something clicked in her and she switched speeds. Cruising down the dragstrip faster than I could process. Tammy started talking tough, trying to talk us into wrestling or fighting.

"You wanna go?" she snarled in a way comical to me and the others.

"No," we all said. I looked at the carpet, brown furled shagginess. Tammy faltered. I don't think she had foreseen the obstacle of none of us rising to her bait. She started calling us, "bitches" and "chickens" and "worthless blood clots". "Fishmongers!!!" She screeched and made a spitting noise at Angie.

I thought it was just a noise until Angie yelled, "Eeeeewwww gross Tammy! I can't fucking believe you. You just spit on me. You bitch. Fuck off."

I sat. Incredulous.

"Yeah. I did. Cause you bitches are chicken cuntfaces."

Then Tammy spat at Darlene. Angie, Darlene and I stood, poised to run. Tammy jumped up, her feet crashing against the floor. She filled up a lot of the basement. The low ceiling grazed her head and she towered over us. She screamed again. We took off up the spiral staircase, spattering in different directions once we hit the ground floor. Tammy charged after us, spitting at our backs. Big, thick horks pelted us, flying through the air.

We were on her turf. Tammy clipped along, quickly bridging the distance between us. I couldn't run fast enough. It was like I was trying to walk through water. Tammy grabbed my dangling arm: wobbly pasta just before it's thrown against the wall to make sure it's cooked. She whipped me around and threw me against the wall in the hallway and held me there. Stuck her face with her pebbled, glossed-over eyes right at me.

One of her horks landed on my shoulder. Another on my neck. A mucous mudslide down the side of a cliff. Even though we had been drinking wine, her breath and horks reeked of rancid banana. I got so mad I wrenched myself free and pushed hard with both hands against her chest. She fell in slo-mo.

"Lezzie freak!" she screamed as she went down. "You perv. You touched my tits, you touched my tits, fucking dyke. Stay away from me!"

Angie and Darlene hovered in the brown doorway across from me. The beige hallway stretched endlessly on either side of them. Tammy lay sprawled on the thick, cream carpet, sputtering angrily. I sent a pleading look at Angie and Darlene, begging them to deliver me to the safety they were enjoying. They lowered their eyes, as if what Tammy had just accused me of was true.

Tammy sat up. I ran up the spiral stairs, gripping the dark wood banister for strength. I heard someone behind me so I ran faster, whipping around the corner.

"Fuck you, Reena! We don't allow lesbians in this house.

You think you can push me around? I'm gonna get you bitch!" Tammy screeched.

I couldn't let her spit on me again.

"Tammy, stop this, cut it out," I wheezed.

"Me? I'm not the lesbian. You're the one who has to be stopped, you cunt-sucking freak!"

I ran so fast I could barely see where, all the while trying to puzzle what Tammy was accusing me of. I'd never really thought about homosexuals before. And I didn't have time to think properly now.

The walls of the hallway hurled past me like a camera whirling in circles. I saw a doorknob. The bright round brass winked at me. I grabbed it and threw open the door, slammed myself inside, as someone pounded against it so hard the door jangled in its frame.

"Let me in, let me in!" someone screamed.

"It's me. Let me in, she's coming!" screamed Angie.

I opened the door and Angie leapt inside. I slammed it shut against Tammy. But not before I saw her face glowing. Lit up like a counselor telling ghost stories with a flashlight held under their chin. I wondered why all the TV shows I'd ever seen had never shown what really goes on at a sleepover party. They made it seem like all anyone did was look cute in their pyjamas, giggle and drink hot chocolate. The most dangerous thing was to stay up too late and have mom chide everyone to go to bed.

This wasn't that kind of party. Tammy rammed into the door to remind us. I wondered if the tiny lock would hold.

Hold her out. I looked around the washroom for something to protect myself. All I could find was a basket of little gift soaps shaped like rounded roses. I wondered if I shoved them into Tammy's eye sockets, would the old lady perfume scent of the soap have a toxic reaction? Did Tammy's mother ever imagine a guest contemplating committing such a sacrilege against her daughter with her decorative soaps? Angie panted where she lay crouched in the bathtub, sweat like water drops on her forehead.

Tammy shrieked from the other side of the door, "That's right, you chicken-ass motherfucking cowards. You hide behind that door. You have to live with yourselves. Cowards!"

Suddenly it went quiet. And then I realized there were only two of us in the washroom. Darlene was still out there. Angie and I looked at each other, but neither of us moved to save Darlene, even as we heard her scream. I heard a loud thump, which I imagined was Darlene being tackled to the floor. Then all I could hear was the sound of Tammy growling.

None of us went home. Angie and I hid in the bathroom for a little while, her laying in the bathtub while I sat on the toilet, resting my head in my hands. We heard the front door slam and then Darlene called from the hallway telling us it was safe. Tammy had gone into the yard for a cigarette. She didn't come back for about half an hour. While we waited, we sat in the living room and quietly watched TV, gingerly sitting on the edge of a salmon-coloured sofa. No one wanted to go back down to the rec room. We discussed calling our parents to be picked up, but who ever heard of a teenager asking to come home early? Doing so would be like breaking some sort of unspoken code. The code of the sleepover. You have to sleep over the *whole* night. You don't leave part-way through, no matter what happens. I fingered the hard plastic of the remote control and knew that as bizarre as it sounded after what had happened, if we did not stay for the duration of the sleepover, it would be pure betrayal. When Tammy came back inside she seemed too tired for more wrestling and chasing craziness. She didn't even seem to remember any of that had happened. She wanted to go to bed. But although it was a five-bedroom house, Tammy made us all sleep in her bedroom. But no one could sleep in her bed.

Tammy, as she put it, "was no perverted lesbo."

"I don't sleep with girls. No way," she said.

For a pillow, Tammy gave me a rolled up sweatshirt of hers. She wouldn't give me a blanket, even when I said I was cold. Instead she got an old beach towel and tossed it at me. The room went black. Her walkman clicked on. I went to sleep, shivering under the thin towel against the hard floor, listening to the whirring gears in Tammy's Walkman.

I don't really remember the next morning. What happened when we woke up or how I got home. With Tammy, I have lots of blanks.

I remember the yellow crescent moon marks on the wall by the garbage can in the kitchen. They glowed in a surreal way, like when you look at a bright light and close your eyes and still see it, etched on the insides of your eyelids, refusing to disappear.

After that night, I tried to get some distance from Tammy without acknowledging what I was doing. When you run from a dog gone bad, the dog will chase you and pounce. Dogs smell fear. It was easy to not return phone calls. But it was harder at school, with Tammy right in front of me. Her hair had gone wild; a Medusa's scalp writhing with greasy snakes. Her eyes were narrowed slivers of broken glass. The other kids sensed something too, and gave her a wide berth. School kids nervously inching past the crazy neighbourhood dog, praying she was securely tied up.

I also managed to avoid Tammy, but in high school, she was hard to forget. Layers of her would appear, covering some filter in my mind, with her blue-gray fuzz. I'd stubbornly peel away the coating and drop it in the trash. I did a lot of peeling, but Tammy always came back.

I was already a few years into university when Tammy walked into the video store where I worked part-time. She looked as cool as ever, still in her biker jacket and don't-fuck-with-me attitude. She shuffled through the store, her Walkman blaring, intent on ignoring me.

"Tammy, it's me, Reena, from school. Remember?" I asked.

Her eyes crinkled as she chuckled, "Heh heh. Yeah. I thought it was you."

Tammy paced while talking to me, loud. She still hadn't turned off her Walkman and fidgeted restlessly, picking up items and reluctantly putting them down in the wrong place.

I got the same feeling I get when people come in the store and I know I should watch them so they don't steal. So I watched, but it was Tammy I was watching, and I felt like a traitor.

Her speech had this weird rhythm to it, blurting out then total silence. Tammy darted her eyes nervously from side to side the whole time we talked. Her neck swiveled awkwardly to get a better view of whoever she thought was trying to sneak up on her.

I don't remember what she said she was studying. Although now, years later, I wish I'd paid closer attention and not been afraid of the gleam of her. Not wished her to dissolve like cotton candy pressed against your tongue. But that's not the way it happened. I ached for her to leave the store and not cause any trouble. She kept switching in mid-sentence to a different accent and dialect. She'd sputter aggressively in a country drawl, then switch to a timid British accent.

The conversation dribbled. I watched Tammy as she walked out of the store uncertainly. Looking like she didn't belong. Anywhere. Once she was gone, my co-worker came out of the back room.

"Boy, was it me or could she not decide where she was from? She spoke like thirty-five different accents," he gushed, always eager to jab customers.

"She's someone I used to know," I said and looked at the floor, to stop myself from crying. Flat licorice plastic runner under my feet. Going nowhere. The co-worker backed into the room without saying anything else.

One day not long after, Angie said, "You'll never guess who called."

But I knew. Angie had the whole scoop. Somehow university didn't work out for Tammy. She had ended up a dope addict living on the streets. Heroin was the rumour. But she'd gotten help, went to rehab. Her parents let her move back home because Tammy had been diagnosed as a paranoid schizophrenic. The scattered jigsaw puzzle pieces that were Tammy fell into place. She wasn't mean. She was ill, that's why she chased us that night. Except even though the puzzle of Tammy was complete, the pieces of me in the puzzle made me sick.

I asked Angie for Tammy's phone number. I wanted to call her. I had intentions of making a place for Tammy again. Back where she belonged, mirroring the place she had in my thoughts, always there, a merry-go-round forever turning and flashing.

I never got around to calling. Just picked at the skin around the splinter that was Tammy until it was infected.

"Chicken!" I heard Tammy scream. "Baby-assed cunt chickenfart."

But I still couldn't pick up the phone. I never called.

And then I was walking down Yonge Street to buy a Jesus night-light as a housewarming gift for Angie. As I approached one of those downtown arcades, I saw a girl sitting on the sidewalk in front of it, leaning against the wall, begging for change. Walkman on. Hair unfurled in its kinky rope curls.

Even before Tammy looked up, I knew it was her.

Before her eyes reached mine, I stared past the space she occupied. Just like the day of the shrimp, I found Tammy's channel changer and clicked for myself. I walked past her. Didn't toss her any change. Didn't buy her any food. Didn't offer to help. Or say hi. Or say anything. I walked past her like I didn't know her. Like I'd never had her over for dinner, never been to her house, never gossiped on the phone with her, never smoked my first cigarette with her.

In the dollar store I didn't feel so good. I bought the night-light. I had to go back. I could stop and talk to her. I could apologize. Explain how it surprised me, seeing her like that. Seeing myself in her shoes someday if things went wrong. I walked back up Yonge Street, to the arcade. But the space she had occupied was empty. Not more than ten minutes had passed.

About a year later this guy from my old high school phoned. He said his name was Howard. He had been a friend to Tammy, but not as "close" as me. Tammy had died. Her family was sitting Shiva this week.

As I visited Tammy's mom and other "friends," I saw the broken shards of Tammy's past sit uncomfortably on the edges of chairs. Her mom spoke wistfully. How Tammy had been going through another bad period. She had to be admitted to the hospital again. That this time it had been Tammy's idea.

"She was such a sad girl. So sad," her mom mumbled in her baby voice.

Because of cutbacks, the nurses were too busy to search Tammy's things. Tammy swallowed all her pills, then buzzed for a nurse. Tammy told the nurse she'd tried to kill herself by swallowing her pills. But that she'd changed her mind. She needed her stomach pumped. Right away. Her mom should be called. Right away. But the nurse didn't believe her. Didn't believe Tammy had any pills to swallow, and she shouldn't have. Except she did.

I watched Angie through swimming-pool-salty eyes, while Tammy's mom went to get photos. I wasn't Angie's friend anymore. I remembered how mean she'd been to Tammy over the years, all the jokes she'd told about Tammy, to me, to anyone who'd listen. Remembered the tone of her voice as she used to tirelessly imitate Tammy's mom howling for Tammy to come to the phone. Now I watched her console Tammy's mom, sickly-sweet pastel Pepto-Bismol coating everything, all plastic politeness.

As I looked at the pictures being passed around, I realized I'd never hear Tammy's mom scream for Tammy to come to the phone ever again. Almost every time I had called Tammy, her mother answered in her high-pitched voice.

"Why hello, Reena. Nice of you to call. It's good Tammy is friends with a nice girl like you. Hold on for a moment dear, I'll get Tammy for you," she'd say in her baby voice. Then every time, she'd yell for Tammy. She didn't pull the phone away from her mouth as she'd scream, *"Taaaaaaammmmmmmyyyyyyyyyyyyyy!"*

I used to picture her words jettisoning up the grand, spiral staircase in Tammy's home. All the T's, A's, M's, M's and Y's in Tammy's name blitz up that spiral waxed banister like unsealed helium balloons, spiraling out of control to

Tammy. If Tammy didn't hear the first time, her mom would continue just screaming Tammy's name until she came to the phone. Then, when Tammy picked up the phone, her mom would switch back to her sugar-coated baby voice and say, "bye-bye" to me.

Looking around at Howard, at Angie, I realized I was only one of the meagre, crappy pieces of Tammy's life. And she'd had no more than that.

I saw so many pictures that day. Tammy stuck out in all of them. A sore thumb in a family of well-groomed, normal-looking people. Tammy was always well-dressed, but her stark eyes stared out to the camera in almost every picture, a mistake you'd catch, like someone wearing toothpaste on their chin. The puppy dog fringe of woolly bangs hung over her eyes in every picture. The ones where she wore make-up, blue eyeliner and frosted pink lipstick, were just wrong.

After the appropriate amount of time had passed, I excused myself from the Shiva. Tammy's mom walked me to the foyer and I caught a glimpse of my reflection in the mirrored sliding closet door. Tammy's mom shut the front door — the one that I had once plotted escape through — behind me as I left.

I didn't cry until I got into my car and drove down a few side streets; I didn't want Angie to see me and come over. I pulled in front of a house that looked more or less like Tammy's, as most of the houses in the area did, and turned off the car. Then I used up most of the Kleenex left in the box.

Now when I walk down Yonge Street, my eyes automatically flick across the street to the arcade where I once may or may not have seen Tammy. I always look for Tammy at this corner, but I know she's not there. Tammy's dead. She's been dead for over two years now. I shake my head. Want to shake the Tammy-sleep out of my eyes, but I can't.

SARAH DERMER

Roped In

Beth and Debbie were the first lesbians I'd ever met. They were living together in a one-bedroom basement apartment on Palmerston Avenue. Sometimes they invited me over to their house or out for coffee. I was offered the occasional drive to class. They thought I was hilarious. I figured if I could keep being funny, maybe they'd call me more often.

I wanted to be invited to go to the numerous Ani DiFranco shows they drove to, or to the parties I imagined they attended, hosted by women from the Women's Centre, perhaps. Or maybe by lesbian activists who ate fire or demonstrated in "kiss-ins" with the Lesbian Avengers. I was ready to be included in whatever lesbian outing they were adventured in — except for being outed as a lesbian. I wasn't ready for that.

Sure, I'd thought about it. About being a lesbian. The longest relationship I'd had was with David Goodman, a sixteen-year-old Jewish boy from Chicago I'd met on a trip to Israel with my summer camp. He was as skinny as me and got into trouble all the time. So much trouble that his parents ended up sending him to an all-boys' boarding school. We lasted three weeks. Then there was Steven. He wore thrift-store clothes and wrote poetry. My crush on Steven lasted a whole year, ending abruptly when he fooled around with my roommate Catherine after a hallowe'en party. Catherine also wrote poetry. Then there was Andrew Katzman, another Jewish boy from Chicago whom I met on another trip to Israel. A theatre major who was planning to move to Israel after he graduated. When I arrived in Chicago to visit him over Christmas break, he revealed that he "didn't think it was working." I left Chicago early. We never kissed, not once. He got engaged to some girl he met in Israel about a year later.

I had been so unsuccessful with boys that on my twenty-second birthday, I decided to let the world know that I was ready and available for any heterosexual action coming my way. So my friends organized a "coming out as a heterosexual" party. My roommates' boyfriends gave me lap dances. My friends gave me erotica and lingerie. Catherine baked me a chocolate cake in the shape of a penis. One especially cute friend with a tattoo on his right arm took his shirt off and fed me broccoli from his mouth. The broccoli boy was the most heterosexual action I'd had since I was sixteen. I went to bed drunk. And alone. The broccoli boy was the last taste of sexuality I would have for quite some time.

On good days, I would tell myself that the "right" guy just hadn't come along yet. On bad days, I knew I was going to die alone. On the really bad days, I would tell myself that everyone thought I was a lesbian.

And really, everyone did think I was a lesbian. After attending a Jewish feminist conference in Toronto, my mom asked me, over a cup of hot chocolate, if there was anything I "needed to tell her." Apparently she thought my attending a "Jews and Homosexuality" seminar at the conference was suspicious.

Debbie definitely thought I was a lesbian. She used to play an especially humiliating game with me, usually when surrounded by a lot of her friends. It went like this:

"Sarah, have you ever been attracted to a woman?"

"No."

"Oh, come on. Not even once?"

"No."

"Not even someone famous?"

"No."

"What about Sarah McLachlan?"

"Sure."

"Really?"

"No."

Alright, sure. Maybe Sarah McLachlan. And my roommate Catherine, who showed me how to be a good feminist and confided in me. And my other roommate Carrie, who made me feel smart and was funny with me and needed me because she didn't have anyone else. And Darlene from *Roseanne*.

And Debbie and Beth.

But I didn't tell Debbie any of that.

I didn't tell her because I couldn't. If I told her I was a little attracted to every woman I'd ever met, then that would make it true. And if it were true, then what?

Plus, I didn't trust her. Her "I know you're a lesbian, even if you won't admit it" game reminded me of the games girls used to play in grade seven.

Janis tells me that she hates Diane.

Then Janis asks me to promise not to tell Diane.

Diane asks me if Janis hates her.

I say no.

Then she asks me again.

I say no.

She asks again.

I tell her maybe, yes. But I'm not sure.

Then Diane tells Janis that I told Diane that Janis hates her.

And Janis says that the only reason she told me that she hated Diane was just to test me. To see if I could keep a secret.

And Janis goes to Diane's house after school to listen to Mini Pops records on Diane's pink record player.

I walk home by myself.

And I stop telling secrets.

But, it didn't matter what I told Debbie. She was the best storyteller I'd ever met. She told stories about all kinds of people. Believable stories.

I knew the stories weren't one hundred percent true. But I didn't care. I loved being let in on those secret stories.

I just didn't want other people to be let in on my secret stories. Secrets I was sure I hadn't told.

One night, she invited me over to her basement apartment on Palmerston Avenue. She was playing a game of Truth or Dare with a group of friends I barely knew.

I didn't want to play. I didn't want to tell secrets to strangers. I tried to convince myself that no one would truth or dare me. Maybe they'd forget I was in the room, I thought. But no one forgot. Thanks to Debbie.

"What about Sarah? Someone truth or dare Sarah!"

No one said a thing. I knew I wasn't exciting enough to be truth or dared. Debbie elbowed the girl beside her — a red-headed woman I recognized from my American Women in Film and Literature class, who smoked as much as she talked and wore more red lipstick than my Grandma Sybil. I admired her outspokenness in class, but her boldness made me nervous.

"Oh. Me? All right, fine…"

Breathe in, breathe out, breathe in, breathe out.

"Alright, I've got one. Do you like boys or girls?"

"What?" Jesus Christ, not again.

"Boys or girls? Which is it?"

My mouth was hanging open. "Um. Boys."

"Really? Huh." She looked at Debbie. Raised an eyebrow. Turned to me. "Debbie said you'd had this 'coming out' party so I just figured that meant you're a…"

Please. No. "What?"

"…big fat dyke."

I wiped my hands on the corduroy pants I'd had since high school.

"No, no, no. It's boys. I like boys. Really. I do. It was a 'coming out as a heterosexual' party. Because I like boys. Y'see? Boys. Definitely boys."

The red-headed woman shrugged her shoulders.

"Whatever." She rolled her eyes and started to laugh. Debbie joined in, giving the red-headed girl a wink.

I went home. Said I wasn't feeling well.

I hated Debbie. I hated her friends. Grade seven all over again. Being tested to see if I would tell a secret truth. Being caught in a lie I didn't know I was telling.

Or maybe I did know. I knew so bad I just wanted someone to tell me what to do about it. And how.

I wanted someone to tell me that it was perfectly normal to be secretly in love with all my roommates. And I wanted someone to show me the ropes. What to wear. How to walk. How to fuck. The lesbian ropes.

But I'd definitely chosen the wrong mentor to rope me into lesbianism. I'd chosen Debbie. Who came out when she was, like, five. Who walked lesbian, talked lesbian, fucked lesbian.

Debbie, who offered me gin and tonic served in Mason jars. Who invited me to sleep over on her living room futon when we stayed up late talking Sarah Schulman and Dorothy Allison. Who would sleep beside me when Beth wasn't home because she "didn't like to sleep alone." Who would leave me in the dark. Waiting.

Debbie. Who had what I needed and was never going to show me how to get it.

I waited for years for another potential lesbian mentor. Watching *When Night Is Falling* didn't help. Reading *Rubyfruit Jungle* didn't help. Therapy definitely didn't help. Finally, I just couldn't stand it anymore.

Got drunk, walked into a lesbian bar, kissed the first girl who hit on me.

I'd roped myself in.

TARA-MICHELLE ZINIUK

This Is Halloween

The "Anarchist Retirement Home" has become the anal-
ogy for all things we want to spend money on and don't
want to have to feel badly about. I'm not sure any of us see
it as a reality; I think we all just see it as something to say
to prove that we still have the drive to do the work we do.
Like saying it assumes we will hold out that long, resist
settling; like saying it ensures that we will return from our
burnouts, will not fall into the offers of complacency many
of us have the options of. As though, when we pursue plans
that have us appear to be sell-outs, artistic interests, alright
jobs, monogamy, natural hair colour; there is still an under-
lying bringing-down-the-system goal.

This woman is ultimately the most socially accepted
being I have ever come into contact with. She is a wife and
a breeder, a homeowner, a car-buyer. She has an air-miles
card, air miles, and vacation days. She has cheque books
and joint bank accounts, domestic help and a Weight Watch-
ers "I lost blah blah many pounds!" ribbon magneted to
her fridge. She knows from car washes and sweater sets
and tennis bracelets. She is blood-related. We have nothing in common. I am trying to tell her about my upcoming
move.

"I found a one bedroom apartment for three-hundred
and eighty dollars, isn't that great?"

"Three-eighty for a one bedroom? You want to live in a dump?"

Click. Grrr.

Tonight we are trying to put together halloween costumes. I comment on how I never wanted to live so long that I was dressing up for halloween in clothes I used to wear out. We dress like sluts and freaks anyways, it's true. Body paint, wigs, fake fur and silver studs. This being the truth makes finding a costume infinitely harder to do. So many of my things are in storage. I knew I should leave out my cat ears and tube of faux blood but somehow I was convinced not to. We are going to go out in black lipstick, fishnet sleeves, shimmer glitter and fake eyelashes and call it "us at fifteen." Someone who is thirty-seven will find this amusing, I'm sure. At least we are trying to convince ourselves this will be the case.

We are not justified in wanting tattoos or weekends off unless there are actions planned for those weekends, paying cover for events that are not fundraisers. We will not contribute to capitalist society. We will not burn out. We must remember that ultimately, we have it easy. We will make sure, that if we do burn out, we will have a place to do it in. Mostly, I want the lives we live not to be kept separate, not to have to call our non-activist friends our "non-activist friends," to be able to carry our megaphones into the independent theatre company rehearsal space, and place our stacks of programs next to our stacks of outreach handbills. It's tiring trying to explain to people how "when we get old" we'll recount our youth from rocking chairs in front of the "Anarchist Retirement Home." Of course, this is where I want to be then; Club Med for the ex-crust-kid generation. But I don't want to have to ask my corporate-logo friends to wear something else when they drive in on weekends. And when I'm eighty, I want to have tattoos I regret that *don't* say anything about how I was a teenage revolutionary.

She wants to know if I'm working. I'm sure she is not asking because she saw the interview I gave on behalf of the sex-worker coalition. Boyfriend? Biologically speaking, no. "Yes." You only date Jewish guys right? Who? I knew a Jewish guy once. Silence. When are you going back to school? To school. Working. You only date boyfriends. You're working to make thousands of dollars. You could be making thousands of dollars; you're Jewish. Boyfriend. could be making thousands. You only go to school right? I cannot believe this woman is related to me. I have easier conversations in line at the grocery store, but for some reason I keep trying.

"I found a bedroom in an apartment for three hundred dollars. The girls are nice, the apartment is clean."

"Three hundred dollars for a bedroom? You could rent a whole apartment for three-fifty!"

Clench jaw. Sigh.

We spent Devil's Night avoiding the outside world, avoiding eye contact, avoiding remembering to be cool enough to remember that it was Devil's Night. We ate mini-Mars bars without thinking about what they were out for when we found them on the table. Our nightly playlist included: Depeche Mode *Stripped*, Rebel Yell, the Runaways, Metallica's *Unforgiven*, Wild Strawberries *I Don't Want to Think About It*. We are not only listening to music from when we were fifteen but music from when someone else was fifteen. "Man, this would have been a great song to be fifteen to." We are listening to new stuff on the radio made to sound like the stuff we liked at fifteen. We like it all fine, really. We used to hate the radio. When we were fifteen. We used to hate everything. We are not indifferent, we just forget. We are our parents calling anything with a guitar and hair "rock and roll." We are not depressed, we just forget to call people back. When we wore black lipstick we were depressed, but not now. Now, we are just quiet. Quietly, we must sneak out of the house like teenagers, make it to the Halloween party, and remember how to pretend to know more music than we do.

The way to outlive capitalism is to create sustainable communities. There is a formula to even the most radical notions. We must ensure that we are not living beyond our means and that our means are most minimal. We must ensure that each member of the community is able to participate to the same extent but according to their strengths and abilities. We must not become communistic about this. We must ensure that we have all of the things necessary for survival and for a meaningful existence. We must not be dry about this. We must either eliminate capitalism or eliminate ourselves from capitalism. We must decide. To decide to make choices ensuring our ability to choose. We must not be privileged, or must not take advantage of our privilege, or must never admit to it… or we must hold ourselves accountable to it… We must remember that we are alternative culture. Sustainable. Community. Many communities came before us. We must remember not to forget to remember to not forget that.

What are you now, nineteen? "Yes." I may as well be. I am nineteen. I am nothing other than nineteen. I exist only as the numeral nineteen. The Roman numeral nine. I am Roman. I may as well be. Nine. As long as I marry a Jewish man. With a career and an income of thousands. Thousands of nineteens. In Roman numerals. "I am pretty heavily involved in political work." I tell her. I out my dissent. Like activism? "Yes." Very much like activism in fact. In fact, that's what they used to call it. I tell her I am not a lobbyest or a letter writer, try to let her in on direct action while the radio spews scares of terror. She thinks about it not even for a second and settles into what she believes from what I have told her, that I am "in trouble with the law." She tells me she is glad I am strong enough to make my own decisions, that she only wishes I would make the *right* decisions. Maybe, she suggests, if I don't want to get a job I could focus on trying to find a *husband* with a job.

"This is halloween. This is halloween." This is the nightmare before Christmas. Passover. Complacency. The most wonderful time of the year.

Light and Shade

"Perhaps twenty years ago I could not have loved you through all the complications of sex and gender, from woman to man to in-between. But if not, I would have been foolish, to lose you for the sake of such a little difference, the wavering line between light and shade."

— *Minnie Bruce Pratt*

I still remember that morning you asked me if I would let you touch me if you were a real boy. You sat next to me on the bed lacing up your boots and I lay in your bed with the smell of sex and sleep still warming us on that cold morning. I was naked except for one of your old wife-beaters which I found on the floor beside the bed and slipped on when I had to get up to pee in the middle of the night. It smelled like you. Like boys like you. Like sweat and boy-smell that, when I get a whiff of hugging boys like you, buckles my knees. That smell is the difference between you and me.

The night before I told you my own girl body was clean of fingerprints from teenage boys. Having never been a straight girl once gained me a gold star in dyke circles. She's never been with a boy. A fact for which I was once honoured furrows your brow. Now, once again, you ask me what side I'm on. I sit facing you with no answer.

I thought of the time I've known you — how far we've travelled. Followed each other across the country, through three states in three years and infinite genders and beings. Even though I didn't recognize your deepening voice, that doesn't mean it's not familiar. Before I ever let you touch me, we'd walked as friends, lovers, butch/femme, boy/girl, mistress/boy, daddy/girl, and finally came to this, casual fuck buddies for the space in between life's significant others, a space pretty rocky at best. After all we've been through together, anything more would lead to one of us murdering the other.

But don't you dare think for a second that I don't know how much my girl body scares you. How I open my girl for you to explore and how its familiarity scares you to death. I invite you to come inside, then rise to meet you. And while looking at me as an equal, you realize I know enough about boys like you to be terrifying. You know...I might be easy, but I'm not simple.

I realized I was a girl late in life. It wasn't until the summer before grade seven. I was twelve years old when I became a girl. My family had just immigrated to the U.S. and I was a one-girl-mission in search of normalcy in adolescent America. Granted, I'd known forever about being a tomboy. But living in a house of sisters and women, I never knew about boys. I came to realize the difference between me and you in a gas station that summer on a payphone, during the period of my life where I existed in a world of diaries, slumber parties and shopping malls. Boys were on the other side. I stayed safely on the girl's side. I was trying to be the perfect American girl, but I was always scared they'd discover I wasn't.

At the gas station that summer afternoon, I ended up alone with Connor Flaherty, a boy from school who was calling his dad. The novelty of being with a boy was sending me into a frenzy of awkward adolescent girlness. And he was just calling his dad to have him come pick us up. On the phone he referred to me as "this girl". Defined me as different than him. And, to my amazement and even titillation, he continued to use female pronouns for me. *She* goes to my school. *She* lives around the block. *Her* parents are at work. How did he know that? At that point I decided boys didn't even speak the same language as girls. That to each other their relations and interactions were from a different planet. And I was a fan of planet all-girl. Boys were weird and I wanted no part of that. I was headlong into the society of note-passers and lip-gloss wearers and secret-whispers. There was no turning back. Connor Flaherty caught me off guard. He knew about my pronoun choice without me clarifying. He could just tell I was a girl. The realization he'd known all along about girls scared me in the most amazing way. Because it was by his definition of our difference that I began to realize what it is to be this girl, and who this girl is in the world of boys.

To this day all I know is that the kinda fellas who don't belong in either bathroom, whose shirts button the other way and who take up more space than they were given, buckle my knees. I play Wendy to your Peter Pan, but we know it's really Tinkerbell to the Lost Boys.

I come from a long line of strong women who taught me what it means to lay down for you. I'm not the only dust my mother raised. She taught this girl what it means to be a girl and to provide as well as seek safety. And I have cut down my own family tree for the paper to write the simplest love story. Girl meets boy.

I think about the kind of girl I am. You couldn't touch me if I were a real girl.

JP HORNICK

Fumble

She told me, "I don't usually like smooth butches."

The breath rushed out of me and I sat there, grinning, thinking, I am *not* a smooth butch. Well, maybe sometimes, just for a moment, and just as part of some larger game or play or seduction. But certainly not always and certainly not sustainably.

It goes something like this:

There's a cute girl, more likely a beautiful femme. This never happens to me with other butches or boys — who I'm just as generally attracted to, but with some different sense of ease. So, there's this beautiful femme standing, sitting, walking, moving, *being*, there and here, a setting contained enough so that she's present and I'm present at the same time and neither of us is going anywhere, at least not for the moment.

She's a looker and I'm looking. See me sitting here, dapper in pressed pants and suspenders, tailored shirt with French cuffs, open just so at the collar. I've got a newspaper, something smart and crisply folded to the most interesting article. And I'm sipping coffee, good coffee, in an eclectic coffeehouse, and I'm looking.

See that sly glance over the edge of the paper where she's sitting, at the counter on a high stool? There's a lot of will in that glance; one can almost touch it, and I wish she would. Always. Wish she'd reach out and touch that pulsating, palpable *will* every time I'm looking like that.

So let's say — and it often goes this way, I swear — she catches that look, returns it with a sly grin. So far, so good, you might be thinking, might be identifying with one or the other or even both of us just about now. But this is where it all goes to hell. A personal hell, permanent parking reserved for innately un-smooth butch boys, with plenty of scenic views for spectators.

That returned glance comes across the room and slides against my skin. Creeps between the fibres of my clothing, nips into flesh, bores between molecules and hits its mark. Like a shock to the whole sub-atomic structure, that look simultaneously jolts coffee from my hand into my lap and across the table as my sly, smooth, glancing eyes light up like Christmas bulbs and my affected smirk is replaced with a puppy's grin.

Are you still watching? Jolted perhaps from your own quiet moment, your own coffee over there? Distracted by my frantic flurry of newsprint sopping up the spill, smart sentences dissolving into a dripping pile of consonants and vowels?

Sometimes, when I'm lucky — and despite, or maybe because of what you know now, I'm very lucky — the reward for my performance (which is truly a mode of being in the world and not a put-on, come-on slapstick show) is hearty laughter. Not "lemme take care of poorlittleboyyou," but a knowing laughter. A laughter that says, "you boys who are easily disarmed by girls still often know what to

do, so let me take care of you, help you clean that up." Or
— just maybe — "let's leave that mess until later."

Never under-estimate the possibilities in that laughter.

I'm not a smooth butch, but I can clean up my own messes, and I know how to pick up a fumble and run without ever really dropping the ball. There's a grace to the goofiness; it just takes a long, sly glance carefully launched, invited and inviting. Like yours now, but more.

She tells me, "I'm not usually attracted to smooth butches," and I start gathering words to wipe up what's bound to spill over. Usually.

Seven Stops Time

Seven is trying to erase his short-term memory.

He swears this to me over cherry pie breakfast on the rooftop patio of Jamie's Brunch Bar and Grill. Our Thursday fag and hag mid-morning ritual. I'm eating off of his plate with my hands squishing each finger into the sugary mess and drawing little brains on the scratched white ceramic.

"How will you do that, hon?" Half-interested. Slow waking.

His mouth moves fast, arms waving in emphatic swirls. "I have a plan, Eve, it's almost too simple."

On the paper placemat is a series of lists and graphs I can barely decipher. I was late meeting him and he busied himself with the crayons meant to quiet children.

He plans to erase his memory in four weeks by adopting a strict regime of drugs, sex, sleep avoidance and Doing As Much of Everything as he can cram into a day.

Drugs are easiest. Close to his heart in a plastic monkey pill box in his front pocket; a myriad of prescribed pills meant to keep him well. Illicit substances are easy to come by.

Kissing many boys, also a cinch, since his charm oozes endlessly. He will watch only the reality television channel; free cable recently acquired through Thursday lover Roger.

He'll sleep in twenty-five minute intervals throughout the day.

"I'm also learning how to do a handstand on only two fingers. It can be done. It just takes discipline."

Seven continues to explain that while being constantly inundated with images and sound and chemical and emotional chaos, he'll never have to think of the next five minutes, let alone tomorrow.

"I can change my relationship to time," he says, preparing a bump of coke on the end of a key and making slight efforts to hide in the shade of a giant plastic plant beside our table. "Dying will have no meaning." This from the man who last month barely survived a rooftop jump from eight stories up wearing only a crash helmet. "I am a t-cell giant!" he'd exclaimed. I dug my nails into my face watching his leap. A gaggle of beer-drinking rooftop friends cheered in shock or pride as he reached the other side of the alley.

This is his May Project. Appropriately ambitious for spring. Unsubtle and completely present-oriented.

I chew each synthetic cherry as though it were an exercise in precision. Like when you repeat a word too many times and it becomes something else, this cherry between the roof of my mouth and my tongue becomes a ticking clock, it's own increment of time.

"What happened to your April project?"

Seven shrugs, grinning, teeth oozing red dye number five. "I don't remember." He winks.

He hands me his Palm Pilot with a crushed red ribbon

on top. "Here, my sister, is the devil. Play with it well."

He purchased this electronic organizer in March, when his plan was to impersonate a business man for fun and profit.

"Can I play *Tetris* on it?

"No."

I put it in the red velvet bag strung over my chair and take a slow sip of my licorice tea. It's 10 a.m. He leaves a big tip for Kimmie, the waitress. He has a vague memory of throwing a fork at her yesterday. Soon, he will have forgotten this.

I've long since learned that having Seven as a roommate is like having a TV you can talk to. He's constantly moving. He's instant gratification with New Wave hair.

I watch him flitter about the restaurant, wondering what happened to his very first monthly project, inspired by a cold winter in which he spent many hours indoors. He began by stapling slices of Wonderbread to the apartment wall in a checkerboard pattern, taking meticulous care to date each addition. "I'm documenting the evolution of mold," he exclaimed while I wiped away day-old liquid eyeliner that had dried while I napped on the sofa.

We've been roommates for four years now. Like sisters you ignore until you're lonely, and then you drag them out to the mall.

We're both spindly, big-eyed and unambitious in the conventional sense, unlike our other roommate Rachel who is a writer and upon publishing her first book tattooed her ISBN number across her left tit. She used to take us to her literary parties until we began playing scavenger hunts with things could steal from said gatherings.

While Seven is trying to render time irrelevant, and Rachel tries to fill time with successful endeavors, I am forever trying to slow it down.

I light a cigarette, pushing away the red-stained, gummy plate. I want time like this with just breath; never frenetic or too occupied. To simply watch the blink of call display, get foot rubs, walk the dog in the park. Never needing to run after anything with a scrub brush and a bottle of seltzer. The arch of my back elastic against the bed frame.

I want to remember that yesterday began with tea on the front porch and pie on the roof. A lazy conversation with the dog in guttural mumbles. Montreal is a city that encourages all day sleeping. This winter I was under the dirty streets hibernating — an umbilical cord reaching out to the pavement. I would have cut it too, if only I wasn't required to be at LSP and Associates twenty-three hours a week.

Being a temp is the perfect job for me, the lullabye lull of no potential. No raising the bar, occasional mumbled praise from someone I don't know about my accomplished mediocrity, the gracious two-cheek kiss of anonymity.

When we leave the restaurant, I slide down the twisted iron staircase and out onto the street. I see three bunches of orange and yellow tulips and one dead squirrel. I sit on the edge of the curb and wait for the bus that will deliver me to my one p.m. shift.

When Seven appears, he crouches to kiss me, my hair

sticking in his lip gloss, his teeth red-stained. "You look lost," he says, unlocking his low-rider and biking off before I can respond.

Falling asleep briefly with my chin in my hands, I dream about being a guest at Lydia Lunch's sixtieth birthday party. Waking up, a truck passes by and exhales warm exhaust around my ankles.

I'm having the world's slowest nervous breakdown.

JOANNE HUFFA

One Day This Will All be Mine

The pebbles are cool and smooth. I place the smoothest on my tongue and close my mouth, then my eyes. The earth beneath me is damp and smells like worms. It rained a little this morning. The ground is wet, but not muddy. Mum makes me wear rubbers when there's mud. Today, I'm outside in sneakers. There are lots of rocks here at the end of the garden. There are also three big trees. One is a maple. Some of the big rocks have snails stuck to them. These are the ones I like best. The snails are slow. Sometimes they don't move for a long, long time. The pebble in my mouth is getting warm. I spit it out and find another, gray and round and cold from the ground. I hold it in my mouth.

Because of the rain, there are worms on the lawn. I know that they come out because the earth swells and then there's no room for them. But after the rain sometimes they can't find their way back into the ground. With popsicle sticks and my fingers, I dig holes. I put the worms into the holes and hope they know what to do next.

I'm sure they do; they have instinct. Just like the snails know that the rocks look like them, so that's a good place to stay if they don't want to be eaten.

The new pebble is warm now. I remove it from my mouth and place it beside the first one. It's good to keep a pile of smooth stones. If they're jagged, they can cut me, and then my mum gets worried and mad at me for putting dirty things in my mouth. I could choke. She doesn't know how good they feel. I don't want to eat them, I only want to let the cool hardness sit on my tongue. Just taste the earth and the rock.

It takes a while to find a replacement, but when I do it's perfect. These ones are the best. Brown and white stripes that are almost as smooth as our coffee table. It looks like mum has polished it, too. It's almost too big to put in my mouth, but it fits behind my teeth and I settle down between the maple and the big rock.

We have slugs, but not on the strawberry patch. The slugs are kind of gross, like when you accidentally hit your thumb really hard with a hammer and your nail falls off. I wasn't supposed to look, but I saw when mum replaced the bandage. I didn't know part of me could just go missing like that. But that's what slugs look like — snails who have lost their shells. Plus they're black and shiny. They're fun to put on your arm and let them slime up and down, but only for a while.

Today, I have a thermos of lemonade, a peanut butter sandwich and some carrots. I take the stone from my mouth and eat some sandwich. It's o.k. I like it better when Jamie comes over with his lunch and we trade half for half. One time his mum gave him pizza for us both. Today it's just me and peanut butter. The lemonade tastes best after a mouth full of sandwich.

Mum lets me stay here for hours. Sometimes all day. She thinks it's good that I'm taking an interest in nature and getting some fresh air, too.

Dangerous Places

M. confessed he was still in love or at least in rebound with S. the first time we hung out together. He slapped me with "S. is the love of my life" right in the middle of one of those let's-get-to-know-each-other conversations that happens way too late at night. He was leaning against my chest, my back was up against a wall, and I was so happy because he was slurring his words from five bottles of beer. Just when I thought he might kiss me, out popped: "We met reaching for the same book at a second hand bookstore."

That was my date with M. At least I call it a date, but now I'm not so sure whether M. would. I had a great time, up until the conversation. I gave the jerk my black flower necklace when we were dancing our asses off at El Convento Rico. Imagine a guy who can get down on the dance floor on your first date. I mean really get down. And he even kissed me, late that night, after the drag show was over, when the music was too cheesy to actually dance to.

Then M. insisted on walking me home through the alleyways and shortcuts I usually take by myself. I laughed a bit at his concern for my safety. I've never been one to shy away from dangerous places. I try not to bother with fear too much.

When I got home, I called on will power and shut the

door on M. I shut it in his face, even though S. was already in bed. I knew because her light was out. I threw myself face-down on my bed with my jeans bagging up underneath me and dreamt of skateboards and smoky bars and boys with curly brown hair.

Earlier that night, when M. told me about S., I thought I was cool with it. But the next morning, when S. came dancing out of her yellow room, I realized it wasn't going to be that easy. She was wearing a purple towel. Her short red hair seemed redder than ever. She saw me heading towards the bathroom and scampered in there before I could react, calling out as she pulled the door closed, "Sorry, late for work. Hope you don't mind."

I minded very much, actually, but that's not what you're supposed to say to a roommate who's in a rush. I sat down on the stairs outside the bathroom and waited for her to finish. The wooden door wasn't tightly closed. It swung open just enough for me to watch her work in front of the mirror. She started plucking her eyebrows. Gross.

I got bored. Eventually, partly because I wanted to make small talk, and partly because I just had to tell somebody, I burst out: "I went out with M. last night."

"Yeah? Where'd you go?"

"Nowhere special. Dancing," I said, already feeling miserable for telling her.

After a couple minutes she said: "M.'s great on the dance floor. So alive."

I wanted to kick myself. I shouldn't have told her, no matter how strong my urge to gossip. I leaned back against the stairs and looked up at the chipped ceiling. I waited five minutes until she finally shoved the door open and came out.

"You two dated for a while, eh?" I asked, in spite of myself.

"Yeah," she said, and her lips curled into a crooked grin. "It's still kind of weird to think he's moving on, even though I did pretty much immediately."

"Hmph," I grunted.

"You know," she said, as she walked past me to her canary-yellow bedroom. "The hardest thing about living here with all you women has not been the line-up for the bathroom."

"Hmm?"

"I think we use it about as much as men would. The hardest thing is actually not being the cutest girl around."

I was squinting pretty hard at her and, objectively speaking, she looked pretty good to me. I wanted to see her naked, but when she went into her bedroom, she pulled the door shut tightly.

In the kitchen, my hair still damp from the shower, I checked that she wasn't around. I poured myself some juice and put the water on for coffee. I was reading my horoscope and munching on a bowl of cereal doused with brown sugar and soymilk when she walked in. She was carrying skater shoes in her right hand and gray wool socks in her left. She sat down across from me and hiked up her taffeta party dress to pull on the itchy-looking socks.

"Like your dress," I said, keeping my head down. I

pretended to be fascinated by my bowl of soggy cereal and the answers to all my Sagittarian questions.

I know I'm not exactly Queen of Style, but her sneakers truly clashed with the party dress. Fashion statement or not, the taffeta had seen better days. The cream-coloured blouse had elbow-length puffy sleeves and the skirt was the colour of red wine. Before she put on the wool socks and skater shoes, she reminded me of Molly Ringwald wearing that bridesmaid's dress in *Sixteen Candles*. That's *not* a compliment.

When she finished with her footwear, she straightened up. "Can't talk long, but the hardest part about living with all you women is the fact that my ego has been knocked down a few notches."

I looked up at her over my bowl of cereal.

She reached up and curled a piece of hair around her finger. "When I was on my own, there was no give and take that way."

I took another bite of cereal.

S. stood up and walked to the front closet. She opened the door and took out her skateboard with the Riot Grrrl stickers peeling off like bad skin. She said, "Have to go now, though. I'm late for work and I need to ride there or I'll be in a crazy headspace all day."

"Sure."

"You know, it's over between me and M. We're not made for each other." She smiled at me and pulled open the front door. "It's just a bit...sloppy."

"Guess it always is."

"When you find a person who's close, but not quite right, you question your decisions. Well, I'll see you..." She started to leave, put her hand on the front doorknob and was pulling it closed behind her.

"Hey S.," I called at the last second. She stopped. "Take the alley-ways. They always help me when I need to think."

"Nothing like a short cut," she said, diving out the door. I noticed she didn't lock the front door behind her. It's a rule we have — to keep the front door locked. But she just pulled it shut and skated off. I walked over and flipped the deadbolt.

The kettle blew hot air. I poured the coffee. The phone rang. I ignored it. If it was M., I was in no mood to speak to him.

I sat down to finish my cereal and my abuelita's advice came to mind. She liked to say: "Los hombres son como aguacates." Men are like avocados. You can never tell a good one until you cut it open. Where's my abuelita when I need her most?

Lately, though, I can't seem to help it. All my dreams are filled with skateboards and smoky bars and a boy suspiciously like M.

Markèd

My daughter just got a tattoo. It's a heart with the word "Dad" in it.

"Happy Father's Day!" she said, her sleeve all bunched up. What could I say? She turned thirteen almost six months ago, and if she can vote and drink, I suppose it would be wrong to try to prevent disfigurement.

"It's *re*figurement, Daddy," Angela would say, has said in the past, and I suppose I should be a little more accepting. It's just a little bit much to process all at once.

I remember last year, Amy and I — Amy being Angela's ovum donor — were talking at a party about how strange Angela was compared with the other girls. This worried Amy.

"I mean, see that girl over there? With those pretty little legs spliced onto her earlobes? Why doesn't Angela get something like that?"

I folded my arms. I had given Angela my old skateboard for her birthday, and felt a little self-conscious about it. But I wasn't trying to clone myself, really I wasn't. There were easier ways to do that. "She doesn't really like the modern styles, Aim."

She couldn't have heard us (she's never had any sense boosters, either) from where she was sitting, but she looked over and smiled at me. Ignoring her friends, who flapped

226

their carnival limbs and whooped, she smiled at me. I smiled back.

Amy saw this and just snorted. "The girl is *so* fin-de-siècle. Just don't blame me."

At least it was an ink tattoo, not those nasty carvings so many young girls go in for these days.

She stood there, arm sleeve rolled up. "Pretty rad, eh?" Angela was hooked on my old collection of skater videos and had adopted the lingo.

"Wicked," I agreed.

She tapped the tattoo once. A naked cherub burst out of the centre and circled, a trail of halo behind it. "I couldn't resist. It was cheap, and it was just this spray-program he put on after the tat. It'll wash off in a few months." She tapped it thrice and three angels joined us, doing a little figure-8 routine.

"Well..." I said, watching the fattest angel retreat into her heart. "I'm touched. Not that you have to do something like that to show you love me, but..."

She was tracing the heart and I could tell from her light touch that it was still a little tender. "Oh, it wasn't just for you. I wanted an old-style tat. Philomina and her crew are always on about what a little girl I am, just because I think their patches suck."

I worried for a moment that she had fallen out with Philomina. She had been friends with her for years.

"I told Philomina her new mouth was fuckin' ugly. She

got this new mouth, and it says everything she says a second later? It's *so* damn annoying. And it's so dumb looking! I was like, 'No, Phil, don't do it' but she did it anyway. Then she asks me what I think. What was I supposed to say?"

I shrugged. I had a little trouble picturing another mouth on Philomina's already crowded face.

"Anyway, she'll see what a *real* refigurement is," Angela said, with her chin out. Her eyes weren't as convinced though. "This is real. They knew how to do it back then. It wasn't all computer-positioning and molecule-shaping. It was an art. Everything sucks now. I wish I was born back then."

I gave her a hug. Tapped the tattoo a dozen times and watched the flurry of low rez divinity cavort around our living room. Thought about telling her that it sucked then, too, and didn't. She needed hope, now, more than truth.

"Hey Dad," Angela said from the couch, "Amy called." There was another person beside her, quite close. They were watching TV, shouting out orders at it.

I put my groceries on the counter. I wondered who the couch-mate was, happy to see that Angela finally had a new friend after the Philomina trouble.

I went to the living room and Angela turned off the TV. "Dad, this is Monika."

Monika turned towards me, a slim girl with short red hair. On her forehead, an eye opened and glowed brighter and brighter until I blinked. "Thirdeye off," Monika muttered. "Sorry Mr. Munroe," she said. "My mom put in this thing to help with my social skills."

I looked at her eyeless forehead.

"It's just a facial recognition/name recall macro," Monika said, shifting uncomfortably, "I mentioned once to my mom that I forgot this guy's name and *wham* guess what I get for Christmas."

"The third eye was a mystical symbol of omniscience, or all-seeing," I said, realizing I sounded like a teacher or a dad but not able to help myself.

Monika nodded politely and my daughter grinned. "Monika's parents brought these for her from Britain," she asked, holding out a pack of joints. I took it. *Hemp smoking causes lethargy*, the Chief Medical Officer's warning read. "They're phat..." Angela tempted.

"Better not," I said. "Amy'll want her dinner soon." I handed them back to Monika. As she leant over to take them from me, I saw a heart on her arm. *Angela*, it said.

In the kitchen, cutting carrots and listening to the girls whisper and giggle, I thought lazily: *Ain't language a virus?* and *Ain't culture a virus?* and *Ain't love a virus?*

LISA FOAD

In Trace Amounts

Eight rolls. Each 24 exposure. They sat undeveloped for months, hidden in the cool darkness of my refrigerator, haphazardly scattered among yeast packets, jars of capers, chili paste. It was a steady accumulation. Roll after roll after roll, each unlabelled, a disorderly archive swelling. My refrigerator door a memorial to memory. Swinging shut, 192 snapshots, keeping *that was then* like a secret. And, invocation, incantation. Me pleading with evidence.

Eight rolls, dewy with condensation. Knocking like knuckles in my purse, icy blue pleather, stud-gunned rhinestones.

I ride the streetcar there. It was a panicked decision, weighty with anxious anticipation and the need for immediacy. I have always hated transit. Crowed, noisy, unbearably hot. Me sitting small arms and legs crossed. Jeans too tight, red lips, and a hoodie pulled up and over messy, matted, over-processed hair, hiding four months of root regrowth and tired eyes. Feigning impenetrability. Willing invisibility. The woman behind me coughing roughly, relentlessly; the man in front making sleasy morning-after talk about the girl he met last night. She was a ten.

Staring too hard out the window, I don't see a thing. Spadina Avenue sunlight streaming eclipsed by the acute feeling that today, especially today, my body will give out on itself. Bones snapping, sharply tearing their way through muscle, the surface of skin. Slippery blood, streaming, pooling. Me screaming those dream-screams where no sound comes out. And wringing my hands around endings. I am a beacon in the middle of a field of winter and my heart is mostly wanting.

Before now, everything was different, incredibly average. Always hungry, never satisfied, but even still, measure by measure, movement threateningly simple. Last night, greens steamed over a bed of rice and, plotting out the art of boldness during commercial breaks, last-minute details over drinks with her, sure hands, lazy smile, partner in crime. Work was inconsequential. The DJ fucked up my set again, leaving me awash in red lights a minute and a half too long, wrong song. Daniel came in late, vodka tonic swirling blue-green in black lights and the usual, *I'm just across the street, the executive suite, the things I could do, I know you want to, your eyes give it all away.*

If only. I can't imagine this man, an oil financer in Armani suits, going home to a sprawling estate in Houston's River Oaks. His wife, a gala wife, a benefit wife, and his five-year old son, hammer-and-nail rich dreams of becoming Bob the Builder. I remember the first time we met. Downstairs in the VIP, $300 for one hour. Red cashmere scarf, eyeglasses glinting, tireless hands reaching. Saying, *you have found yourself a fan.* That was a year ago. I'm losing patience these days. Being someone's favourite wears thin quickly.

On the way home, the cab driver made small talk about Marilyn Monroe. His favourite movies: *Some Like It Hot*, *The*

Seven Year Itch. He hated *Bus Stop*. Yonge to Wellesely to Bay to Bloor, his eyes darted back and forth from the road to my reflection in the rearview mirror. As I was digging out my fare, he turned to face me.

You look like her.

I paused, confused.

Like Marilyn, you look like Marilyn Monroe.

I handed him the money, a crumpled ten, and said an awkward thank you as I reached for the door handle.

I didn't think she was very pretty, he called out as I shut the car door. I stood there for a minute too long and watched his cab disappear west along Dupont, leaving me alone in the three a.m. empty quiet. Counting out the eleven paces to my front door, *I have never been further away than closer to home.*

This morning though, seismic shifts. It was still early, a breezy softness floating in through the windows. Me cranky with coffee, purring cat wrapped in my lap. The phone ringing, unanswered. And ringing. And ringing. And finally, *hello*. A series of bruised voices, blistering voices, one call after another. A series of exposures, indictments, familial fracture. Secrets I've abandoned, unraveling.

And me chain-smoking and wide-eyed thinking: *Don't think.* Feverishly scratching notes in a spiral notebook, committing allegations, accusations to paper. Feeling home slip, homesick. Thinking: *this is not happening*. Thinking: *anything you say can and will be used against you*. And my jaw slack, lungs pumping panic, everything suspect. It was then I knew, without question, that I had to develop these eight rolls. Searching out the impossible return through 3-1/2 x 5 white-bordered boxed confessionals. Clues, codes, a trace. Something to fill in the gaping gaps.

I have always been a compulsive picture-taker. Each time, I tell myself: *this is the time of your life*. I imagine a roll teeming with unaware smiles and faraway looks, blurry mid-sentence mouths and lipstick smudged. Snippets of white-blonde toughness. A fleshy girl glowering. But I am almost never in the picture.

When I do appear, my caught-in-the-act renderings are always ridiculously posed. Ramrod straight and chin up, arms stiff. A statuette leaning into slate-gray landscapes, the bluest sky. Vanishing points. No sign of the girl that tells herself she is tattoo full of red words, notions that glitter and one-way tickets out. No sign of the girl who tells herself she is one-thumb-high at the side of the road. Instead, a shuddery girl, strangle-wide smile and eyes empty. Like I was never there.

The truth is, I am mostly faking. I blot my lipstick on return tickets, always return tickets. And I wait. In line-ups for change, for my turn.

I'm one of those girls, cliché-ridden, roll-my-smokes-in-tears tragic. Spurred on by the spectre of loss, I thread myself together with bits and pieces. Bottle caps, coffee-stained napkins, the last bite, the longest of looks. Fodder for stories I'll tell myself later. That I have warmed my hands over tragedy, blown perfect kisses, heart-shaped goodbyes. Romancing ruins, drunk reunions. Pretty girls make good graves, I've been told. Sometimes it's art but mostly it's trash.

Today, trash for sure. Attempting to avert structural collapse with collections, compilations, 24 exposure. Making it all up through time stopped, time caught. The voice in my head a dull thud, echoing. I am a girl in trace amounts.

At Harbord, a hulking man, rough-shaven and red-faced, sits down beside me. He is wearing a brown winter parka. Stained and torn. Sweat beading along his brow, his upper lip. He's digging crumpled pieces of paper out of a soiled A&P bag. Flattening one piece at a time against his lap. Meticulously smoothing out wrinkles with scabbed fingertips, muttering. He arms himself with heavy metal scissors. Folding. Snipping. Folding. Snipping. Dull and achy-breaky, the scissors skid and tear, gouging sniprip holes in the paper tearing, torn.

Asks me, low and hushed-like, if I play the lottery. *Wednesday's jackpot is the big-time. Thirteen million.*

I shake my head no because my own throat feels engorged.

Well, you've got to play to win. If you don't play, you don't win. Snip snip. Rip rip. *Listen*, his words tumble, water rushing. *If you win this week, could you set me up in an apartment, because I just lost mine, nothing fancy, just a room even...*

I tell him that I'd give him a million.

For the first time, he turns to me. Foggy blue eyes, yellow speckles. Grabs roughly for my hand. Shaky. Breaky. *If I win, I'll give you a million, too.*

It's a deal.

The swell of safety swiftly rises up within me. Tucked tight against the smeared streetcar window, I suddenly feel protected, armored by this man snip snipping, rip ripping. I have always sought armor from others. Girls who, footfall-firm, walk the curb while I step safely, shielded by their sureness on one side, bricked buildings on the other. Even there, sidewalk-safe, I feel the fear of falling. The any-where, anytime threat of collapse. A rawness that can't centre itself.

I swarm forward and back, lulled by the sounds of snipping and ripping, through the void of makeshift space that is memory. Sentence fragments, words that tirelessly circle the perimeters of *that was then*, the parts that I can't ever remember. And while my mind inks weary vignettes, the same old same old, I know there is more to this story.

Like last summer. A family wedding.

We converged, tense and anxious, like a bomb about to go off. Fifteen hundred miles of twisting highways and turbulent air space temporarily disappeared, a two-week shift in our disparate geographies. My grandparent's home, the central axis point. Brown-bricked. Unassuming. Quiet.

It was the last two weeks of August. Sticky hot. My mother and sister four hours late. Missed their flight. They haven't been home in five years. This home that is not one. I've only stayed away one year. Doing my best to avoid collide and collapse with markers of busyness and sheer unavailability, 365 days of stale excuses. After all, me and the brown-bricked house, just an hour apart by car. Distance offering up the myth of safety. This myth and others like it, the cheat list that keeps me moving. And stalling.

The wedding. A good excuse. The only excuse.

There are no ritualistic route markers beckoning a way home. No wish-imbibed candles, red iced rosettes atop a two-tiered cake, Happy Birthday in cursive. No looming fir tree strung with mini-lights and blinking plastic Santas, red and green buffet littered with pine cones and punch, loaves of stale fruitcake, Kenny and Dolly crooning.

These days, it is only my grandparents who believe. The promise of Armageddon a welt upon their lips, an apocalyptic heart ticking too quickly, the end is near. Fistfuls of scriptural revelation, condemnation. Lungfuls of shame and disappointment. Their only language. Sacreligious, they all used to say.

We — mother, sister, aunt, myself — one by one, on the run. You would think that by now we would have built bridges, made plans, formed an army. But we are suspicious girls. Riddled with secrets, smack-down, tear-your-heart-out secrets. None of us knows what it feels like to have nothing to lose.

In August, the first night back. Seated in the backyard, bony plastic patio chairs, waxy vinyl cushions, lemon yellow. Three generations of silence. A thick doughy dusk. The air breathless. Nightfall swarming. Almost undercover. Saying, *what's new with you?* Smiling, good-game smiles. We all look okay, but mostly we all look away. This is the great cover-up. There is no safety in numbers.

I am: vinyl-pinched thighs, restless. Carving out to-do lists on the palm of my hand: bills to pay, dishes to wash, manifestos to write, shoes to buy, girls to kiss. Imagining the words smudged, the letters bleeding, lazy blue threads tracing lifelines, heart lines. I have never been a palm reader. I keep my hands balled up into fists. Blotchy white knuckles feigning readiness.

And, faltering. Blood rising, skin buzzing, head swimming, I wonder what my body will give away. Things like one and two and three and four and hips grinding, legs spreading. The scent of pheromones never washes off. Top secret terror that I will suddenly tell all, blurt out *smashshitjunkpunkfuck* and what if I can't stop? Inside me, a landslide of heart-wrenching beats fluttering. My cheeks flushing red and redder. There is nowhere to look but down. I am, lungs hard and tight, two fistfuls of diamonds, stone cold crumbling. My body, dangerously volatile, working against me. And my body often betrays me. Throat closing, breath barely, I vow. Cross-my-heart deliverance pacts with the voices in my head. Close my eyes and jump.

The snip rip, snip rip man beside me is cutting out reindeers. Christmas in June. Across from us, a woman and her daughter. The girl, frail, bony, dusty pale, sleepy red-rimmed eyes fierce with need. Squirming and sobbing, her crimson dress bunching up around her waist. Lost her doll.

Puh-leeze, she's in your purse, the wail is a siren, tiny hands grasping for the black leather bag.

And, the mid-forties crown of graying feathered hair

shakes hard left, hard right, no. Snatching the purse away, out of reach, pushing hard at the flailing girl with, *stop it, sit up straight.*

The girl, crying heavy, throaty, insistent, *I want Rosie! She's in your purse!! Just look, please, look!*

And the mother, cool and unfettered with, *no, she isn't in my purse. You left her in the waiting room. I told you to take care of her, but you left her anyway. On the chair right beside you.*

And the girl crumpling, defeated, crying softly now, silent screams of emergency. A gaping wound.

And the mother, smooth and hard like bone, salts insistently, *I watched you leave her. And now she's gone. Just like your doll in the cab, your book at the restaurant. They're all gone.*

I am dream scream dramatic. I'm having horrific fantasies that this mother has really pilfered and pocketed all the toys. That the young girl will find them buried spider-web-deep, in the basement storage closet when she is twenty-seven. A well of trauma housed in long-gone dolls, books and McDonald's figurines. The slip quick ground will yield beneath her, and she will fall for what feels like forever, through twenty-seven stories of heartache and fever. A furious bottomless crashing. A flood of memories, tidal wave torrential. Things like bedroom doors opening and, eyes wide shut, the well of darkness lit sporadically by car headlights, a kaleidoscope across the walls. The scent of Aqua Velva stinging her nose, skin tingling, ears ringing. Heavy hands reaching, breeching. And, after each time, a toy, a good girl gift of thanks. How her mother knew, but couldn't let herself know. The toys, then, testimony she took away. The toy closet a cache marking the erasure of evidence. Lost and found.

When my sister and I were young, he gave us silver heart-shaped lockets. She swallowed hers.

The snip-rip man offers a reindeer to the teary-wet girl. She reaches tentatively, hopelessly hopeful.

And the mother, shielding her daughter's hands with her own and shrinking away, declining, *we don't take things from strangers.*

I crunch myself smaller, fearing atmospheric combustion, heart attack.

But it's just a reindeer. It's an animal. He is pressing the reindeer into the girl's tiny lap. And the mother, sighing hard, looking. Away.

The little girl, slight smile, whispering, *thank you.*

And, seconds later, they are gone. And, seconds later, he likes my smile, so I get two. Names them for me, John and John. Fraternal twins. And, leaning in close, one eye winking, *the real Rudolphs.*

They feel, crinkly whispers, fragile. In my hand, paper-thin possibilities. And one and two and three and four, resisting the urge to crumple fingers into fists. Palms carefully, cautiously, open.

And, back then, August. In the well of night, sneaking out for cigarettes. My sister and I sprawled out along the grassy slope of the backyard, sheltered by a nest of stars, heart of hearts. The sky moon-drunk, the sharp scent of hibiscus swarming. And, lie after lie, no big deal, stupid things like, *yeah I'm good*, and, *no I don't like that band*. We could probably teach each other a lot but we don't. Instead, we blow smoke rings and say fuck a lot.

Inevitably we argue. The same desperate fight. The kiss-me-quick code we can't crack. It has been years, that feeling of forever, that these gaps have existed. We are, one tough love moment to the next, without a net. Two weary girls fighting for air, averting eye contact, keeping our secrets clutched close and closer. No one wants to be the first to give it all away. I am almost sure we want the same thing. But there are too many interruptions. Hours, months, years, residue from *that was then* that just won't go away.

Time has always worked against us. A two-hour time difference, an eight-year age gap. The day they left the country, mother father sister, I stood at the edge of the boulevard watching them, 4x4 loaded down with boxes, drive away. Her face was pressed tight against the rear window, her eight-year-old body sobbing, hand waving, grasping, helpless. She was the only one who looked back. She has not done so since. I, on the other hand, have never learned to look away.

Underneath the stack of letters we don't write, the words we won't say, two hearts of glass. We reel backwards and forwards through emotional forgeries. No idea what battles are worth fighting. Who is who. What we're protecting.

Our late night words are small and wilted. Timid facts falling flat, fast.

And she, picking at the scuffed rubber soles of her

white platform sneakers. Swelling with hostility. Turns to me with a slow pan of gray rage. Lets it smolder, leaden and loaded. And, *what do you want from me*, her voice is a hiss and her hiss is a dare.

I want. I want. I want to tell her. But expectation and desperation crouch deep in the crevice of voice, string up language so there is none. Instead, the sound of my fingertips tapping out SOS on thighs just short of collapse, and I wonder, *where did bravery go?*

Cool glare. Hot stare.

I feel her hatred carving out words like liar and coward on my skin, and I bristle. *I want you to tell me*, I scream. Liar. Coward.

Her head already shaking yes, no, the pile of hair knotted loosely atop her head, threatening to come undone. And, eyes narrowed, her voice hard like boulders crushing, bits of gravel spinning out, *we have never ever been close.* Flicks her cigarette with finality, a glowing ember on its way out.

I nod imperceptibly. Bobbing for words. Biting back the rush of tears. Wondering dumbly, numbly, what else I have lied to myself about.

And *fuck it!* Her body collapses quickly, swiftly. Turns away the face that is framed by a humidity-induced halo of baby-fine frizzies, the eyes that are pooling with tears. And just like that, it is over. We both give up, give in. Holding her in my arms, this is as close as it gets. Palms open and empty, we drift in the well of lonely that lives between us. Some things are best left unsaid.

And *fuck it*. I pull her body down with mine, nestle her head to my chest, stroke her temples softer softest. Tears receding and, *I love you*.

I keep it quiet, the tide of memory. Things like his breath, muggy and whiskey-stale, a damp cellar of secrets sweeping across the nape of my neck. Slithering. Slathering. His fingers, gnarled and misshapen, missing the left pinky. Sweaty hands reaching. Breeching. Saying, *shhh*. Saying, *Maddy, you're my favourite*. Saying, *Annie, you're my favourite*. Mixing us up. All the time. It didn't really matter. It was both of us. All the time. But this one is not true, mostly true. Neither of us have really ever been anyone's favourite.

Today though, the pictures. Developed finally and telling a different story. Talking, trash, the story I'll tell myself later.

This one roll. The roll that I can't stop looking at. August, my sister and I, during our two-week wedding-based August reunion. We fled midway, a two-day escape to Toronto. One photo to the next we are, lips moving wordless, two girls in trace amounts. On the bus ride up, over-exposed self-portraits. And, making faces over eggs, bacon, rye toast. And, traipsing across pastures of pavement, Yonge Street, College, Queen. We have flowers in our hair. And small talk over sushi, scratching Bingo tickets at the Second Cup. Shutter snap smiles. I remember thinking, *it can't get much better than this*. But we were mostly faking. In between all the right answers, we don't know each other at all.

And so now, College and Bathurst, one shaky breaky

foot in front of the other. Feeling further away than close to home. I squint hard, imagine overgrown ferns, a pile of dishes in the sink, sunburned squares of linoleum, the floors always clean. Hold close my paper reindeer. Try my best to forget there is more to remember. Close my eyes and pretend I am perfect.

KATHRYN PAYNE

Straight Peters (a monologue for cellphone on streetcar)

Anyways, so I'm telling Tanya last week about how easy straight boys are but, y'know, I can't just proposition the pretty ones on the street and besides, I want them to work for it. So, I've got to be a straight girl for a night, but I need my "girlfriend" to come cruise with me, cuz straight girls don't even go to the bathroom alone. Tanya's tickled by this, right? We joke about it for a while and decide to pretend to be het for a night.

Why not? I mean, it's pretty common, how hard can it be anyway?

Yeah, I know. So, I call my sister right away and say, "Babe, be my straight informant. I want to pick up, where do het girls go to do that?" After claiming not to know that kind of stuff — whatever — she finally admits that the music was o.k. at this place called Atomic Weight.

Yep, on Queen, with the silver paint. Yeah, that's it. Then I called Tanya back and we decided to meet at her place Friday night for drinks with Sandra and go straight from there (ha ha). We both wore mini-dresses — I have this light blue one I used to ho in. Never fails! And Tanya wore this low-cut black number. We totally looked like bookends — two cute short-haired blonde chicks with good legs, right?

Anyways, drinks at Sandra n' Tanya's are always delightful. We were all quite taken with our little passing scheme and once well into the Caesars we decided that real straight chicks would go check out some of the meat markets on the College St. strip. So, with slightly-sloshed farewell kisses for Sandra, we set out into the night.

Once we get to College, we can't pick which place we ought to try, so we just start at the first one we come too. It was called Kalendar or something else over-decorated. When we got there, I began to worry we'd overlooked a variable in our scheming. Really, it was like the straight people all know each other or something. You'd think it wouldn't take more than a couple minutes before some guy'd be all over a table with two cute babes "alone" at it. Hell, they come in droves when you're only interested in having drinks with your date!

Yeah, yeah, just like that. But no, they all stood around in little swarms talking to each other and long-haired girls. I couldn't even get any of them to play those cruisey eye-contact games D'Arcy taught me. We sighed, sipped our drinks, discussed using wigs next time and checked the lads out. The selection wasn't that phenomenal, really.

Just as we agreed to leave after the band — what?

Oh, I dunno, some group of boys wailing a bit. Not bad. Not great.

So, just then, it gets interesting. This guy Peter drifts over. Tall, light brown, white shirt, black pants, like maybe he's a waiter just off work. He asks nicely if he can use our ashtray and then sits down with us in the way chatty men do, introduces himself and makes conversation. We tell him we're trying to pick up and we're not that impressed with the crowd. He asks me to repeat this, looks a bit surprised and then says maybe he can help. We laugh, and he says no really, look at us, a couple of lovely ladies, if he didn't have a girlfriend, we'd already be picked up, but he does, so the least he can do is assist.

Nah, not really, I mean, of course it was, but it was charming too.

So, we start looking around the room for a guy we — well, more like I, Tanya wasn't wanting to stay in character all night, I don't think — anyways, a guy I want. And there's this one with kinda longer hair, you know, that jawline length that makes them look boyish and pretty. I was trying the eye stuff on him earlier, and he'd almost come over (walked towards, lost in crowd, didn't reappear, you know how it goes). So I point him out and Peter says "No! Not that one. You could do so much better than that."

Seriously! Weird, eh? Now me, I'm astonished — why would someone offer to help and then question my choice? "I want that one," I tell him again.

"Look, believe me, a good-looking girl like you, you could do way better," he says, "Don't you want to take a stroll around the room and see what else is out there?"

"No," I say, "we already looked around. I want that one."

And, he's like, "You're sure?"

"Yeah. Absolutely"

"Totally sure?"

So, I'm going, "Yes!" Geez, I'm thinking, like it makes that much difference.

"Ok," he finally says. "I'll go see what I can do."

Yeah, so off goes our new friend Peter in the direction of my lust-object. Tanya and I watch as he wanders over to sexi-guy, shakes hands, and proceeds to gab, both of them smiling, gesturing towards me, and so-on. I worry, for a second, that I might be being made fun of, but when I ask Tanya if that's what it looks like to her, she laughs.

"Does it matter? Like we'll ever see any of these people again."

There I am, mulling over the enormous license that ano- nymity gives us, when Peter comes chugging back to the table. He sits down without saying anything and Tanya and I stare at him all expectantly.

"Well?" I ask, knowing it's not great news or we'd be across the table from sexi-guy by now.

"Well," Peter looks rueful and says, "He says you're really cute and he'd love to, but that girl over there (he points to this teen-magazine-looking chick with long dark hair) is his fiancé."

"Damn!" I say, making an exaggerated-but-girly oh-pooh gesture, "Figures."

"Aw, he wasn't for you anyway, trust me." Peter con- soles, "See anything else you like?"

"No, not really." I'm really disheartened now. You know, I'd forgotten about that whole game of straight relation- ships and affiliations — they didn't matter when I was doing straight guys as a ho, so I forgot that they matter when you're just another chick in the bar.

Tanya sees my disappointment, and tries to help, "How about that one," she points to a skinny long white guy who's doing a real seventies look, "he's kind of pretty."

"Nah, too skinny."

We try this a couple more times, Tanya or Peter selecting a candidate and me rejecting him: "Too hairy, too drunk, too goofy."

Tanya's finding this pretty funny after a while, "Might be that the secret is not to be too picky" she offers, laughing some.

"Nah, no point going to all this trouble for substandard goods," I explain. Peter looks stunned, like he didn't imagine women were this mercenary about sex, and doesn't know what to think of us.

"We need a bigger pond," I tell Tanya, and turn to him, "Peter, what other bars are there around here where straight guys hang out?"

Peter pulls a puzzled face. Belatedly, I realize that I've specified straight guys, when everyone knows that heterosexual women don't do that — to hets, everyone is het and you only specify orientation if someone's queer. Clearly, I've got to lay off either the drinking or the talking.

Tanya pipes up, "Yeah, we accidentally went to this gay bar before this. Really cute guys — what a waste!"

Yah, yah. You know how they say stuff like that, isn't she clever?

But this Peter guy smells a rat, "Y'all aren't lesbians

just having a good time with me, are you?" he asks petu-
lantly.

Tanya says "No" real emphatically, at the same time
that I say "Close," cuz we're both mostly bi, right?

He looks really confused now and says "What?"

And Tanya says — deadpan — "Come on! Please! Do
we look like lesbians?"

Now this is so fuckin funny that I nearly spew my drink
and fall out of my seat. But he's looking reassured, so I try
to hold still and swallow. We need a local informant, clearly,
if we're going to have any luck tonight. "Really Peter," I
lean into him, "Where should we go? Where would you go
if you totally wanted to pick a girl up?"

"That's easy," he's still a bit spooked, but playing again,
"my girlfriend and her friends always complain about getting hit on at the Granite Gong."

"Great!" I almost cheer. "Let's try that place."

It turns out the Granite Gong is just a few blocks down
the strip.

So off we stroll, carefully not arm-in-arm, giggling about
Peter's question. I pay the insanely high cover at the door
and we head for the bar at the back. We haven't even
placed an order before we've got a guy each, clearly pals,
flanking us.

Oh, I dunno really. I can't describe guys so well. Like if
it was a butch, or some kind of dyke, I could do better, but
I don't think I can tell the types of white guy apart, really.
Not-great but not-bad looking, dressed in your basic jeans
and shirts, shaved and shiney, because they were out on

the town, nothing special. Likely suburban guys downtown for some Friday night action.

And they had it all worked out. The heavier-set one — who'd clearly assigned himself to Tanya — took the lead. He introduced himself and paused for his friend to step in. Then they stood there making tres boring conversation while we waited for the bartender to bring our drinks. Tanya giving me really clear "Get me out of here!" looks the whole time.

As soon as Tanya and I both have our drinks, I bum a smoke from the guys and use my first few puffs to try to figure out how to nicely ditch them. Tricky, since they have positioned themselves to kind of corral us in to our little section of the bar. We could be polite, stay there enduring the small talk, but I definitely don't want either of them. So, they're just standing literally in the way of my evening of conquest. Resolved, I got a firm grip on my glass, smiled my biggest and said a charming thank you for the fag, grabbed Tanya's hand, ducked under the bar-leaning-arm of the guy on my side and made a bee-line for the lounge area at the other end of the place, just fast enough that it'd be humiliating for our new buddies to follow.

I dunno, I guess they just stood there and watched us go. Beats me. Would have blown it to look back, eh?

So once we're at the other end of the room, we plunk down at a table and giggle wildly. Tanya thanks me for saving us, we look unhappily around at the rest of the bar and complain cattily about sleazy guys. I'm getting frustrated, and drink my drink too fast.

"I'm afraid to go anywhere else around here." I tell Tan.

"This is the wrong kind of pick-up scene," she says. "Too calculated and just too, well, *straight*. Hell, those guys were talking about their jobs and definitely looking for wives or wife-substitutes. Where's the fun in that?"

No kidding, man. Can't hide from it anywhere!

"Let's try that place my sister recommended," I suggest to Tanya, who's polished off her drink too, "Maybe it's more the sort of place our kind of straight chicks hang out."

"Or, more importantly," Tanya reminds me, "our kind of straight boys."

So, with a "Touche," we head for Atomic Weight. In the cab, joking with Tanya, bemoaning how long this is taking, I realize I am decidedly drunk now. When I tell Tan, she snickers, and says "All the better to pick you up with" in a witchy voice that makes us laugh uproariously until we arrive at the club

As we cross this overpriced threshold, I turn to her, grin and yell, "Here we go!" over the music that's finally good music, trippy techno bass-driven, already making my feet twitch and hips wiggle.

I head like a bullet for the DJ and wee, makeshift dance floor at the back. The dancers are mostly guys, a few girls, many of them freaky looking. Ah, I think, that is more like it. I sidle up near the dance floor and Tanya goes to get drinks. By the time she returns, the DJ's playing something that moves me and I'm up and dancing, every other step sticking to the gummy floor.

I feel drunk, pretty and anonymous, with a bit of that sense of being special as a girl in the straight world because I don't carry around the same weight of self-consciousness and insecurity most of them do, know what I mean?

Yeah, like I know I'm cute, I know I'm a good lay, and I don't need a boyfriend, thank you. There I am, surrounded by posing and strutting guys ten years younger than me, one of the only chicks on the floor, with the luxury of knowing I'm one of the better dancers, knowing I'm sexy.

So, I am finally having a blast! I'm watching the guys around me out of the corner of my eye, checking every few minutes to see where Tanya is (sitting near, dancing with difficulty on the gooey floor, talking to some guy), but mostly I'm just giving my body to the music, letting the lust that inspired the evening's endeavours flow into my legs and arms and spiral into my torso.

Then I notice I'm kind of dancing with some guy. He's cute, tall, with that to-the-jawline haircut, nifty glasses and genuine rhythm. I'm smiling at him, my "that's good" smile, my "welcome" smile, my "uh-huh" smile. I'm having fun and he is touching me "accidentally," tentatively. I play with him, moving in close and gyrating, backing off and waiting to see if he'll follow. The music's still good, the air's smoky, Tanya's dancing with some other guy to my left. Eventually, I need to catch my breath, and so I move off to the side of the floor.

Dancing boy follows, you know how it goes. I end up sitting on his lap, both of us sweating. I don't remember what we talked about, or how, but it was just surface dialogue anyways. The subtext was the important part: "Now I'm going to sit on your lap and see how you react to such familiarity and proximity" and when he reacted well, big hands balancing me there, I asked/didn't ask him, "do you want what I want" and somehow he indicated yes. His body comfortable against mine, his hands easy on me, the chemistry effortless and drunken.

Yeah, just the same, it's amazing how that doesn't matter, really, eh?

After a bit, Tanya wandered over, to see how things were going.

"Are you wanting to go soon?" she asked, all tired and hopeful.

I'm like, "Yeah, I guess," and turned to my dancing-boy — "Wanna come home with me?" It was easy to ask — our bodies already knew the answer.

"Sure," he says. No dummy, him.

No kidding, eh? So, we tumbled out onto the street and grabbed a cab. Peter — honest, that was his name — tucked me under his arm, and I draped myself into him. We dropped Tanya off and headed back to my place.

No. She was off at meetings in Ottawa that weekend.

Yeah. Oh, I'll tell you about that later, let me finish the story first!

So, it turns out I've picked up table tennis player from Bulgaria, who, he claims, often gets mistaken for — and I quote — Huge Grant.

No, I kid you not! Seriously. I got into trouble because I called it ping-pong. "Its' proper name is table tennis," apparently, "ping-pong is the Chinese word for it." And, get this, he called me an older woman. He's twenty-five and when I told him how old I was, he says, all proud, "I always get the older women. They're drawn to me, I guess." Isn't that the cutest!

Really, he was a lovely lay — big handed, sweet, attentive and eager-to-please. He tried to go down on me, but it was the typical sloppy slurping, so I put him to work at things more suited to his, um, innate abilities. Hell, he didn't even give me grief about the condom. The best part (other than the earnestly knowledgeable history of Bulgaria delivered in the drunken horizontal nude) was that he woke me up at six, fucked me nicely again, and then left to meet some pals to watch a World Cup game — without even asking for my phone number.

Yeah, heh, so, I got to wake up much later alone, well fucked and with this *great* story!

Oh, shit, I gotta switch to the subway here, call you back when I get home.

What Price Freedom

Your house is silent at this time of night. Your insomniac roommates have gone to sleep. Your crackhead neighbours have stopped bouncing around. Even you are no longer expecting me; lost to dreaming. It's around five a.m. Not dawn, but close. The night is almost over, but I still have dark cover for long enough to get what I want.

You mumble in your sleep and twist slightly as I lean over you in bed. My pocket is bulging, full of promises to end your troubles. I have something for you baby, I say to myself. I'm getting you out of this shit. I can't resist, and kiss you once as I stand back up. You are so little in your sleep; your mouth pouts and your eyelashes flutter. There's none of the bravado and stress I'm used to seeing—just rest.

I remember the day we were wandering the east side, searching out graffiti and abandoned buildings to fuck in. You were having trouble breathing and I made you stop and lean against a wall. "Are you sick? Do you want to go home?"

"No, my asthma's getting bad."

"Where's your inhaler? Let me get it."

"I used it all up...I can't get a new one right now."

This translates easily: I can't buy one right now. I don't have the fifty bucks I need to breathe. "We can walk slower." I said apologetically.

You leave your jeans crumpled on the floor by your bed every night, so it's easy enough for me to find them and take your wallet from the pocket. Carefully unsnapping the chains from it is harder, but once accomplished, I slide the red fold of leather into my bag. Finding your credit card statements is much more difficult. You don't organize, never did, and gently tugging at the piles of papers in your room leads only to toppling and noise. You stir in your sleep and I freeze.

I once thought I could accomplish anything through sheer force of will and my joy. But the truth comes out: we are not chosen, not sacred — at least, I'm not. After learning this, I went to work, work being the thing that brings us closest to holiness. Daily life being the thing that comes between us and work. Us being the thing that ruins our ability to get paid. Paid being the thing that is holy. Will you be a sacrifice for me? No, girlie, you don't have the money.

There, amidst the tumble of comics, newspapers and phone bills is your statement. I slide it out and tuck it in with your wallet. Looking at the old you for the last time, I walk out of your house before I light a cigarette, not wanting to irritate your asthma-riddled lungs. At the corner, I feel around in my pocket for the wad of freedom nestling there. Almost six a.m. I get in a cab uptown, to my neighbourhood.

Let out on the corner, I walk to your bank. Taking your card out of my bag, I use it to open the securi-door and enter. I insert it into the ATM and using the code you gave me months ago, access your account. I am aware of the camera right above my head. This time, it's recording more than someone taking their last $20 out for a night of cheap boozing; more than some upstart withdrawing $100 to impress and hopefully bed a lady; more than a mom seeing $80 and having to decide whether to pay the phone bill or buy groceries.

I knew working at that shitty temp agency would pay off. It did when I got that contract processing mailed statements for your bank. First, find a regular depositor; pick some guy who has lots of money already, who gets lots more every two weeks. Watch their funds—if several chunks get withdrawn in early spring, they're probably on vacation somewhere. They'll never remember where they spent what, what the exchange rate was, where all the receipts are. Siphon off some of the fat. Don't get greedy. Just a few grand from each one. Create a new account for the money, and transfer. From that ghost account, transfer to someone who needs it. Close the ghost account. Bada-bing. Nobody needs signatures anymore. If the computer says yes, it's a go. All done while managers are lunching, wanking off, or working out at the company gym.

Looks like $3,000 will do the trick. Your phone bill account — update payment, $182. Your bank's credit card — update payment, $1,643. Your hydro bill — update payment, $113. I leave $1,062 in your previously empty savings account for good measure. This won't fix you for life, but it's a little bit of freedom for a few months. No more thirty days until the collection calls, no more ten days until the phone's shut off, no more late payment charges. For now.

I exit your account, pocket your card and transaction statement, and hail a cab. Getting back into your house is easy. After re-attaching your wallet to its chains, I leave the statement in your front pocket, where you'll find it while digging for bus fare in the morning. I consider getting into bed with you, but don't. I'd love you to taste the relief on my skin, but I wouldn't want to ruin the surprise.

Something or Nothing

The first time Jill met Keith, he said "Did you ever have nuclear dreams when you were growing up?"

That was his favourite icebreaker at parties. He was taking a poll, he said. He was born in 1960 something and his theory was that childhood nuclear dreams belonged to his generation and his alone. "I had them all the time," he said, "and sometimes I still have them. Dreams where everything is going up, all mushroom clouds and ashes."

Jill has had only two dreams where she was dead.

In the first dream, she was hiding from stormtroopers in Nazi Germany. It involved a long and complicated plot with false identities and lots of running and hiding. In the end, she was caught and shot dead. Jill woke immediately, sitting bolt upright, her heart thumping in her throat.

In the second dream, an intensely bright white light was engulfing the room. She's a kid in this dream, at school with all the other kids who were taking cover under their desks, but the light came, and she stood up to look at it. Then the light was gone. She knew she was dead, but the odd thing was, she didn't wake up right away. She kept dreaming about being dead, and there was no light, no sound. There was nothing, and the nothing went on for so very long. It was the most peaceful feeling she'd ever had.

This was the dream she told Keith about. It was at the

beginning of their brief, unhappy friendship. It was 1989 and Jill was nineteen.

The nuclear dreams became a theme. Wherever he went, Keith left mushroom clouds in spray paint or black magic marker. Jill would follow them around the city until she found him, sitting alone with his beer at the local watering hole or at one of the punk parties that happened on Vancouver's East Side. Jill felt slightly out of place at these parties. She wanted to be a punk rock girl, but she was too earnest. Deep down, she wanted to save the world.

When Jill looked at Keith, with his big black Mohawk, pierced nose and forlorn face, she saw how he was going through the motions of everydayness. He had *no future* burnt into his eyes. She wanted to hold his hand and show him this wasn't true.

Jill was hanging out with Sarah a lot back then, Sarah with her bright orange hair who, at twenty-three, had never had a boyfriend.

"Even my parents think I'm gay," she said. But she wasn't. She was just a bit asexual was all. It wouldn't occur to anyone that she was interested in sex. But she was.

It was Jill's idea to get a cheap place where they could all live together to save on rent. As it happened, Keith was getting kicked out of his old apartment. It seemed logical. Sarah, Keith, and her. Jill had the idea that they could be a family, all of them together.

Jill saw the little green and white house on the corner of East 6th and Albert, with a white picket fence and the *For Rent* sign in front, and she thought, *that's the one*.

They'd been looking for three weeks already, traipsing through houses and filling out application forms. Getting rejected each time. No one wanted to rent to kids with weird hair and no jobs. But Jill had a feeling about this house. She took out her nose-ring and put on a long skirt to go meet the landlord. She projected responsible grown-up vibes at him. After she had looked at each room, she turned to him and said, *yes, I think this will do.* He rented it to her on the spot.

The three of them moved in and set up house. They borrowed a car to move their stuff, which wasn't much. Keith had about a dozen boxes of comic books. He had his own cat to add to Jill's and Sarah's. Sarah had twenty boxes of vintage clothes she'd bought at the Sally Ann. Jill had a suitcase and a typewriter.

Later, Jill could see the landlord was disappointed in her, when each month he'd come to collect the rent and there'd be beer bottles and cats everywhere. They were not supposed to have cats; it said so in the lease. He never said anything about it though, and she felt badly about deceiving him. That was Jill's way. She empathized with everyone. She went around smiling at the bums on the street to make them feel better.

The neighbourhood was called Mount Pleasant. The irony was obvious. Girls wearing highed-heeled boots and too much make-up walked back and forth on the street outside. Sometimes, the police would get ready for a raid in the parking lot next door. From the dining room window, Jill could watch the policemen put on their flak jackets and run into an apartment building halfway down the next block.

They got their groceries at the Kingsgate Mall on Broadway, which was full of crazy people who wandered around muttering to themselves. One lady quacked, not continuously, but often enough that you knew she did it. Jill smiled at all of them.

It's my kind of neighbourhood, Jill thought. She felt right at home.

In less than three months of living together, Keith began to drive Jill mad.

He complained constantly, it didn't matter about what.

He brought people over at all hours of the night. Jill would come downstairs in the morning to find the living room full of strangers passed out on the floor.

He left toast crumbs and butter smears on the kitchen counter, and never did his dishes. He started eating all the food in the fridge, and never bought any more.

And finally, he lost his job cleaning buses, and fell into a deep hole of depression. For days, he didn't get up off the couch, ignoring Sarah and Jill's efforts to cheer him up.

Then, the final blow. Sarah decided she was going to split for Mexico with a boy she'd just met. He had a VW van and wanted to kiss her in it.

"What about family?" Jill said, her heart cracking.

"Don't worry, I'll find you a new roommate."

But it was too much for Jill. She'd had enough of Keith's dark mushroom clouds exploding in and around the house all day. It was getting so that she'd slip up into her room when Keith came home. If Sarah wasn't going to be there to cheer her up, then would she slip down into some sort of black hole as well?

They gave notice on the big green and white house, and the landlord happily let them off the lease.

The end of Keith and Jill's friendship came soon after that. It was over the damage deposit and the fact that there wasn't any, since the landlord kept it all to clean out the mess they and their cats had left behind. Keith got angry and accused Jill of keeping it. Jill hung up on him and except for one time, three years later, they never spoke to each other again.

Before it all disintegrated though, there was a brief time when they did seem like a family. Jill came home early one day to find Keith cleaning the kitchen and Sarah baking a cake. It was her twentieth birthday.

"Happy Birthday!" They shouted.

"Hey," Keith said. "I was hoping to be finished before you got home."

Jill looked at the gleaming counters and freshly washed dishes drying in the dishrack. If only this moment would last, she thought.

Happiness and clean kitchens are so fleeting.

The last time Jill spoke to Keith was on the corner of Davie and Granville. Jill was waiting for the bus, and he walked by.

"Hey," he said, like three years hadn't just passed.

In the few minutes before the bus came, she learned that he'd gotten a job at a video dating service, doing what, she couldn't imagine. She was going back to school, she told him. He grinned and waved at her as the bus came and she got on. She remembered thinking he looked a lot happier.

She didn't think about him much after that. Five more years went by and Jill never wondered what he was up to.

The news of his death came to her by e-mail. E-mail barely existed when she first met him. *Keith, you bastard,* she thought. He had died of a heroin overdose. *What a fucking clichéd way to go.*

The e-mail said that a service would take place that Friday at three p.m. She imagined him in a casket, with his piercings and tattoos and big black hair, reclining against white satin lining. Keith was dead, and what did that mean?

It means you are no longer anywhere, that I couldn't call you up even if I had your phone number, and your phone hadn't been disconnected because you couldn't afford paying the bills. It means I won't run into you, no matter where I am, ever. But suddenly, I see you everywhere.

There you are, crossing the street, and there again, loitering on that park bench. You welfare bum. Heaven might be an all night drinking-hole and you would be there until closing time, checking out the angels. Or maybe that would be hell because nothing would have changed.

Jill thought about it a lot, trying to be sad because that was the emotion called for. But there was nothing inside her, nothing that had any words. Not sad or angry or anything, and the nothing went on for the longest time.

The End Of The World

I have this dream, actually it's more of a daydream. It's the end of the world and everyone is dead except for me, my dog, and this girl. It's always the end of fall. A few leaves still cling to the trees, and the rest just lie where they fell, covering the yards and sidewalks. The dead people have all just disappeared. There are no nasty surprises, not a single human form, dead or alive, besides the two of us.

Everything is always quiet in the dream, no more cars or yelling kids or barking dogs. We don't say much, the girl and I, because we don't have to. It's the end of the world. There isn't much to be said. She's my age, sixteen, or maybe a little older, with long coal-black hair, and blue eyes that turn gray sometimes, like the sky. I don't know her name but names don't matter much anymore. We always know when we're being spoken to.

The girl and I spend our time wandering empty streets and exploring abandoned houses. We walk a lot. We take bicycles out of people's yards and ride them down the middle of the street, between the yellow lines. The dog runs after us. He's big, with shiny black fur, ears that always stand at attention, and a tail so short he can barely wag it.

The girl and I break into any house we like, any house

that interests us. We go through people's cupboards looking for food. After the first few days, everything we eat is
canned or frozen. We don't mind. Both of us particularly
like canned spaghetti. We always heat it on the stove, never
in a microwave. The girl thinks it tastes better that way.
(You might ask how the electricity is still running, but it's
dreaming, you can choose which details to overlook.) She
doesn't eat meat or fish or anything that was ever alive, so
neither do I. She doesn't mind feeding meat to the dog
though, says he can't help it that he's a carnivore. He's
acquiring a taste for Spam, Chef Boyardee, and smoked
oysters. It's all I can do not to grab whatever meat-laden
entree he's eating and run with it...but I'm a vegetarian
now that it's the end of the world and I've gotta stick to it,
for the girl. She's all I've got.

We play a lot of video games. Tomb Raider is her favourite, but she gets mad at me when we play it because I
always spend my turn coming up with new ways to kill off
Lara Croft. We drink other people's booze and smoke their
cigarettes till we're dizzy and drunk. We sleep in other
people's beds. We sleep together, and no one cares. There's
no one left to care.

In one of the houses we find a bag of marshmallows.
She says she likes them burnt on the outside and gooey on
the inside. I agree. I take out my Zippo and set a kitchen
chair on fire. We stand around the chair and roast marshmallows, letting them catch on fire then blowing them out,
till the whole place smells like burning wood and scorched
sugar. Several marshmallows later the kitchen drapes go up

in flames. We beat a hasty retreat, stand across the street in a pile of leaves while the house burns. Neither of us wants to think about what might happen if the house next door, and the next one, and the one after that, catches fire. It would just go on and on. The whole world could burn down and there'd be no one to stop it. We stand in silence and watch the flames. She squeezes my sweaty hand. An hour later the house is a pile of smoldering rubble on a tree-lined street. The houses next to it are blackened with soot but still standing. We stare at the charred remains. There are plenty of other houses just like it. We move on.

Sometimes we dress up in other people's clothes. She looks good in black. We find a house where a teenaged goth type used to live. Posters of Nine Inch Nails and The Cure on the walls. Short black skirts, leather trench coat, fishnets, matching black lace panties and push-up bra, and big black boots in the closet. White powder, black nail polish and mascara and eyeliner, red eye shadow, and clove cigarettes on the desk. Rings with skulls and spider webs and crosses, spiked leather collar, studded cuffs, thick metal chains on her dresser. KMFDM in the stereo. Beetlejuice doll on the bed. The girl and I think we might have liked her if we'd met her. The girl's eyes turn gray. I dress her in a leopard print mini, a black tank top, fishnets and the boots that make her look like tank-girl, all huge boots and skinny legs. Paint her face till she looks the part. "If these were really my clothes," the girl says, "I'd be dead." Her mascara is running down her cheeks, black on white. "We're still here," I tell her, "I'll prove it to you...."

She has tattoos all over her arms and she cuts all the sleeves out of her T-shirts. It's the end of the world; she doesn't have to hide her arms anymore. I want tattoos too. One night we find an artist's home, paint and clay and India ink. There's a pack of razor blades in the bathroom. I take off my shirt (someone else's shirt not so long ago) and hold out my right arm. "Do the whole arm. Shoulder to wrist," I tell her. She nods. It takes seven hours and four razor blades. I can hardly breathe by the end of it, the pain is so bad. Blood and every colour of ink everywhere. I don't even look. When she's done, I go to a mirror. I never knew the girl could draw.

I'd never slept with a girl before, never slept with anyone else, never will, I guess. I don't mind. She's never told me she loves me, but I tell her every time. The words fly from my mouth whenever she cries out. Sometimes, afterwards, she breaks down. I don't know why and I don't ask. She's crying now, shaking. I hold her till she falls asleep. A few hours later and I'm still awake, watching her breathe. It's still dark when she wakes up and slips away, and I don't follow her. I dream that she's drowning in black water. The next morning when I wake up she's lying next to me again, sleeping on her back. Her black hair is tangled and damp and everywhere, spread across her face, her shoulders, the pillow. During the night she carved a tattoo across her chest. It's a mess of blood and blurred ink, but I can read it anyway: *I'll love you till the end of the world.*

Why You Hate Me

An excerpt from the novel *I Am Kasper Klotz*

1. BECAUSE I KILL PEOPLE. Well, that should be pretty fucking obvious. Most people aren't too fond of a murderer. Even though the people I kill completely deserve it and bring it on themselves.

2. BECAUSE I TELL MY VICTIMS WHAT I'M GOING TO DO. Yeah, I'd say this makes you even madder. It's one thing to go around killing people, it's another thing to look people in the eye and say "Hey, you're going to die." That's the one thing people don't like. I don't understand it, what's the big deal?

I'll admit there's not much thrill in killing other artists. A lot of them are already completely into death and dying because their art is all about that morbid stuff. The same goes for lower-class types, who just don't have the money to keep death away. For them, disease and death are just normal parts of everyday life.

But middle class people are fun to kill. "I'm murdering you," I say. "You are going to die." This completely freaks out the suburban types. After all, their lives are devoted to staying alive, to ignoring death. That's why they always keep the suburban streets clean and free of "homeless" types. They don't want to be reminded that *life is short and painful*. Yeah, killing the middle classes is great. It's fun to see the terror in their eyes as they confront death for the first time in their stupid, corny, pointless, cowardly lives.

3. BECAUSE I LOOK, WELL, DIFFERENT THAN YOU. That's always a problem, isn't it? I'm not pretty. I'm big and ugly. Everything I own is in bad taste. And I smell. And I'm a bit effeminate, which doesn't go with my shaved head. I wear army pants, and I have disgusting tattoos. If I were a nice, clean-looking murderer, then you wouldn't hate me so much.

4. BECAUSE YOU LIKE HATING SOMEONE. It's all very well for you to deny this. I know, you're a very loving person, and you're into having warm feelings about everyone. Crap! You gossip about your friends. You tell dirt about people closest to you. You're very competitive, and you feel inadequate. (I don't know — it could be sex, it could be your job or lack of one, it could be anything.) And the only way you feel better is by nurturing nasty feelings about others. I'm a repository for all your jealousy and fear. "It's Kasper's fault." "Isn't Kasper ugly and horrible and evil, don't you just hate him?" Go on, hate me. If I didn't exist, then you would have created me. Actually, you did, didn't you? But

God knows you don't want to admit that you hate yourselves. That would be too honest. So choose me instead. Go on, spill it all on me. You'll feel a lot better.

Distant Relations

Sylvia is an angry one. Every moment is sharp. Standing back from the living room window she watches the yellow Toyota sit at the end of the driveway, engine running. The door opens on the driver's side, then closes. The door opens on the passenger's side. Someone leans over the door to talk to someone else in the back seat. Finally they are all in the car and it rolls softly through the snow and down the street. The empty, blank street.

The family downstairs has left again. Sylvia goes about the house trying to do things. She looks through old newspapers for articles to clip, then hurls the remains into recycling. She sprays the plant that has invisible bugs. Each jet of water is squeezed out in bursts. The bugs will surely die this time. She locates the cat, but the cat is sleeping. She opens the fridge and then closes the fridge. Opens it again, then closes it absolutely. As she opens and closes, crashes and stomps, she frets and searches for something to occupy her. Why doesn't the phone ring? She lifts the receiver in case there's a message, then slams it down at the steady tone. And all this time, she listens for them to get home.

She watches the women downstairs all the time, like a spy. They are her landladies, which sounds ridiculous because they are women, lesbians, somewhat butchy. Her landpeople. Never landlords. She is their tenant, she tells people, so she doesn't have to think of an appropriate adjective. She watches as they follow each other around the backyard — first cutting the grass and trimming the lilac bush, then collecting fallen leaves into garbage bags, and now scraping the ice from the windows of the car. She knows when they are listening to music, watching TV, laughing, reading aloud and even cooking. Their lives seem full. She knows it, too. She knows because they occasionally invite her down into their warm, comfortable home. They give her wine when she says yes to water. The kids come in and stall so they don't have to go to bed. At Christmas time, their tree is a fairy tale of lights and presents.

Today she is angry because they have gone away and left her. A cold winter, weekend day and they have left her alone in her top floor apartment. Sylvia decides that she will ignore them. Ah, but that is what they really wish for, she imagines. "Can't she find anyone else to phone, visit and spy on?" they must wonder.

Do they know she spies?

Her crush started after three months. The pleasure of triangles. She has a crush on them both, as a pair. They talk to her, on those late evenings, about their troubles: crises at work, lasting and hateful entanglements with a past partner, older parents getting ill... She sees them snipe at each other sometimes and once even witnessed the edges of a fight. It was on one of the few nights when Sylvia was out in a restaurant, catching up with an old, visiting friend. Her back was to the window in order to view the busy restaurant with a certain pleasure. So this is where the people are, she thought to herself. Then suddenly she saw one of them, the one with the smoother, more open face and the curly, blond hair. She was dressed up, preoccupied, rushing through the crowd and out the door. There was no eye contact. Then, ten minutes later, the other one emerged from the midst of the crowded restaurant: short dark hair, stocky walk and incongruous make-up. This one came towards the front of the restaurant more slowly, with her face set. A little grim. Unlike her partner, she saw Sylvia and stopped at the table, asking which way her lover went. A momentary excitement! Sylvia felt like a part of them, playing a role. She conveyed valuable information and asked about their welfare. It was a rush. She replayed it over and over for the rest of the dinner, as her friend talked about a new, lackluster job. The next day she tried to get it back and even ventured out into the yard to ask one of them again: "Is everything alright?" The answers were vague. She had no place in it now, so she patted the dog who is always happy to see her.

Oh yes, the dog. But even the dog is fickle. Sylvia took care of the dog once, and that day she realized the truth — that the dog's excitement, the wagging tail and leaping paws, was a result of her being a temporary novelty. When it came down to extended contact, he simply pined for them to come home. "You and I, dog," she whispered to him one day, "we are both in love."

Today, when they finally come home from wherever they were, it is later than usual. It is about 8:30 when the car slips down the driveway and the sensory light snaps on. The dog barks. They pile out, making a gathering of footsteps in the new snow. She stands in her darkened kitchen and peers for clues about where they've been. The eight-year-old boy bends down to make a snowball, but the snow's too fine and it slips into a puff of dust. They come in the side door, stamping their feet. Suddenly her floorboards are muffling voices again. They're getting ready to take the dog for a walk, she suspects. Sometimes, on dog-walks, they have phoned up, to invite her along. Sylvia does not check her e-mail, so that the lines are free. She does not start anything new, just in case. She listens even more carefully, at one point even lying on her living room floor, ear to the smooth wood just to be sure. She waits, but tonight they do not call up to her. Instead, she hears them all, now on the front porch, now the door slamming behind them, then their voices, increasingly far away as they move together past the quiet neighbours and down the street.

Sylvia picks up the phone again, then puts it down. She keeps the TV off and tries to read a book of short stories she was given for her last birthday. She listens for when they come home.

Delivery

An interesting party was interrupted by the delivery of four party-sized pizzas with hot peppers, extra cheese, onion, black olives and anchovies.

Glen refused to pay since he did not order them. Other guests confirmed and backed his story to the delivery boy.

"What am I supposed to do?" the delivery boy asked. "Look at the order sheet. This is your address and this is your name."

"It must be a prank or something," Glen said, glancing again at the receipt. Several people squeezed past. He slapped one of them on the back of the head. "It is a party," he added, looking over his shoulder.

"Shit," the boy said, bracing the four large boxes in his arms.

A girl with pink hair arrived at the door. To Glen she said, "Everybody swears they didn't order anything." She looked over at the delivery boy. "Even Dave."

Glen looked at the boy and shrugged. "Sorry, man." He closed the door. A guy on his way into the party whooped and pumped his fist in the air as he passed.

The boy took the boxes back to the car. A girl was sitting in the front seat, watching him.

"Could you drop me off at the subway station?"

The boy shook his head and then looked around him. A jeep was pulling out of a driveway.

"Please! It's late and I don't want to walk there. No one else will give me a ride."

She was pretty, and he didn't entirely believe her. Opening the back door, he put the boxes on the back seat. Maybe *she* ordered the pizzas, he thought.

"Oh boy, those smell great," she said, looking over.

There was a vague gesture with his hand, aborted, as he got behind the wheel. The engine didn't start. Staring at the dashboard, with the coat of dust noticeable even when unlit, he sensed she was watching him. Another try and it caught. He looked at her for a moment, then backed the car out.

"My name is Helen." She extended her hand.

He grasped at her hand awkwardly. "Hi Helen."

"What's your name?"

"David," he lied. "I'm going to drop you off at Summerhill."

"That'll be super. I really appreciate it." She drew her coat together, the heavy collar rising against her neck.

He could've gone on the amber but didn't and immediately regretted it. He looked in the rear view mirror.

"Were you at the party, David?"

He looked over at her. She was smiling.

"No, not really."

"It was a beautiful party. Glen's friends are just so lovely. How do you know Glen?"

Turning he realized it wasn't the right street.

She peered out. "You could just go straight and turn right over at — "

"Yeah." He did so.

"If you don't mind me saying so, I didn't see you at the party. But then again it was a pretty big party."

Just before he had rung the doorbell, amidst the music and general noise, he could make out a singular laugh — sounding extraordinarily carefree. At one of the windows above the door he could see the silhouette of a woman with a drink in her hand. With her other hand she made a motion like she was waving. Something sad occurred to him, unexpectedly.

"I left early," he said

"Oh really?" she said, more animated.

"As great as the party is, I have to go meet some people... and I completely lost track of the time."

"Another party!" she said.

He nodded, watching her. With her left hand she touched the opposite ear then reached down to scratch her ankle.

A passing streetlight flickered out.

"A girl on the go," she said quietly. She laughed abruptly, almost to herself.

He glanced away. They arrived at the station. She got out.

"Thanks so much... I hope it wasn't too much out of your way."

"It's okay," he said.

"Good night." She closed the door and stumbled back a step.

He did not watch her go inside. A couple of blocks away he saw three kids smoking on the steps of a Gap store. Stopping, he leaned across and called out to them. He got out then and took out the two boxes. They finally approached.

"What's on them, man?"

He told them.

"That's gross," one of them muttered.

They inspected the pizzas.

"There's nothing fucked up with them?" It was more like a threat.

He shook his head, watching them. One of them, a girl, looked remarkably like the one at the party. She looked at him and then at the car idling behind him.

They took all four boxes and went back to the steps.

The cell phone rang while he was driving. There was another delivery. He didn't mention the prank call.

"I'm on my way," he said and clicked off.

The streets were unusually empty for a weekend night. In the lane beside him was a new-looking truck. The driver was on the phone. A young girl in the back seat looked at him.

The smell was getting to him. Before he turned into the back alley of the pizzeria he dumped the pizzas into one of the many trash containers that lined the alley. It was not a clear night and a mass of clouds glowed in the centre. Inside the harsh light hit him behind the eyes and he was perspiring. He counted out the money for the pizzas and paid for them while the next delivery was being boxed.

"Hey, it's the same place," the owner yelled. The radio was set to the twenty-four hour news radio station.

He looked at the receipt.

"They must be real hungry."

He nodded. "It's a big party," he said, taking the three boxes.

"Yeah? Nice cars in the driveway, huh? It's a fancy fucking neighbourhood."

"Yeah. A really nice house."

"Shit."

He stood there looking at the order sheet. Glancing up, the owner was looking at him.

"See ya."

He waved.

Just before leaving he caught something on the radio. A streetcar had derailed, some passengers were injured and traffic was snarled. He unlocked the doors and threw the keys onto the passenger seat. He stowed the pizzas, got into his car. He checked the receipt, replaced it on the seat next to him, and took the keys. Hands resting at his lap, he looked ahead. The possibility of an alternate route occurred to him and he brought the keys to the ignition.

MARNIE WOODROW

Foreword

It's an interesting thing to re-visit one's "old" work. Moments of cringe and moments of delight alternate. You note that some of your youthful concerns continue to be concerns, even if they've morphed or, hopefully, deepened. You see themes that will dominate your creative push for much of your life in this early work. If naiveté equals geekiness, then this work represents me at my geekiest and most joyfully dark: I knew nothing about the rules of the game, nor about publishing as an "industry." I loved Toronto, I loved being out on my own, and my obsession with restaurants as symbols of life and living was only just beginning. Best of all, I was twenty-two and lived without armour, without reserve. At some point even a super-geek learns to put her helmet on in order to deal with life — and most especially with the writing life.

At heart I will always be that geek, inspired by persons just outside the edge. The day I write about a regular gal pinning her whole existence on domestic normalcy is the day I'll quit writing. That said, this particular piece is very much the work of a long-ago self, and thus bears little resemblance to the way I write now. Or so I like to believe.

— MW

Reasons To Waitress

1.

Sociologist or waitress? I wondered on the brink, of *destiny* they call it. What'll it be, paper cuts or gravy stains?

I opted and now carry my tray with the same grace as I would a diploma in peopleology. My skirt swishes hello and snags on the tables as I pass in the small room my Career.

Where there is smoke, there is coffee.

I want to remember always the first shifts of this life's choice. When I didn't know the menu and demands for extra this/less that made me shy and crazy. I practiced a smile sufficiently bulb-bright and my fingernails were kept clean enough to pass the Inspector's mighty swab.

In two shifts I realized: there is no Inspector. There is only finesse and a kind of willing servitude. How you set down plates, how you balance three coffees at once on dirty lunatic saucers. Smile is *all*: smile and ask them how they are today/tonight. Plug your ears when they grunt their answers. Even they don't care how *they* are.

I love people too much to become a sociologist ever.

There are two basic food groups when it comes to people. Individuals can flux back and forth between the groups. One gang sit pretty and reduce themselves to bags of skin that need filling: the stomachs. Patient at first while at your mercy, waiting. Once you get some food into them, they control *you*.

Gang Two enter restaurants in an effort to avoid thinking about their stomachs *at all*. Planning their consumption is too vulgar for them. If they have to make it; if they have to lug it to a table at home; even if they have to make a choice about it. It disrupts their thought processes. Why should genius be reduced to self-service? Get them coffee, don't ask them too often if they need anything. They *do* need, but they haven't come into a restaurant to get it.

2.

Imagine a small room full of bellies. All expectant bellies that seek your favour. Trembling when you swoop near their tables. Some are actually very hungry and others are just idling there between shifts of social productivity. Soup would go down well and club sandwiches and falafel. Foods for soft teeth and foods to cuddle the psyche.

Imagine that it is you that provides the steaming bowls and pre-arranged platters. You don't do garnishes but you are the Royal Presenter: you have the glamour of handing out gastronomic Academy Awards. Whatever it be, Best Supporting side-salad or the bottomless coffee, you have an edge. The Academy Awards happen only once a year. You are the constant presenter. Daily/nightly.

You are in charge of bellies, ashtray distribution and alcoholism in its public pursuit of unhappiness. Bellies you recognize and those you see once and never again.

Though they shit on your nerves and ten per cent you, be proud. Under their cruel crusts those bellies need you.

They may never smile, may snap their requests, but they need your ten-minute nurture.

Some of them eat just to see you.

3.

An indigenous man came in, wanting soup.

I took the ladle and the Styrofoam to go cup and kept one eye on the dining room. Careful I wiped the lid and turned to him.

And I said that's two thirty-nine with tax.

He smiled, fished in deep sea pockets and handed me

a dollar coin

and a bullet.

He smiled harder when I said he owed me one fifty-six more.

"I don't pay tax," he said.

I looked at the bullet, explained with my practiced whitesneer.

"You don't want it? It's my last one, it's valuable."

I wondered where the other bullets had been spent. It was a biggish bullet.

He took it back and took the soup from my same open palm.

"You should be honoured," he said over a shoulder. "I ate the others."

4.

On the calm Mondayest afternoon shift, I resent and treas-
ure being stuck with it. I imagine in these emptier after-
noons that I in fact own the place. Not a chain of them nor/
not a resto-empire but this one, being special and famous, is
mine. I own the chef talking all day on the telephone to his
large wife. I own the menu design and all the food in the
freezer. Even the bags of too-soft tomatoes. They look good
on Mondays, being mine.

I have no appetite when I am at work but on Mondays,
when the place is dead and the unemployed tea-sippers
come in and stare me down. Then I eat. I start by stealing
slices of avocado; end by snorting curry through a two-
dollar bill. I get that desperate and that ruled by my stomach, by ownership. Somedays I'm a ginger-junkie, cutting
off hunks of the root and letting them rest against my teeth
until I can't talk from tongue-numbness. Anaesthetized.

I polish the salts and peppers because I feel I own
them. On other shifts, when they are not mine, I let them
get cakey and watch the roaches dance on their lids.

I see the whole place differently on these quietest days
and the word *dump* never enters my mind. Nor is *shit hole* a
palatable word spoken or thunk. Not when *I'm* pseudo-
owner. When I'm not, when it's Tuesday, say what you
like. I'll agree with you.

5.

One night I covered somebody else's shift so it already had
that borrowed feel. I did double did my rounds my duty

and listened to the same tapes over and over at an accept-able volume. I would have liked to crank it up, but people were eating.

Pretty eventless situation as nights go.

A woman came in, drank three pints, fell over in a coma of a kind. That sort of thing I don't much mind. She looked happier on the floor than she had upright. The red carpet kind of flattered her skin tone.

A couple stormed out without paying. My guess was it's their regular gig and they hit all the restaurants. They argue about the ingredients in pesto, she throws the first beer bottle and hits the same toughened spot on his eye-brow. He shouts and chases her out the door

forgetting to pay.

My blouse got caught in the frozen yoghurt machine and the cook tried to help me by breathing down my back. He smelled of hummus, his lips were grainy like couscous.

I don't want you, I remind him. He seemed to have a short-term memory. Mostly uneventful. At two-thirty in the morning a university jacketjerk fell into a chair and promptly puked, hitting my shoes as I poured him coffee, black. Such are the occasions when we earn the privilege of screaming. There on the carpet for our viewing enjoyment, a puddle. I began my tirade against late-night imbeciles like him. Whose fathers pay for their binges. Whose fathers have probably never had to clean up their baby's recycled beer. To make a clearer point, I slammed my hand flat on the table beside him, pressing my palm into the crumbs and wood.

He looked the drunk Mama's boy. His big eyes focused blurry on my flat hand.

He brought a fork down on it fast: nailed it to the table.

I felt the nauseating burning all through my veins and fell. Fell fast in a heap next to the woman who'd had three quick pints.

I woke up in someone's arms, hand in a bandage and punctured straight through. They were a woman's arms, cradling. A strange apartment, not mine, or my mother's where cradling happened still, in times of need. I felt only two things lying there. My hand throbbing. And breasts, surrounding my skull.

At mid-day she fed me soup and drove me to the subway. Favours returned made me love my job. It was the woman who had heaped herself on the carpet. She told me she'd be back for coffee and to watch out for me. She merely changed bars, but I'm grateful still.

ANNA CAMILLERI

Compass

I never called my uncle Pietro. Sometimes *Zi* or *Zio*, but mostly Frog. His friends joked that he was so ugly, he looked like a frog (even though none of them had ever seen a frog). When they bet on who would fuck Gina first, throwing down wrinkled dollar bills on the concrete backyard like it was monopoly money, they called him frog prince and made puckering, lip smacking sounds. Frog would tell them to kiss his hairy ass and called them faggots or cocksuckers. They'd talk about Gina's rack and whether she puts out or not. Frog would say "I had her — she purred real nice like that bike I'm gonna get."

"In your dreams big man." They'd grunt back in unison, "The only thing you got between your legs is a boner."

"Down to here man, down to here," he bragged, while smacking the inside of his thigh. Frog always had a quick come back. They'd slap each other on the back and throw back their heads laughing until old Signora Rossi who lived next door started singing: "Our Father Who Art in Heaven" through her kitchen window.

The first summer I remember them out in my grandmother Zara's backyard was in 1975. I was five and they were thirteen. Captain & Tennille were at the top of the charts with "Love Will Keep Us Together," and I thought my uncle Frog and his friends were the coolest. For that whole summer Signora Rossi implored — *raggazi, per piaccere* — boys, please. They didn't even bother to glance at her; they carried on as though they hadn't heard a thing. She complained to my grandmother too, but Nonna said they're just being boys and besides, she figured it was better for them to be in the backyard making noise than on the street running around doing God knows what. By the time August rolled around, Signora Rossi was done with trying to goad them into being quieter hellions. She would slide open her kitchen window with a loud bang and yell *ziti* or *ti maze* — quiet or I'll kill you — over and over again as she caught rivulets of sweat on her embroidered handkerchief. They didn't pay attention to that either. They were on top of the world, and there was no place to go but higher.

The leaves turned. They moved their sideshow indoors when the cold came. Signora Rossi had resolved to come up with a new tactic during the crisp winter months. "Ave Maria" sung in a vibrating soprano with all the zeal she could muster usually worked like a charm, unless the boys were drinking beer out of Coke cans.

They'd toss beer caps across the yard like they were skimming rocks on a lake. I never tossed the caps myself, but I watched them from behind the metal bars on the porch. Every so often Spoon would call over to me, "Hey Professa, did you see that? I kicked Frog's ass." I had a secret crush on Spoon. Sometimes he winked at me when the others weren't looking and said, "You're gonna be a pro at this soon, just like me." He was a bad boy in the grown up world where I wasn't allowed, but I knew he was kind underneath all the cussing and fighting; he let me sneak sips from his can, and never said a word to anyone about it.

"Oh yeah, watch this!" Frog hit the top of the wooden fence at just the right angle, and the cap popped up and hit Signora Rossi's window with a clank. She retreated into her house screaming *disgrazie-* bastards! He strutted around with his hand up shouting, "Who's the man?" and they clapped hands with rounds of high fives, low fives, and super-fly handshakes.

No matter how many times the police knocked on the door about busted up phone booths, parking meters, or pilfered candy bars, my grandmother considered them to be good boys. And anyone who said anything to the contrary, including priests, teachers, or cops, got a piece of her mind.

There were two things I was sure of at the time: first, if I got into half as much trouble as they did, I'd spend half my life digging myself out of a giant shit pile, bare-handed; and second, my uncle wasn't ugly, not even a little bit.

When he was just a wriggly newborn, my grandmother Zara held him up to the window so she could have a good look at him. She was struck by his beauty. It could be said that every mother thinks her baby is the most beautiful, perfect child. But Zara was an exception. She thought her first two kids were the ugliest things she'd ever seen. Raisin-like wrinkly little things. Not Frog though; with Frog she was breathtaken. Nevertheless, she gave his bum, which was smaller than the palm of her hand, a good hard smack. Of course, he cried for a long while. She wanted him to know what life was about right away; that it was hard. And besides, there was something about Frog — something different from Lina, my mother, and Giuseppe, her middle child.

Superstition and magic rule my Nonna's world more than religion or reason do. I can't say exactly what her magic is — what it looks like, what she does — but I do know it's rooted in the earth, in the fields she farmed as a girl child in Naples. Rooted in the elements that devastated or raised up crops rich with green. Magic that was whispered between women through villages, surreptitiously carried in small pouches on cow paths under a studded sky. Magic that became diluted upon immigrating to Canada, to Toronto, where for all but a couple of weeks in the winter when snowfalls slowed traffic to a crawl, the world operated on different principles — ruled by clocks, bus schedules and science — rather than the body's language; mysteries of the earth; faith in the unseen and unknown.

Zara saw colours around Frog, mostly violet and dark shadow. She was so startled by her vision, she nearly dropped him. *La maladetta*, the curse; she saw it in Frog. She had only seen *la maladetta* one other time, in a little girl who died in her sleep a short while later. She spit into the palm of her hand, rubbed his face gently, pressed him to her breast and invoked the Virgin Mary and a host of spirits for protection. Behind her back, she pressed her two middle fingers into her palm, with thumb, little finger and index pointed outward: the *corno*, another invocation to ward off harm.

Destiny, when taunted, when disbelieved, could grow deeper, more set; it could take a turn for the worse, like the eye of a tornado devastating everything in its path.

Every full moon, Zara prayed for answers. How could she protect her boy without knowing where the harm would come from? All she heard in response to her implorations was this: *Love your child, love him as best you can. He will be lost in a forest without a compass. Love him so he will find his way home, even when your heart is broken, love him. This is the only principle, the only magic, the only law.*

A long time ago, before I was born — before I was even an idea or the heat that swelled in my mothers breasts down, down, down through her body like a falling star in the night —you were running into the wind. This is how I imagine you Frog, even now that the thought of you running, running anywhere, is hard to picture. You in your big boots, beer belly bursting against and over your belt, a drink in one hand, a smoke in the other. A forlorn expression on your face wrinkled and lined beyond your years, nose and brows pulled into an unmistakable 'don't fuck with me' scowl. The gravity of you so heavily pinned to the ground. The weight of your presence cast a shadow, even in your mother's house, especially in your mother's house, where you raged quiet and sure, where you grew to mythic proportions. At fifteen you were six feet tall and everyone thought you were done with it. No one in the family is taller than five foot ten, except Rocco, and he's not blood related. You grew and grew and stopped at six foot four, at seventeen years of age. A whole head above the rest of us.

I have pictures of you. Snuck them from Mom and Dad's house after Lucy's funeral. Mom said a hundred times over the years, "I'll make a nice album for you Professa." But she never did, and wouldn't let anyone near them. Dozens and dozens of envelopes filled with prints and negatives carefully taped into freezer bags and stashed inside the *crystalleria* where the alcohol was kept. I tip-toed across the hallway, took what was most valuable — a few prints from each envelope, the ones I liked most. I suppose it was my way of trying to keep some of you, or get to know you. After they took you away, I didn't know if I would see you again, or if I would want to.

On Sunday December 5, 1993 our family came apart like an old, threadbare sheet. Nonna had gone to church as she did every Sunday morning. Mom and Dad and I went over to Nonna's house for lunch, and Zio Giuseppe and Zia Rachaela dropped by later with coffee cake. It wasn't particularly unusual that you and Lucy and the boys weren't there, and to be honest, I was relieved — not that Lucy, Sam and Peter weren't there, but that you weren't. My stomach turned every time you yelled at the boys, and picked at Lucy about and what a 'fat slob' she was. You'd pace around the kitchen table, down the hallway to the front door, and back through the kitchen. Without fail, Nonna set a plate for you even though you never ate anything. She'd pat the chair next to her and plead, "Pietro, come sit. I made the chicken nice, just the way you like it."

Mom said the things the rest of us were thinking, but never said.

"Look at you Frog — you got the shakes and you can't wait to pour your next drink."

"Mind your own fuckin' business Lina."

"Well stop making it my business. Why don't you go to a bar instead of coming to Mom's house — oh right, I forgot — the booze is free here."

And then you'd screech out of the driveway. Nonna would sit there wringing her hands, glass-eyed, muttering to herself, or to God. She would not, could not, be consoled by us. The only tenderness she accepted was from Chico, purring, swishing and circling around her ankles until she reached down to stroke his ginger coat. We'd cover the leftovers with wax paper, wash the dishes, say our goodbyes with kisses on both cheeks, and drive Lucy and the boys home in silence. We knew there would be hell to pay, but we weren't the ones you'd be going home to.

All those years Nonna had been praying to keep you safe. She never imagined that someone else's blood would spill, that you'd be the one left standing. That you would drive away from the house with a stained bread knife in the passenger's seat, and your sons behind you screaming Momma. That the neighbours would walk in through the open front door, find the boys pulling at Lucy's arms, trying to wake her; already lost in the reverie of grief that would score their lives, all our lives, indelibly.

Time stopped that day and became a compass; a road to every place thereafter; a cool north wind, dawn from the east, fire from the south, twilight from the west. We did not grow stronger like the cliché about tragedy bringing a family closer together. We scattered like beads from a stretched necklace. One went this way, the other that. We continued to have lunch together on Sundays with CHIN radio humming in the background; exchanged words about the weather, the specials at K-mart, anything but you. Nonna continued to set a plate for you as though you'd stop in any minute, and even Mom knew not to say anything about it.

You were a child once. It would be easy to forget this in light of who you are today. The smiling little prankster, always working on a foolproof scheme, building bigger and stronger fortresses, is all but gone. Where did you go? You were a boy once, curls raging against the summer breeze. A smile that sailed me into the next day that came, and came.

Eraser

Suzanne said she would like never ever be a stalker and she had no idea where Jason had come up with that idea, and she ran home and erased her history so no one would ever know who she could never be.

The next morning, Suzanne walked to the kitchen table, half asleep, cross-legged and dreamy. When her Mom saw that pieces of Suzanne were missing and that she could see through the bottom of her daughter's left calf, she was concerned. Up until that day Suzy had never appeared transparent and although Mom's routine had always included pills of many different colours, she couldn't be sure that it wasn't the pills at work; that she wasn't hallucinating her daughter literally disappearing before her eyes. That the pills and calm-in-a-highball were not fucking with her head. She didn't say anything, and instead carried her concern to her hair appointment and then to the doctor's office where she accidentally left it with the back issues of *Homemakers* and *Good Housekeeping*.

At school the next day, which was Wednesday, Suzanne's best friend Charlene noticed that Suzy's fingers did not hold her pen the way they used to. They seemed awkward and it was taking much longer for S. to write back to her on the three-hole punched old-school way of communicating. Suzanne's index finger on her right hand was missing and this made her handwriting nearly illegible, which was bad since they were working on a project together. At lunch, after chocolate milk (bigger than small but not big enough to be concerned about hips and thighs) Charlene said, "Suzanne? It's about the finger."

Suz, shrugged and laughed a little like she had no idea what Charlene was all on about. Like it was no big deal and that she, Charlene, should be more concerned about how she was going to document the effect of Big Box stores on the economy and the disappearance of Mom and Pop Shops using the colour scheme they had come up with. Colours they felt represented the tragedy of the corporate takeover of American ideals and apple pie. Black, with a shock of gray. C. backed off, as she had learned to do, and with a similar look in their eyes they got up from the table. Without speaking.

Leaving the cafeteria was no easy feat for Suzanne. Her left leg was considerably weaker than it had been earlier in the morning. As she pulled up her pant leg to see what was going on, she made sure no one was looking. Head turned left right and then left again. It seemed as though with time, the rest of her leg had become translucent. Not quite gone, but certainly not in the fine form that it once was. Like the elasticity of skin after years of drinking, or the last year of a marriage that was once the talk of the town. There, although not really. With her left leg weakened from the knee down she was slower-going and as she passed Jason's table she looked off to the side so he wouldn't see her. She chose the institutional green outfit out of her closet this morning. Made it easier for her to blend into the sur-roundings; easier for her to go unnoticed by Jason. He didn't notice her—which she thought would be good but was turning out to be bad—and she wondered whether she had gone too far, whether she was still even there at all.

After her "escape" and a one-handed high-ten goodbye with Charlie, more commonly known as five, she walked up the stairs to the front foyer of Canning High School and turned left. At the pay phones she waited in line with everyone else and eyed the vending machines, wondering whether the new space in her leg would be good for stor-age and how many Payday's she would be able to carry with her at one time. As the line moved forward, Suzanne reached into her pocket for change. Two dimes and a nickel.

Her middle finger dialed home; her mother answered and she asked for a ride. She wasn't feeling well and all she wanted to do was come home and check her e-mail. Buy a sweater online and maybe see where Jason was tonight even though she knew she shouldn't. When her mom an-swered the phone she said she didn't know anyone by her name and she must have the wrong number.

It wasn't the first time Suzanne had woken her mother from sleep. A land where Mother was not a single mom but just single, and where she had a different name and her hair was naturally chestnut. It seemed o.k. that on the other end of the phone was a woman who had never heard of her before and so she walked through the front doors of Canning High and took herself, along with her wobbly leg, and stood at the bus stop.

Sitting on the west side of the 65 bus on its way through town, Suzanne saw everything she had always seen. The gas station and the Hodge Podge stood as still as ever. She got off at her stop. Walked three blocks down and one around the corner to her house and unlocked the door. At 3 p.m. her mother watched *General Hospital* and today at 3:23 p.m. she wept on the sofa. Over her mother's shoulder Suzanne could see Brenda lying in Sonny's arms; she wondered whether Brenda remembered Lily, who died in the same arms. Loved the same man. Died for the same reasons.

Upstairs S. shut her bedroom door, changed from her jeans to her sweats, and started her computer. All musical and machine-like, the monitor became bright and welcoming and she sat down in front of the keyboard to begin her search. Even though she said she wasn't a stalker. Even though her blood boiled hot and her stomach ached and her face flushed when J. called and told her to leave him alone. Called and said you're crazy. And I have proof. And I know where you've been and you've been on me. You've been all over me, Jason said to her. I am suffocating.

It took Suzanne only a minute to find him. She was a pro. Or so it seemed—here right now but clearly not forever. When she found him, hanging out where he usually was, she changed her name and her profile so he'd never know she was there. And so he would talk to her. Tell her what his plans for the night were and see if maybe, since they lived in the same town, they could hook up outside The Strand. No one ever went inside. Too old and mouldy and smelly. But outside was right next to where the cool kids hung out, and just close enough to Suzanne's house that she could look outside her window and see him waiting for her. Or for someone he did not think was her. And she would see how long he would wait for a stranger that was everything he wanted. Like she was. Just not her.

Tonight, before she gets into bed and after her shower, she will erase her history. For the same reasons as yesterday. And tomorrow she will see how much of herself she can hold on to. How much she still carries with her. No past. Only present.

MICHELLE TEA

Rap Video

It's a giant full moon, wicked bright, so bright it hurts your eyes, burns its shape onto them until a swath of Transylvania-style clouds waft past by and dull the fluorescent glow. It's a full moon and people on the streets are going insane. This morning it was nothing but Jehovah's Witnesses, millions of them, like a league of nicely-dressed zombies staggering corner to corner, shaking their little pamphlet bouquets and nagging passers-by about the Bible. Then tonight it was everyone screaming *fuck* at the top of their lungs, then *bitch* and *whore*. I was behind the guy walking his dog. I thought it was sort of cute how he had old-fashioned suspenders on, and his dog was a sort of fluffy girl and they were jogging together. As I passed them the man rose his fist into the air, popped his middles finger up and started screaming *Aaargharghaaaarghfuck-youcomebackmotherfucker-I'llfucking kill youaaaargh*! A psychotic cab driver had nearly smashed into the delicate haunches of the man's dog; it sped off down Chavez leaving him howling like a lunatic. *Excuse me*, he said, composing himself. *No problem*, says Vito, who often yells things at cabs. I thought it sounded like the man had been waiting quite a while for a cab to almost run over his pet so he could finally start screaming in the street. A pair of tiny twelve year old girls rushed by hollering frantic *fucks* from their deeply glossed lips, shrieking with glee at the sound of the word leaving their throats.

That was at the start of the night.

Later we're all bunched together in 16th Street filming a rap video. The song is about lesbians getting harassed on the street by men, and we have been instructed to look like we're very upset. Street harassment is very upsetting. We are a group of queers, mostly female except for the ones who aren't anymore, and we are all concentrating on looking upset and also very tough. I was instructed by Vito, the rapper behind the song, to not dress slutty, and it was in fact very hard for me to do that. My clothes ricochet between bluntly slutty and oddly conservative, conservative in a costume-y way, like I am portraying a campy schoolmarm in a drag act. After a woollen dress and a plaid wrap-around skirt got nixed I tossed on a flashy skirt that slunk down my calves, and felt jealous of the two girly girls, Veronica and Wendy, who showed up in fishnets and miniature skirts, big clompy boots, and decorative jackets.

They are selected as bait for many shots — to brashly cavort down the street, attracting the harassing attention of drunken males. "Why aren't you bait?" asks Mack, a trannyboy whose sleeveless hoody is extra baggy because he just got his nipples tattooed onto his new tranny chest. "I was told not to dress slutty," I said mournfully. "Oh, to butch it up, yeah we were told that too," pipes Kelly, from within her own hoody. "I bound my tits," I shrugged, and people laughed. People are Ronnie who just got a Hedwig tattoo and has solved the pronoun problem by abolishing them altogether, which makes speaking about Ronnie a very grand experience as you are never allowed to shorten Ronnie's name to he or she and must always call Ronnie, Ronnie. Sentences like: *Ronnie just got a booty call on Ronnie's cell phone* and *now Ronnie is wondering if Ronnie should take a bus to the Haight*, or *if Ronnie should call a cab*.

Jenn is wearing the most insanely punk rock outfit like she pulled it out a 1977 time capsule, all studded and shredded, but she brought one of those ginormous puffy hip hop coats to cover it all up if it turns out that her hip hop look is more appropriate for the video. There's Tracy and there's Vito, who is in one of those plasticy track suits the men on *The Sopranos* wear, and his hair is all long and curly-wild and his mustache is darker like maybe he hit it with the mascara before we left. On his chest lies an abundance of gold, mostly fake. Tommy's directing it and there's a brief posse of punk boys at her command with the camera. We set out to be harassed.

Vito wrote the song before he transitioned, when he was a transdyke who wanted more facial hair, some sideburns, a sleazy moustache. He wrote this righteous anthem about all the bullshit dykes absorb when they're hanging around together in public, stuff like double-headed dildos and how guys always say *Oh can I come and watch*, crap like that. *I'm a lesbian trapped in a straight man's body*. Once after Vito performed the song in Texas a very serious transguy came over and had to process how it was offensive to transwomen to say that, the straight-man-trapped-in-a-lesbian's-body part, and Vito was like, Really? That's how you perceive transwomen? I don't think of transwomen that way at all. Straight guys say that shit to dykes all the time so what are you going to do, not report it? One year and twenty-four boosts of testosterone later, Vito is really a guy, not so much a dyke anymore, and it's sort of funny to watch him lip synching this angry dyke anthem. It's like he's this really sensitive straight guy with lots of lesbian friends. We stomp behind him down 16th Street and I try to keep an irritated look on my face but it's hard not to laugh, especially when I think of how totally feeble and non-threatening I look, so I work on not thinking about myself at all which means I start spacing out, looking around 16th Street at all the lights and the marauding losers, people dashing in and out of the fluorescent grocery store, small, tailored foodies clattering by on their way to tapas.

I remember the camera is still on me and snap back, look into the lense, arrange a bored and distasteful look on my face. I imagine I've ruined the video because every scene will have footage of me sort of staring blankly at my surroundings, like some weirdo who wandered into the shot. Yeah. Mack is smoking, Tracey is smoking, *Sorry I'm smoking* Mack says and I tell him it's fine, it makes him look more intimidating: he has no fear of death, no fear of lung cancer or smelling gross, you want to fuck with a guy like that? And if it irritates me I'll just use it, as they say in film. Do they say that in film? I feel very white walking down 16th Street to the hip hop beat. I do not dare to raise my hand in a hip hop salute, fearing the limp swish of my wrist on camera.

Jenn is fearless — first she had this giant chrome hunting knife out and was swinging that around, now she is doing those wide-arm jabbing-hand rap motions at the camera. I don't think I can even really walk to the beat, so I sort of lope along sheepishly toward the back. The Bait are boldly singing along. When we get to the corner of Valencia a man swings wildly around the corner, plowing into us. *Get this!* I yell urgently to Tommy as he angrily tries to shove Wendy, but we are walking into horrifying guyville, and soon I will not be able to stop yelping *get this!* at the camera people. Blondie's is in full swing. Sometime I like to tell people that Blondie's used to be a dyke bar, just to see them gasp and scowl suspiciously.

It's been a long time since I've braved this gruesome corridor — honestly, I thought all these people had gone home, had fled the city when they lost their jobs a year or two back. I realize that most of my social interaction is conducted via e-mails with friends, where we talk — no, type — about the city saying things like: "It's getting better," and I started believing it. Now it looks as depressing as ever and we're pushing through a crowd of people who are going to be totally stoked dude when Gavin Newsome becomes our mayor. We clear the scary crowd and prepare to plunge back into it again. There's a gang of white boys in Polo shirts hanging around the parking meters on the curb. I don't like this part of the eighties revival. The white boys in the Polo shirts. Tommy asks them if they want to harass girls in our video, they know how to harass girls, right? *Yeah!* their leader hoots bravely. But they are too drunk to be able to take direction, or it's too real and we are too traumatized, and we walk back to the boarded up shop down the block and clog the sidewalk, wait around as Vito and Tommy plan some shots. "Wait, those are girls?" Polo Shirt gasps as we depart also traumatized. A guy from Veronica's work, a hapless little man, just passing by, is recruited to lean against a spaceship-sized SUV and leer at The Bait as they saunter past. "Walk like girls," Mack hollers. The man makes an inebriated face, scrunches his lips, begins to drool and make hand gestures. Everyone claps. He's a pilates instructor, Veronica explains. Now we're stalled.

We're wondering whether or not to plunge back into the scary male Blondie's overflow for more footage of actual harassment. It's like a reality show music video. Jenn is clutching the crappy little boom box that plays the tinny rap song, Vito's voice not yet so testosterone-soaked, a bit higher. I tell everyone how I saw Spike Lee on 18th Street today. I walked by him on the way to grab a Rice Dream at the expensive health food store and thought, that's Spike Lee. Then I thought, oh yeah Michelle, a Black man with a camera and it's Spike Lee, God you are so fucked up, and then I walked back again eating my Rice Dream and I looked him right in the face and it actually was Spike Lee. So I sort of loitered on the street for a moment thinking maybe he would notice me and use me for a shot or something, but he just ignored me and I longed for the days when I was younger and my hair was blue. People paid more attention to me then.

Now we dive again into the awful throng. Some of them are martini-drunk from Blondie's and the rest are margarita-drunk from Puerto Allegre. We strut behind small Vito until he stops, and then we pose behind him menacingly as he gesticulates in his lip-synching frenzy. Behind us is a wall of losers, a real line-up. One of their girls jumps into the fray for a minute, haggard before her time, long streaked hair —they call it chunked on the do-it-yourself L'Oreal boxes at Walgreens — and mall-bought, modern hippie clothing. She throws faux gang symbols at the small video camera cupped in Tommy's hands, then bounces back to her friends. Is this a Fifty Cent video? Another reads from the silkscreen sewn onto the back of Jenna's armoured denim vest — *Shoot rapists not heroin*. Wendy informs them that it's a video about street harassment and they all did a really excellent job. They stare at her blankly. They are easily confused. We march over to our safe space, the boarded up storefront. It is a doomed bit of real estate on that evil block.

It was once a Beatles-themed restaurant called Mop Tops which served ghastly British food and had Beatles cover bands on the weekend. Kansas, who lives upstairs, discovered that the oysters were actually canned oysters they slid into old oyster shells; they just stacked the oyster shells in the dishwasher and kept using them. Maybe they found them on the beach in the first place, or went to a real restaurant for real oysters and pocketed the fishy shells, who knows? This information was eventually tagged onto their front door in a big sharpie, and then the graffiti was reported by the local paper and Mop Tops disappeared. It was replaced by a health food store started by a woman who used to work for a big snooty health food store and stole lots of money from the register there to go off and start her own empire, which I thought was very admirable and I liked to purchase iced tea and homemade soup from her little bad karma venture, but it soon shut down because, as I said, the space is cursed. Now an orange sign across the front reads Tandoor and I fantasize briefly that it will not be a tandoori restaurant but a self-tanning boutique with those tans they spray paint onto your naked body with a car wash-like contraption. Everyone leans against the boarded up windows, and they do a middle finger wave, each angry, harassed queer flipping the bird at the camera in a choreographed line.

Jenn demonstrates the femme way of flipping the bird — middle finger straight up, the rest of them balled tight like a fist — and the butch way — a slight crook in the middle finger, the rest of them sort of bent in a knuckly crouch. It does look more butch. We trot back up to 16th Street for one more ride, but not before Vito dashes over to the party trolley, which is illegally parked in the center of the street. He gets a little footage while hanging off the brass railings. Drunk secretaries shimmy behind him in their slacks.

Back on 16th Street we march solemnly by the Albion, which is no longer the Albion, but I can only remember the name it had back when I used to drink there; back when it was better the way everything is before it changes and you can no longer recognize it. We march past the old Albion where the cocaine used to flow; it's now called Delirium and there is no more cocaine. They advertise the "Service for the Sick" sign, that glows above the bar, by putting the same phrase on their outside sign and all their flyers — like they're so proud such a funny sign hangs inside their bar.

But the thing is when it was the Albion it really *was* service for the sick, and the sign simply glowed its red glow above the bar and nobody made a big deal about it. Crackheads would be ejected for stinking up the bathrooms with their plasticy smoke, though an ex-FBI agent turned crappy cocaine dealer was allowed to sell bindles in the ladies room. They permitted smoking in the back pool room — where a roach once fell from the ceiling onto my head, long after the no smoking ordinance passed. They sold booze to people deep into the later stages of alcoholism, and everyone got along pretty well: the cokehead straight girls; the bruiser bull-daggers; the scuzz-bag skater boys and their perpetually pregnant and teary-eyed girlfriends; tweaker trannies and guys who looked like salty old fisherman; drugged-out strippers and hip hop dudes; and moms from Daly City who will tell you all about their knocked-up teenage daughters after a few lines of the government cocaine.

Everyone got along except that one really sad alcoholic who would always start a fight around last call, and sometimes yuppie girls would get their credit cards stolen. And there was the time we chased a bunch of boys out for saying faggot — even the bartender came over to help us, pulling his cock out of his shorts and waving it at the offensive guys. We concluded that the bartender was almost certainly looking for a reason to show the lesbians his penis. We forgave him. He ignored our cigarettes and sometimes gave us free beers. That was the Albion, that was Service for the Sick, not this neon-lit faux-dive hipster joint we cruise by, a crowd of dudes smoking out front. One of them catcalls "Look at the art students" and I swear, I can't believe I was called an art student; it's the worst incident of street harassment I've ever experienced.

We pick up a new cluster of queers, the stunning highlight of them being a transgirl named Queens who has hair like thick black frosting, stuck with a flower, and a face full of lush make-up. She's a drag king, she says, and this really fucks people up. Her transguy friend is rolling his bicycle along and when we explain that this is a rap anthem against the harassment of queers by men, he says he was beat up by an Oakland cab driver last night and holds up his elbow. It's discoloured like a banged-up banana. I feel super shallow all of a sudden, like we're traipsing around making this big show of harassment, sort of daring all these potentially violent guys to fuck with us for art, having a good time, and here's this kid that just got his ass kicked.

The bruises fade up into the tattoo on his upper arm. Then he smiles. "I jumped his fare though," he says sort of proud but sheepishly, like he knows he's a real bad-ass, "You gotta pay if you're gonna play," he shrugs. Kelly, who had also been really concerned about some psychotic Oakland cab driver freaking out on queers says, "Oh that doesn't count then," and the kid says "Yeah but he didn't have to beat me up, he could have just called the cops."

I think of how scared and desperate I feel about money lately, and how there's this depression happening but no one will call it a depression, I mean on the news or in the papers or whatever, like it's not being officially deemed a depression, barely a recession, but it's so scary. I mean Vito cannot find a job and he is now more hireable than ever before; every day his standards sink a little lower and he's dropping off resumes at Starbucks and hopefully getting on welfare and food stamps. I think about how everything feels like so much scarcity and people are in this fearful survival mode; the cab driver has to pay rent on that cab, and if some little punk tried to stiff me I'd probably chase him down and bruise up his elbows too. I decide to boycott this kid in solidarity with the cab driver and stop talking to him. Then I think about how I used to feel like the world owed me everything and how I loved getting drunk and doing things like stiffing cab drivers and stealing and vandalizing — generally being an asshole. When did I get so moral? God I was really turning into a little grown-up! But I am still haunted by the thought of the ripped-off cab driver.

Later, Vito goes to the Castro with everyone, to be tortured by evil faggots who are, he tells me, misogynistic, ignorant and horrible. I believe him. And he says that the kid with the bruised elbow was actually wicked-nice, so sweet, bought him an overpriced four dollar bad-faggot juice at the bar, the best kid, so I said okay and I guess I should just let it go.

Down the street it's UFOmer who I used to heckle and

harass years ago when he'd climb onto the stage at the Chameleon and sing these terrible songs and say vaguely offensive things. Back then he was a little whacked-out but basically together enough so you could harass him and not feel like you were picking on a retarded person, an easy target, but UFOmer has really disintegrated. He hangs out in doorways with that same acoustic guitar and he sings in a voice stripped dry from smoking God knows what or maybe just not having enough water or something. He sounds very dehydrated. He's got his guitar slung around his back and he's holding a tub of popcorn and hurling handfuls of it at everyone saying "I'm a terrorist, I'm a popcorn terrorist." The popcorn is pretty stale and rains on us like little pellets while UFOmer cackles. His face is tanned and deeply lined; his hair is longish, like an unintentional mullet, and today he is wearing a very long zebra-striped jacket that swings down the legs of his dirty jeans and almost sweeps swanky 16th Street.

Tommy is filming his giddy proclamations while tough yellow nuggets of popcorn bounce off the camera. Tracy loves him. "He's David Johanson, he's totally New York Dolls, look at him, he's David Johanson," she says. I start to say, no he's not, he's just a homeless guy with a bad haircut and today he happened to find this zebra thing to wear and tomorrow he could be in a flannel hunting jacket or a Corona T-shirt. But then I stop and think yeah, UFOmer does look like David Johanson and what do I know about his wardrobe anyway, and he's got that guitar. Why not let him be David Johanson? Because he used to be this asshole drunk guy I thought was my enemy, but that was ten years ago and look at him now, off his cake and flinging popcorn. Why would I want to be his enemy?

UFOmer wanders off before Tommy can get him to sign a release.

Excerpt from **Lenny Bruce is Dead**

After Frieda was gone, Chick would use the barbeque to cook all his meals. It was like he just couldn't go in the kitchen. Sometimes he would start grilling hamburgers at four in the morning. He would silently flip them on the grill with his head tilted like he had just forgotten what he was going to say.

They sat in the synagogue basement and the rabbi told him about the time he met the Rebbe in Altantic City when he was a boy. The Rebbe had told him he would have to move halfway across the world in order to do his work.

"This was at a time when the Rebbe didn't have as many followers," he said. "You could actually have a sit-down with him."

As he said this, the rabbi slammed the table with the palm of his hand.

"The Rebbe is a five-star general in the army of God and we're just privates. The Rebbe has told us that redemption is about to happen. Every moment the Moschiach is not revealed means there is a greater likelihood he will be revealed in the next moment. And we belive that the Rebbe *is* the Moschiach. Our heart breaks with every second we have to spend in exile."

It would be awful if there was a bully and the bully made me take off my clothes. It would be just terrible if this was on the street where a little girl could see me and ask her father if I was the same kind of monkey that Tarzan had in the cartoons.

"Love Kay," it says at the end of the letter, but it's written on top of liquid paper. He only notices the liquid paper later, after he had read the letter several times. He holds the letter up to the light and sees through to the words. "Rock on." She has never used an expression like that before, not even ironically.

Then one day she calls him up and leaves a message on his answering machine.

"I'll be home at eight," she says. "No, wait, I'm lying. I won't be home until nine." *No, wait, I'm lying?* What the hell is going on here?

Two weeks later he is sitting on a park bench with Kaliotzakis. All the way down the street he sees Kay. She is with a man. As they get closer he tries to decide what he should say. Kaliotzakis is a kidder. Josh isn't in the mood to be kidded.

When they are several feet away he realizes Kay is with his father. He forgets what he had decided to say.

They just keep walking. Neither Kay nor his father look at him. It isn't like they're pretending or anything. It's like they really don't know him.

Later, just as he is going to bed, the phone rings. It's Kay. She's asking for Theodore.

"Theodore speaking," he says.

He goes right along with it.

It is as though, being raised on a farm, Reggi often had to spank the pigs to tenderize the bacon.

His laugh is so smug and invincible, it's like he has a pipe clenched between his teeth during the opening song of his own Christmas special.

When Frieda used to make dinner there were a million and one side orders. Now, when his father grills a streak, it's just steak. Sometimes he would put baked beans in a bowl at the center of the table. That bowl of baked beans would look like the loneliest thing in the world.

He once read a book where things went on forever. That book was only 312 pages.

About The Contributors

Debra Anderson is a four-eyed femme award-winning writer who has been published in *The Church-Wellesley Review 1997-1999*, *Fireweed*, *Tessera*, *Periwinkle*, *Zygote*, *Hook & Ladder*, dig, and *Acta Victoriana*. Her animated short film, *Don't Touch Me*, screened internationally. Debra is busy on her novel-in-progress *Code White*, an excerpt of which was published in the anthology *Bent On Writing: Contemporary Queer Tales* (Women's Press, 2002).

Kristyn Dunnion is a saucy tart who likes big boots and loud music. Her first book, *Missing Matthew*, is published by Red Deer Press, 2003. She is currently finishing *Mosh Pit*, a punkrawk novel for young adults

Anna Camilleri is a Toronto-based writer, performance poet, curator and co-editor of *Brazen Femme: Queering Femininity* (Arsenal Pulp Press 2002) which is a finalist for a Lambda Literary Award. She co-founded the performance troupe Taste This with whom she collaborated to publish *Boys Like Her:Transfictions* (Press Gang 1998) to critical and popular acclaim. Anna's next book, *I Am a Red Dress*, will be released by Arsenal Pulp Press in 2004. Visit her website at www.annacamilleri.com.

R. J. S. Carrier-Bragg lives in Toronto and has been writing since Mrs. Bielby's journaling assignment in grade 7 English.

Rose Cullis lives in Toronto. She most recently won an award from the Harold Greenberg Fund (script development program), to develop a screenplay of her play, *Baal*. Playwriting credits include *Baal* (Buddies in Bad Times Theatre, Toronto), *Pure Motives* (The Theatre Center, Toronto) and *That Camille Claudel Feeling* (the Toronto Fringe Festival). Her writing has appeared in *UnderCurrents, The Church-Wellesley Review,* and *torquere.*

Lynn Crosbie is a Toronto writer, whose latest book is *Missing Children* (M&S).

Sarah Dermer is a nice Jewish lesbian living in Toronto.

Lisa Foad is a Toronto-based writer and video artist. Her work has been published in *Xtra!, The Women's Post,* and *The Chicklist* (which she co-edited), and workshopped through Nightwood Theatre. Her video screenings include Barcelona's 25hrs, SAW Video's Independents Online Web Streaming Project (2003), the Images Festival, and the Inside Out Festival (2002).

Camilla Gibb is the author of two novels, *Mouthing the Words* (2000 City of Toronto Book Award), and *The Petty Details of So-and-So's Life* (Doubleday, 2002). She was the CBC Canadian Literary Award winner for her short story in 2001. "House Contents" was originally published in the Hart House Review (1999).

Sky Gilbert is a writer and theatre director living in Hamilton, Ontario. By day, Sky is an assistant professor in Theatre Studies at Guelph University. ECW Press published Sky's first collection of poetry *Digressions of a Naked Party Girl* in 1998, and his theatre memoir *Ejaculations From the Charm Factory* in 2000. His first three novels: *Guilty* (1998), *St. Stephen's* (1999) and *I am Kasper Klotz* (2001) were critically acclaimed. His fourth novel *An English Gentleman* was published by Cormorant Books in September 2003, and his second book of collected poems *Temptations for a Juvenile Delinquent* by ECW in November 2003.

Jonathan Goldstein is a contributing editor to Public Radio's *This American Life*. He is a co-recipient of the 2002 Third Coast Audio Festival's gold prize. His writing has appeared in *The Carolina Quarterly*, *The New York Times Magazine*, and on Transom.org. He lives in Montreal.

Hadassah Hill is a spoken wordsmith, textile artist, fashionista, and ex-pat currently living in Toronto. Her work has appeared in various anthologies and magazines over the last eight years. She loves kitsch and riding her bike.

Paul Hong is in the process of writing a dissertation and lives in Toronto. His short stories have appeared in *Blood & Aphorisms*, *Broken Pencil* and *Kiss Machine*.

JP Hornick is a writer, teacher, and geeky American expatriate living in Toronto. She's been a housepainter, exterminator, editor, vacuum salesperson, and sometimes outlaw. JP is obsessed with words and how they fit together. This is her first piece of published fiction.

Joanne Huffa's obsessions have changed very little since she was a young girl in the late '70s: Shaun Cassidy, headphones, kitchen-sink dramas, Mars bars. Add to that her sweetie Brad, red wine and friendster.com and the world is pretty much complete.

George K. Ilsley is the author of *Random Acts of Hatred*, a collection of short fiction published by Arsenal Pulp Press. He lives in Vancouver.

Greg Kearney's fiction has been published here and there. His plays include *The Betty Dean Fanzine* and the upcoming *Yay, Hooray!* For the past five years he has been resident humour columnist for *Xtra!* His collection of short stories, *Serviette*, will hopefully drop in the near future.

Leah Lakshmi Piepzna-Samarasinha is a Toronto-based queer mixed Sri Lankan writer, spoken word artist and local hero. Her work has been published in *Colonize This!*, the Lambda Award nominated *Brazen Femme, Dangerous Families, Without a Net*, and the periodicals *Bamboo Girl, Fireweed, Bitch, Anything That Moves* and *big boots.* She has performed her work widely, most recently at the 2nd Annual Asian

Pacific Islander Spoken Word Summit and Yale University's South Asian Solidarity Conference. She is founder of the Toronto's browngirlworld spoken word series. Her first book, *consensual genocide*, is out any day now.

Derek McCormack's books include *Dark Rides*, *Wish Book*, and, most recently, *The Haunted Hillbilly*. He has published two chapbooks, *Halloween Suite* and *Western Suit*, with artist Ian Phillips and pas de chance books. He lives in Toronto.

Jim Munroe has written three science fiction novels and does a CD-ROM zine called *Novel Amusements*. His video game column in Toronto's alt-weekly *eye* is called "Pleasure Circuit." His website (www.nomediakings.org) is home to his projects as well as many do-it-yourself articles on movie and book making.

Eileen Myles lives in California and NYC and is working on a novel called *The Inferno*. She's written thousands of poems since 1974 when she first showed her face in the world.

Taien Ng-Chan is the editor of *Ribsauce: a cd/anthology of words by women* and a contributing editor at *Matrix Magazine*. Her poetry and fiction have been published in a number of anthologies and journals, and she has written drama for the stage and CBC Radio. She runs <wagpress.net> with her partner Joe Ollmann, and currently lives in Montreal.

Heather O'Neill lives in Montreal. Her short stories have appeared in such publications as Toronto Life and The Journey Prize Anthology. She is currently completing her first novel.

Kathryn Payne is an educator in the community college system. She is Creative Editor of *Torquere: Journal of the Canadian Lesbian and Gay Studies Association*. Her poetry and prose have appeared in numerous anthologies. She has published a book of poetry, *Longing At Least Is Constant*, and is working on her next.

Karleen Pendleton Jiménez is a soft butch Chicana writer teacher person, originally from L.A., happy to be living now in Toronto. She has published stories in numerous lesbian and Latina types of anthologies, and in her children's book *Are You a Boy or a Girl?*

Emily Pohl-Weary edits Kiss Machine (www.kissmachine.org). She co-authored *Better to Have Loved: The Life of Judith Merril*, a book about her grandmother — the "little mother of science fiction is a finalist for the 2003 Toronto Book Award and a Hugo Award. She is currently editing an anthology of cultural essays, fiction and art called *Girls Who Bite Back: Witches, Mutants, Slayers and Freaks* (forthcoming, spring 2004) and is also attempting to write a novel.

Rebecca Raby is a long-time member of the Stern Writing Mistresses, a sociologist and a novice pool-player. She likes to dabble in gardening.

Moyra Robson plays bass with the Richard Kikot band and has had work published in a variety of magazines and anthologies.

Stuart Ross, a fiction writer, poet, editor, and creative-writing instructor, has been active in the Toronto literary scene since the mid-1970s. He sold 7,000 copies of his self-published chapbooks in the streets of Toronto during the '80s and co-founded the Toronto Small Press Book Fair. Stuart is the author of several poetry collections, including *Hey, Crumbling Balcony! Poems New & Selected* (ECW Press, 2003). His fiction includes *The Mud Game* (a collaborative novel with Gary Barwin; The Mercury Press, 1995) and *Henry Kafka and Other Stories* (The Mercury Press, 1997). Stuart's online home is www.hunkamooga.com.

Trish Salah lives and works between Toronto and Montreal. She is a writer, activist, educator, doctoral student and editor at FUSE Magazine. Her first book of poetry, *Wanting in Arabic*, was published by TSAR in 2002.

Emily Schultz is the author of *Black Coffee Night (Insomniac, 2002)* and the editor of *Outskirts: Women Writing from Small Places* (Sumach, 2002) She is currently working on a novel called *Joyland*.

Abi Slone has had work in *Kiss Machine* #6 "Girls and Guns" and #5 "Cars and Religion", *Fireweed*, *Brazen Femme: Queering Femininity*.

Michael V. Smith is a novelist, filmmaker, sex columnist, stand up comic, *Globe & Mail* freelancer, an MFA grad from UBC's creative writing department, and a performance artist who does stand-up improv audience-participation nudist drag. In 2001, *Loop Magazine* named MVS one of Vancouver's Most Dangerous People. His novel, *Cumberland*, published by Cormorant Books, was nominated for the Amazon.ca/Books in Canada First Novel Award. Find out more at www.michaelvsmith.com.

Joey Stevenson is a white high femme queer girl living in San Francisco. She has been published in numerous anarchist zines and the upcoming feminist anthology *The Fire This Time*. Joey is an organizer, activist, burlesque dancer, writer, filmmaker, BMX rider, performance artist, and hairdresser.

Mariko Tamaki is the author of the novel *Cover Me*, a collection of short essays called *True Lies: The Book of Bad Advice* and has another collection forthcoming in 2004. She is a member of the performance troupe *Pretty, Porky and Pissed Off*.

Michelle Tea is the author of three books, most recently the memoir *The Chelsea Whistle*. She is co-founder of the all-girl open mic and road show Sister Spit, and continues to curate cabarets and performance tours of the United States. Her freelance writing pops up in places such as *The Believer*, *the San Francisco Bay Guardian*, and *Girlfriends* magazine.

Sherwin Tjia is the author of *Pedigree Girls* and *Gentle Fictions*, both with Insomniac Press.

Patricia Wilson has been lucky enough to read with Bill Bissett, Eileen Myles, Stuart Ross, Mariko Tamaki, Zoe Whittall and other very talented writers. She has a few pieces published in a couple of issues of *UNarmed.* and has written a thing or two for *Xtra!* Patricia is a musician and plays guitar for a band or two. She also has worked at Buddies in Bad Theatre for ten years.

Marnie Woodrow is the author of two outta-print short story collections (*Why We Close Our Eyes When We Kiss; In The Spice House*) and one in-print-so-far novel, *Spelling Mississippi*. She prefers to think of herself as a geeky outlaw who has seen the film, *The Misfits* at least six times when not muttering, "I'm a hustler!" in between projects.

RM Vaughan is a Toronto-based writer and video artist. His books include the poetry collections *A Selection of Dazzling Scarves* and *Invisible To Predators*, the novels *A Quilted Heart* and *Spells*, and the plays *Camera, Woman* and *The Monster Trilogy*.

Marlene Ziobrowksi hailing from points northern and remote, has settled in downtown Toronto. A technical writer, editor and researcher by day (see: www.lucidtech.nu), she is presently working on a collection of short stories that, so far, seem to be about sad kids having occasional out-of-body experiences. She writes with the Stern Writing Mistresses and has performed her work at Clit Lit, Strange Sisters and Mayworks.

Tara-Michelle Ziniuk is a writer, performer, activist, warrior and princess. She is half the spoken-word-cello-sex-noise+politix project "Black Licorice Theory' and former programmer/host of "Pink Antenna" queer news radio. She writes the (new and very dirty) column Lydia Lane Is Not My Name for *Trade: Queer Things* magazine and currently has work upcoming in the anthologies *No Such Thing: Writing by Jewish Women of Mixed Families*, *Raking the Moon*, *Burned Into Memory*. She has recently moved from Toronto to Montreal and is working on her first collection of poetry.

About the Editor

Zoe Whittall was born in the Eastern Townships of Quebec and now resides in Toronto. She is the author of a book of poetry called *The Best 10 Minutes of Your Life*. (McGilligan, 2001). Her work has been anthologized in *Brazen Femme: Transgressing Femme Identity* (Arsenal Pulp, 2002), *Ribsauce* (Vehicule, 2001), *Bent* (Canadian Scholar's Press, 2002) and *She's Gonna Be* (McGilligan, 1998).

A longtime promoter of cultural events in both Toronto and Montreal, she currently works as a curator for Buddies in Bad Times Theatre. She is a freelance arts reviewer for a variety of Canadian magazines and is currently finishing her first book of short stories.

She would like to thank Suzy Malik for her endless patience, shoulder massages, advice and support throughout the editorial process.

Many thanks to Ann Decter, Gillian Bell for the cover illustrations, Jonathan Kitchen for computer love and all of my friends and family.